YOUNG RICH WIDOWS

A Novel

KIMBERLY BELLE · LAYNE FARGO
CATE HOLAHAN · VANESSA LILLIE

sourcebooks
landmark

Published by Sourcebooks Landmark, an imprint of Sourcebooks
P.O. Box 4410, Naperville, Illinois 60567–4410
(630) 961-3900
sourcebooks.com

Originally published as *Young Rich Widows* in 2022 in the United States
of America by Audible Originals, an imprint of Audible, Inc. This edition
issued based on the audiobook edition published in 2022 in the United
States of America by Audible Originals, an imprint of Audible, Inc.

Cataloging-in-Publication Data is on file with the Library of Congress.

Manufactured in the UK by Clays and distributed
by Dorling Kindersley Limited, London
001-342819-APR/24
10 9 8 7 6 5 4 3 2 1

To all the women who have our backs, listen to us, lift us up,
make us better, and love us.
Female friendship is a formidable thing.

THE PARTNERS

It sounds like the opening of a joke: Four lawyers die in a plane crash.

But no one is laughing inside the brand-new 1985 Cessna careening toward the dark, icy Atlantic waters. One engine is already on fire and the other about to blow.

On the manifest: three men, one woman, and a screaming pilot.

"MAYDAY, MAYDAY!"

All four partners. The only partners. The foundation of the firm.

This group has never traveled together before. It's like the virgin who gets knocked up on her wedding night: it was just one time. But once is enough to end it all.

Black smoke spews from the flames of the left engine. The plane rattles and reverberates—the champagne flutes now on the floor, the briefcases scattered, the bowls of nuts spilled on the carpet, and the leaflet with directions for an emergency mocking them as it lies unfolded in the small aisle.

Though they will die together, they feel alone. Buckled in their leather seats, faces terrified and yet resigned in the hellish glow of the red emergency lights.

"MAYDAY, MAYDAY!" shouts the pilot again.

Their lives are different. Their loves are different—for the most part. But it is all ending the same.

Full circle, in fact, since they were all born in the same place, the smallest state. The same Rhode Island hospital even. They signed their names to be in business together. More eternal and binding than marriage. Divorce is one thing, but dissolving a law partnership is far more complicated.

And their partnership is dissolving, isn't it? Over the ocean, with the lights of New York City at their backs, dark night all around.

It's strange how their whole lives feel distilled to this moment. "Crystallizing the argument," to use a phrase each of them has written in a legal brief before. But that word, *crystallize*, the way heat forms the rocks, has never been more apt only moments before the other engine will explode.

One partner—the one with the best suit and worst marriage—begins to cry. His life is already in shambles, and now this. To leave this earth with everything so much worse than before. *She'd kill me if I weren't already dead.*

One partner desperately wants to say goodbye to the love of a lifetime. To say sorry about the finances or lack thereof. The partner can't look away from the burning engine. The flames light up the dark sky. No prayer is offered, but there is truth: *This is what I deserve.*

The partner who's been the quietest knows before the others that there's no way they'll survive the impact. This one grasps a bottle of whiskey tight, like it's the plane throttle and they'll miraculously lift up like in the movies. A long, burning swig full of regret. A prayer: *Don't let her find out.*

One partner would do anything for a line right now. To go out swinging and smiling. To have said, *I love you.* To have said, *I'm leaving.* To have finally made a choice and stuck with it. Even now, even with death here, the words will not form.

You spend your whole life wondering what this moment will feel like, and it's even worse than you ever imagined.

"MAYDAY, MAYDAY."

The pilot is screaming. None of them was prepared. Not for death or even life after what they've done today. Not that they'll have to face it. There are women waiting for them who must pay this price.

Last thoughts instead of last rites:

I didn't get caught.

I should never have betrayed her.

Now that I'm gone, they'll kill them.

This crash is no accident.

The headline will read: FOUR LAWYERS DIE IN A PLANE CRASH.

They think of the ones they love. They think of the four women they are leaving behind.

What will people say about these women?

At least they're still young.

At least they'll be rich.

As the other engine combusts and the dark sea swallows them whole, they leave behind widows all.

JUSTINE

Color fades in poor places. Back in New York City, over-head train tracks or bubble-letter graffiti would have sig-naled my destination. Such markers aren't part of Providence though. The only indication that I'm where I need to be is the washed-out nature of my surroundings: an abandoned parking lot packed with industrial icebergs of gray snow; a laundromat's once-orange sign heathered by exposed metal; the blackening brick of a firehouse.

I park the Mercedes beside the only visible tree, a leafless maple pruned to allow the passage of power lines. Cold has stripped this specimen's bark to an ashen shade. Its remaining branches form a V shape, bare arms outstretched in a desperate hallelujah.

I notice trees now. One of New England's major attractions for concrete jungle dwellers is its jewel-toned foliage. After receiving the job offer, Jack made a big deal of the importance of leaves: the peace to be gained by monitoring seasonal changes through their life cycles, the need for a little boy to grow up with piles to rake, fall into, and scatter. Born and bred in the city, I'd never considered nature a childhood necessity. But Jack had successfully argued his case, as always, convincing me that we'd all grow closer from afternoon forest hikes and nights nestled around the hearth of a real house.

We have not *all* grown closer. Jack has hardly spent a day inside our new-to-us century-old Colonial with its sprawling hickory in the yard and emerald hedge of boxwoods. The need to prove he's worth the partnership interest rouses him early, returning him only after Jack Junior is fast asleep and dinner has long been tucked in tinfoil.

JJ and I, on the other hand, have hardly left our new neighborhood since moving eleven months ago. Most days, I bundle us both in too many layers and then wheel him along Blackstone Boulevard to the swings and slide at Lippitt Park, pointing out details along our lonely woodland stroll. That's a black gum. That's an oak. O-A-K. Oak. I haven't had so much as a *go-see* for a modeling gig in months, but I can tell the difference between a birch, a beech, and a balsam fir. So there's that.

I pocket the car key and then stretch over the console toward the little body strapped into the booster seat. His breath whistles from the neck warmer that has slipped over his mouth during the short car ride. I stifle a curse. A nap is bound to spoil my evening plans. I'd hoped to keep him awake so that he'd conk out shortly after the sitter arrived to stand guard while Jack and I attended his firm's annual Christmas party. Mister Rogers was supposed to occupy JJ while I slipped on the sequin bustier dress that I'd bought in hopes of showing my husband that work isn't everything.

"Hey, buddy." I jostle JJ's little knee. "We're here."

His head rolls to one side, shaking the brownish-blond curls that fall to his brow and around his ears. Jack wants me to cut them. He complains that JJ resembles Greg Brady with his '70s perm. Which is fair, but I don't want our son to lose his curls. It's the sole physical trait obviously from me. His hair color is closer to his dad's blond than my midnight-brown shade, and his eyes are all Jack. JJ's olive complexion is a mix, a blend of his Irish American dad's pink skin and my own yellow-brown tone. Color is often a mishmash. My skin is a mash-up of my Ashkenazi mom's porcelain complexion and my African American father's chestnut hue.

JJ is Jewish, Black, and Irish. In Providence, that translates to Italian—*Neapolitan, not Sicilian. Don't worry.* Romeo, a founding partner at Jack's firm, pointed out the distinction with a broad smile, as though I should take it as a compliment. At the time, not knowing much about Italians except that this guy was one, I'd smiled and thanked him, assuming what he'd really meant was that JJ was so good-looking he deserved to be claimed as one of his own. It wasn't until later, after looking up the difference between

Neapolitans and Sicilians in our *Encyclopaedia Britannica*, that I'd realized the backhandedness. Sicily was occupied by the North African Moors and mixed with them over the centuries. They're the so-called Black Italians.

I shake JJ's knee again.

"Hey, buddy," I repeat. "We're here."

JJ raises his head and blinks his long, dark lashes. His eyes open, bright blue against the car seat's navy backdrop. He turns toward the window. "This not the *lie-berry*."

He means this is not *our* library. The Providence Athenaeum is located about a mile from our house. Its building—a McMansionized Temple of Dendur—hosts an expansive literature collection divided by two-story Doric columns, each crowned with a gleaming, alabaster bust of some conquering Roman or American. And the children's section has a phonics sing-along on Wednesday mornings.

"This is not the library we've gone to before," I correct. "But it's a library, JJ. This is the one where Mommy is volunteering. Remember I said I would do that?"

He scrunches his nose as though smelling something funny.

I lean farther into the back seat to unbuckle him. "Come on. Let's check it out."

My voice is unnaturally high, a consequence of faking excitement. In truth, I'm nervous. This excursion is about much more than me imitating LeVar Burton for an hour by reading to some kids.

I grab JJ's gloved hand and lead him across the street to the firehouse turned library. The smell of books, trees in yet another form, hits me as I enter the room. They lie somewhere beyond the metal detector that I guide my son through, past a long desk manned by a middle-aged woman with a checkout stamp.

The librarian/guard's graying hair is pulled back into a tight bun.

"Good afternoon. I'm Justine Kelly."

My name doesn't elicit any recognition, though the woman does look down at my son before returning her attention to my face.

"I volunteered to read in the children's section on Fridays."

The librarian's expression switches from suspicious to smiley. "Oh yes. How nice. Just a moment."

A little door in the counter swings back, freeing its occupant. My son's gloved fingers dig into my bare palm.

"And who do we have here?"

She hunches over, an attempt to bring herself to JJ's level. He retreats behind my legs. I bring my hand forward, taking my son with it. "This," I say, patting his shoulder, "is Jack."

The woman greets him in an animated fashion. He opens his mouth to say hello, but no words emerge.

"He's shy."

Her smile fades as she straightens. "And what will you be reading today?"

I pull my Coach bag to the front of my torso, slip out the thin book tucked in its front pocket, and hand it to her. "*The People Who Could Fly*. It's a collection of American Black folktales. It came out a year ago and won the Coretta Scott King Award."

The librarian nods along, seemingly satisfied with my choice. "Let me take you to the children's section."

I follow her through a reference area to a modest room surrounded by windows. Waist-high bookcases line the walls. Each is filled with the bright, primary colors of kids' book covers, a literal reading rainbow. There are half a dozen children inside. Some sit around toddler-size tables, staring at board books and sounding out words. Two young boys run through the room, making tight turns around another little boy perched atop his mom's lap.

Everyone is some shade of brown. The fairest woman is actually a bit lighter than I am, though her box braids announce her racial affiliation in a way that my natural hair does not, especially given the popularity of curly perms. Even so, I feel relaxed for the first time in months. To reference *Sesame Street*, I am not "the one thing not like the others." Or at least I'm a little less obvious. My son, however, is a blue balloon in a sea of red ones.

I lead him to the children, aiming for the little boy with his mom. She cradles him between her arms with the book on his lap, hugging him tighter as she reaches to flip the pages and kissing his buzz-cut head.

"Come on, JJ. Let's make friends."

The pressure on my hand increases as I reach the pair.

"Hi." My voice is high and soft. Since moving, the demure tone has become my default. "My name is Justine, and this"—I pull forward the arm being tugged behind my back—"this is JJ."

The woman smiles, though there is something pained about the close-lipped expression. Perhaps she's not keen on conversation. "Hi, JJ. I'm Raquel, and this is Denise."

I look down at the little boy with the feminine name and realize my mistake. The shaved head made me think "boy," but closer inspection reveals this not to be the case. Patches of brown shine through a dusting of black covering the child's scalp. White clouds the pupil in one of the girl's doll-like eyes. Denise is not well.

"Hello." My voice catches on the second syllable. "JJ, say hi."

My son sticks close to my side. I press his hand, an attempt to transfer some shyness-defeating strength while also signaling that I will not abide disrespect right now. We can't have this little girl thinking he doesn't want to be nice to her. "Jay," I warn.

He croaks a hello, and the girl returns a small smile.

"I'm going to be reading today." I address the comment to Denise before turning to her mom. "I picked *The People Who Could Fly*. Do you think it's too old for them?"

"I've read that one to her." Raquel grasps her daughter's hand and swings it back and forth in front of their torsos. "We do a lot of story time, don't we, Nissie?"

Denise leans into her mom's chest. "At the hospital."

"I'm sorry." The platitude comes out as tortured as JJ's hello.

Raquel kisses her daughter's head. Before I can say anything else, a young boy whooshes by us.

From somewhere in the corner, a woman shouts, "Robbie, you best get your behind over here. I told you to stop running."

Denise pulls her mother's chin toward her small mouth. "Robbie's in trouble."

Raquel leans toward her daughter's ear. "Well, Robbie knows better than to make Auntie Michelle yell."

The librarian reacts to Michelle's scolding with her own barked call for attention. "We all have the pleasure of welcoming Ms. Justine Kelly." She claps her hands together. "She will read from *The People Who Could Fly*. Isn't that right?"

I answer by assuming my position atop a small chair at the front of the room and accepting my book. The kids gather in a warped semicircle of crossed legs. JJ throws the arc off alignment by nearly sitting on my shoes.

"My story today is 'A Wolf and Little Daughter.'" I flash a big smile, letting it rest for an extra moment on Denise. "The tale is about a little girl who outsmarts a mean old wolf."

The kids are rapt. I'd once hoped to transition the modeling to an acting career, and I infuse my live reading with all those long-dormant performer instincts. I lower my voice to a growl when imitating the wolf and transform my tone to a sassy squeak when impersonating the girl. I sing. I gesture. I commit fourth-wall-breaking offenses to help the kids understand the jokes.

"Little daughter slips inside the gate. Shuts it. CRACK! PLICK! Right in that big, bad wolf's face!"

Laughter erupts, the high-pitched squealing kind of delighted children. My big finale has even shaken JJ out of his shyness and post-nap stupor. He's grinning at another giggling kid. The moms hanging on the sidelines seem pleased that their children have been so well entertained. Inwardly, I congratulate myself.

And then Robbie falls. A moment before, he was sitting on his haunches, a coiled spring ready to fly the moment his mother signaled his release. But now he's on the ground. All the pent-up energy has somehow electrified his body. He convulses atop the colorful rug, jerking back and forth.

I jump past JJ, drop to my knees, cradle Robbie's head, and then gently turn it to the side, acting on some memory about swallowing tongues. Before I can attempt anything else, Michelle is taking her son from me. She clutches him to her chest. "What happened? Robbie? Robbie? What happened?"

This last desperate question is aimed at me. Instead of trying to explain, I rush through the room's opening to the checkout desk. The same librarian reads behind the counter.

"Call 911! A little boy is having a seizure!"

She drops her book and grabs a nearby phone. I sprint back into the room. Raquel is shouting instructions at the other moms. They need a wet towel. A napkin. Juice. Though her volume is elevated, she is calm. This is not her first time handling a health crisis.

Robbie cries into his mother's chest. Michelle's body

language indicates that his spasms have stopped. Her hand cradles the back of his head, keeping his face in her bosom, out of sight of the staring children.

I hug my son to my thigh. "The ambulance is coming." I say it to Michelle, but only Raquel makes eye contact. "Is there anything I can do?"

Raquel shakes her head and moves away from Robbie's mother and toward me. "This is how it starts." She speaks under her breath. It takes me a moment to realize that she is not talking to herself. "All these kids—"

A siren silences her. Michelle rises from the floor, her son wrapped around her torso like a backpack.

The librarian enters a moment later. "Story time has ended." She claps her hands together. "Feel free to continue reading."

The moms and kids begin dispersing. I take JJ's hand and start toward the exit. He leans into me, sensing that it's too soon for questions.

"I swear, it's catching," one of the mothers mumbles.

"How many kids is it now?" another asks. "Five?"

I lengthen my stride to catch up to them. Are other kids having seizures? Is something going around?

The librarian stops me in front of the doorway, blocking my path to the other women. "Thank you." She exhales through her nose. "We sure earned our pay today, didn't we?"

She must know that this gig is volunteer. "I just hope the hospital can help."

She darts a glance at JJ. "I'd be happy to call your boss and tell how you helped. I'm sure she'd be pleased."

I pull JJ closer to my side. "This is my son."

"Oh. I'm sorry. I didn't mean anything…"

No one ever does, do they?

I think it but don't say it. Too much has happened to argue about stereotypes. "Not a problem. He takes after his daddy."

I swoop my husband's mini-me into my arms. He's too little to walk fast, and I have to get him home, calm, and tuckered out in time to get ready. To Jack, I've just been JJ's mom for far too long. Tonight, I'll remind him that I'm also his wife.

CAMILLE

I t's over."

The words chase me up the stairs to the bedroom, echoing through my head for the thousandth time today. Peter at the tail end of an argument—that much was clear from his tone, shouted from behind the half-closed door to his office. Two little words that, even though they weren't aimed at me, stuck the air in my lungs and my feet to the floor. I couldn't move, which is why I heard what came next.

"You really want to be involved with this kind of garbage? There's proof, you know. I thought you were better than this."

I scurried away as he slammed the phone down hard enough to leave a dent, and he barreled out the door without so much as a kiss goodbye. All day long, I've been spiraling with worry about what was over, if I'm the garbage Peter was referring to, if he'd found the thong I'd tucked in a top desk drawer, and if he was planning to whip it out at the party tonight.

The party I'm about to be late for, thanks to Peter's words and some fatal accident on I-95. The traffic made me late for my nail appointment, which made me late to the hair salon, which leaves me racing around the bedroom like a crazy woman, getting ready in twenty minutes when I really need forty-five. Tonight has to be perfect. *I* have to be perfect. There is no other option.

I touch up my makeup and add a little extra. Extra mascara, extra blush, extra red lipstick to match the dress, a skintight velvet number I bought especially for the occasion. When I tried it on for Peter, he said it made me look like a movie star.

From deep in the house, a voice yells my name like a curse. "*Camille.*"

Peter's only child, his fifteen-year-old daughter, Kimberlee with two *e*'s. That's how she's constantly introducing herself. Heaven forbid you ever get it wrong.

Once upon a time, I would have skittered down the hall to her room, an overstuffed, overdecorated explosion of pink and purple ruffles she was fine with three years ago, when her father bought this place, but now hates. I would have slapped on my prettiest smile and rapped a timid knuckle under the KEEP OUT sign, asking ever so sweetly what she needed. I would have prayed my coddling and fussing would melt away some of her icy demeanor whenever I walked into a room. But those days are long gone, discarded like the shoes and empty food wrappers she leaves all over the house. Teenagers are like predators; they can smell your desperation from a mile away.

I suck a lungful of air, of restraint, and step out of the closet. "In the bedroom."

I don't have time for Kimberlee's drama right now, and I definitely don't have the energy. Not after fighting the frumpy Krystle, wife of one of Peter's law partners, on the catering and decorations. And definitely not after obsessing about the snippet of phone conversation I'd accidentally overheard this morning.

Because it didn't sound like business. It sounded personal.

Angry stomps barge through the bedroom door without knocking. "I can't find my boots. Where did you put my boots?"

Hair teased halfway to heaven. Chunky jewelry weighing down her neck and both wrists. Crop top and tiny mesh skirt. Nowadays, Kimberlee with two *e*'s takes her fashion cues from Madonna.

"The black ones?"

What am I talking about? They're all black. Everything is. Her clothes, her shoes, the pencil she uses to draw those thick rings around her eyes, even her chipped nail polish. Peter says it's a phase, no matter how many times I tell him it's more like a protest—for his divorce from her mother, Mindy, for our marriage, for the move to the East Side of Providence, for the surge of teenage hormones raging through her bloodstream. She drapes herself in gloom and fury, and I'm to blame for all of it.

"I think I saw a pair by the door to the garage." I wrap my hand around the carved balustrade of the four-poster bed and turn, sweeping my hair to one shoulder. "While you're here, do you think you could zip me up?"

An angry puff of air, and then she's gone.

Hallelujah and mission accomplished.

I slide the zipper up my spine myself, then pad on stockinged feet to the bathroom, glancing out the big bay window onto the darkening yard. Like the majority of things in our relationship, this house was Peter's choice, selected mostly for its amenities—high ceilings and crown molding and wall-to-wall carpeting, a kitchen of dark wood and shiny appliances, a second staircase so you didn't have to walk the fifty extra feet to get to the first. He certainly didn't buy it for the view, a plain stretch of lawn that ends in a privacy fence, surrounded on all sides by neighbors.

"For the kids," he said with that smile of his. "And look, we can put a sandbox right there, right outside the kitchen window."

That was back when I was just gullible enough to think we'd actually have some. I hadn't yet learned that's how Peter operates, by promising the universe only to demur and litigate, stonewalling until you put your foot down, then giving in *just* enough to string you along for a little longer. They're skills that serve him well as an attorney.

Also? He forgot to mention the vasectomy.

There will be no children, no family—not with Peter anyway, not anytime soon. And honestly, let him. Let him keep making those half-baked promises; let him keep thinking I don't know they're as empty as the seed he leaves inside me. Like my once-desperate attempts to make friends with his daughter, I'm done trying. There are other ways to get what I want.

And then it's inevitable. I think these things and I think of *her*. The other woman. The wife. My competition. I think of how beautiful she is despite the fact that conversations with her are as painful as a root canal, how perfect she must look in lingerie, like a present made for the unwrapping. I think of them kissing, his hands roaming her perfect skin, touching her in all the same places he touches me. Does he think of me when he's with her? Does he compare my body to hers? I think all this, and something flips over in my stomach, a spool of twine uncoiling before I reel it back in.

Do not think of her. That is the only way any of this is sustainable, by pretending she doesn't exist.

Which is impossible, since she'll be at the party tonight. She's one of the firm wives. Her husband is one of Peter's partners. And seeing as there are only four of them, there will be no avoiding her.

And tonight, when Peter takes my hand to twirl me around the dance floor, I will feel her eyes not on him but on *me*, studying me, resenting my easy smile and head-over-heels glow, while I wonder what is so incredible about her that he can't seem to let her go.

Downstairs, a doorbell rings—the town car, here to whisk me away to the party—and I grab my bag and fur and race for the stairs. As I'm sliding onto the cool back seat, I picture the moment when the four partners strut into the lobby, shedding coats and exchanging greetings with the crowd, and a shiver of nerves, of anticipation prickles my skin because now I'm picturing the moment when he looks up and our eyes meet, and I will know this red dress, this stupidly expensive sexy lingerie, it will not go to waste. All I need is a few minutes with him alone.

Because tonight.

Tonight, he will look at me and not think of her.

Even if only for a few minutes.

MEREDITH

Time to become someone else.

The thong is the first to go—replaced by modest black panties and a matching bra. Then I cover it all up with a blouse, buttoned high enough to conceal my cleavage, tucked into a skirt that cinches around my knees. A structured jacket, sensible shoes. *Pantyhose.*

I exchange my fake gold hoops for real diamond studs, and the transformation is complete. I look demure, professional, respectable. Like a woman who's never broken a rule, let alone the law, in her whole damn life.

Robin had better appreciate this.

My makeup is still too heavy though, remnants of the smoky eyeliner I wear on stage clouding the corners of my eyes. I lean closer to the mirror, scrubbing some of the darkness away with a tissue. Better.

"Damn, Mere. I almost didn't recognize you."

I turn to find Frankie, the strip club's newest bartender, leaning against the doorframe. Technically only dancers are allowed back here, but as far as I'm concerned, Frankie's one of us.

Which is probably why I told her my actual name. To the rest of the club's staff, I'm Tina—more alluring than Meredith, but normal enough to let customers think they might be getting the real deal.

"Brought you something." Frankie holds out a martini glass filled with syrupy liquid even redder than my lipstick. Most of the other bartenders are content to sling the club's standard overpriced shots and champagne, but Frankie's like a mad scientist, always coming up with new concoctions.

"I shouldn't," I say, but I take the glass from her anyway and try a sip. The drink smells like cinnamon and burns all the way down. "Jesus, what's in this?"

"A lady never tells." Frankie steps over the threshold, and the door falls shut behind her, muffling the thump of music from the floor. "So what're you all dressed up for?"

"Just some party."

Frankie perks up. "Yeah? What kind of party?"

"Not our kind." I turn back to the mirror, setting the martini glass down on the counter. "A bunch of stuffy lawyers congratulating themselves on how many people they screwed over this year."

"Well, then you need a drink even more than I thought."

There's a heavy knock at the door. "Francesca, you in there?"

Before Frankie has a chance to answer, the door opens. It's Arti, one of the security guards, and he looks pissed. Frankie tenses. She's only been here a few months, so the mob guys still make her nervous. But the truth is they're glorified guard dogs. You just have to know where to scratch them.

"Something wrong?" I ask him, fluttering my eyelashes. "Frankie was just helping me with my zipper."

Arti's eyes bug out a little at that mental image. "No, uh… it's just getting kinda busy at the bar." He gives me a lingering once-over. "You cutting out early too, Tina?"

"Got a date." I toss my teased-up brunette curls over my shoulder and cock my hip. Even with my ass covered by a layer of tailored wool, his eyes go right to it. It's almost too easy.

"With that lawyer lady again?" he asks.

I nod. Everybody at the club knows about me and Robin, because this is where we first met. She came in one night with some bespoke-suited finance guys, playing up her usual just-one-of-the-boys angle to win their business for her law firm. In my experience, women like that can be even worse than the assholes they're trying to impress. They laugh too loud, drink too much, and tip like shit. Once some hedge-fund bitch from Boston smacked me so hard during a lap dance, I had a bruise for a week.

Robin wasn't like that. Not at all. I actually thought she was a man when I first spotted her through the haze. With her swept-back copper hair and slim-cut suit, lithe body lounging in the chair, she looked like *The Man Who Fell to Earth*–era Bowie. I couldn't take my eyes off her, any more than she could take hers off me.

And now, I'm keeping her waiting.

One more glance at my makeup, then I tuck my imitation Balmain clutch into the quilted Chanel Robin gave me for my birthday and start for the door.

"Your drink," Frankie calls after me.

"You finish it."

She does, knocking it back like a shot, her own darker lip color layering over the print I left on the rim. She already seems calmer. "Have fun at the party," she says.

Arti stands aside to let her leave the dressing room, but when I try to follow, he blocks my path, arms braced in the doorway so I get a flash of the piece strapped to his side. Bet he doesn't even know how to use that thing. Working at the club is entry-level at best for these guys—not much for them to do, since all of us girls can take care of our own damn selves.

He grins down at me. "What's Lawyer Lady got that I don't, huh?"

We've done this dance before, and usually I shoot back something crude, like "great tits." But tonight I'm running even lower on patience than I am on time, so I tell him the truth.

"*Money.*"

That wipes the grin right off his face. I duck under his arm and head for the exit. His eyes follow, but he doesn't.

Outside the club, the wind whipping down Chalkstone turns my breath to crystals in my throat. I tug my coat tighter and trudge the block over to Douglas, patent leather pumps clicking on the pavement, so I can call a cab from a pay phone out in front of a convenience store instead of a strip club. I'm not in the mood for any more questions from men tonight.

It's not until I'm ensconced in the back seat of the taxi that my nerves really start flaring. I've been avoiding it all day: thinking about this party, this night. All the ways it could go wrong. The fact that, even if it goes exactly right, it's going to change everything.

I'm still amazed Robin agreed to this. It's been almost three years since she came to the club and slipped her business card—folded inside a crisp hundred-dollar bill—into my G-string, and I haven't met a single one of her coworkers.

She always had her reasons. Good ones too. At first it was that she was afraid of alienating conservative-leaning clients. Then it was that she didn't want to rock the boat while she was trying to make partner. But she's been a partner at the firm since June, yet I remain trapped in the closet with her.

At first I didn't mind being Robin Calder's dirty little secret. Hell, those first few months, I would have let her tie me to the bed in her College Hill town house and keep me there indefinitely if she wanted. The woman swept me off my Lucite heels like a goddamn romance novel hero. First it was a flood of flower arrangements, so obnoxiously large the club dressing room looked like a greenhouse. Then designer dresses in my exact measurements, diamond jewelry shining like stars in night-sky velvet boxes. And eventually the five-star dinners, the luxurious spa weekends—but never in Providence. Never anywhere someone she knew might see us together.

After a while, it started to wear on me. The excuses, the subterfuge, the broken promises. The outright lies. So a week ago, before she left on her latest business trip, I gave her an ultimatum: take me as your date to the firm Christmas party, or it's over. Robin flinched like I'd slapped her, that peaches-and-cream complexion flushing crimson. But she said yes.

The truth is I don't even want to go to this stupid party. I don't care about meeting her boring lawyer friends. Robin complains about her colleagues so much, I feel like I know them— and their stuck-up wives—already. But I can't stay with someone who's ashamed to be seen in public with me. I've tried that before, and it didn't end well.

The cab pulls up to the law firm's front entrance, and I pay the driver with a fistful of wrinkled singles. As he pulls away, spewing exhaust, I stay frozen, staring up at the imposing brick facade. I've passed by the Turk's Head Building many times, but this will be my first time inside.

I exhale a cloud of steam, then square my shoulders. It'll be fine. Robin's waiting for me. I'm going to stand at her side and link my arm through hers, and whatever happens, however her coworkers react, we'll face it. Together.

As I get off the elevator, the heat hits me first—all those bodies crammed into the event space on the top floor, plus candles flickering everywhere in an attempt to give the buttoned-up space some ambiance. I'm less than twenty minutes late, but the party is already in full swing, a dozen overlapping conversations competing with the jazz combo playing Christmas music in the corner. I pause in the doorway, searching the crowd.

Right away, I spot a familiar face. But it isn't Robin's.

Fuck. He's seen me too, and now he's sauntering in my direction, a mostly empty martini glass clinking against his Brown class ring.

"Well," Rom says, leaning down with a leering smile. "Fancy meeting you here, Tina."

KRYSTLE

I will not murder this woman over pizza.

"It's a new place I read about in the *Providence Journal*," Camille says as she drops her fur into the arms of the door guy.

The elevator swooshes behind her, and I whisper a prayer for patience. The jazz band in the corner continues their epic rendition of "Have a Holly Jolly Christmas," and I'm having neither at the moment.

"I told you, Caserta's pizza is a tradition," I say. "People who've been coming every year to the firm's Christmas party expect it. You wouldn't know that, would you?"

It was a petty dig, her being the second wife.

"Actually, Peter said the new clients expect something... better." Camille waves across the room with her perfect red nails at the corporate client crowd she's referencing. "He said this party desperately needed an upgrade."

My face flushes because she's not wrong. I glance around the stuffy Turk's Head Club, which is on the top floor of the building where we have our offices. Or rather our husbands do.

"You must like the flowers," Camille says coolly about the tall clear vases of roses with sparkling feathers sticking out. They're dramatic and chic and not my first choice, but she's right. "Anything is better than pots of chrysanthemums, Krystle."

"Well, you are an upgrade expert," I say.

Her eyes narrow. "Does anyone even like Caserta's pizza? It's like a brick. Maybe it's gourmet for *you*?"

I think about slapping her across the face, right here in the middle of this fancy Christmas party we planned together. That would remind her that I grew up on the Hill in Providence, an Italian neighborhood where we took care of one another but also didn't mind stepping in to take care of something in another way.

Instead, I say, "Your dress is festive. Making sure everyone sees there's jingle in those new bells?"

"We can't all be Mrs. Claus."

"So true, but ho, ho, ho does apply." I put my hands on my twice-as-thick-as-hers waist. I wish I wasn't wearing this black dress with too much shoulder padding to try to even out my hips. I've been hitting my aerobics class three times a week. Juice cleanses nonstop. If I even see a carrot, I'll ralph.

Still, I've been told I look like Bette Midler four times tonight. Not an insult, but not Daryl Hannah either.

I take a breath, a long one, that only reminds me I'm wearing a girdle. The net under my skirt itches, but I ignore it.

"Is that a new wedding ring?" Camille asks.

"Today is our twenty-fourth anniversary." When her eyebrows shoot up, I can't help myself. "We were married at ten, if you're counting. Child bride."

She leans toward my giant sparkler. "Why this anniversary?"

"Romeo gets me a new one every few years. We could only afford a chip when we were married."

She gives me the most genuine smile I've ever seen from her. "I'm guessing when he slid it on your finger, he forgot to mention it's a CZ."

"A cubic zirconia?" I stare down at the two-carat solitaire. "Get outta here."

"Let me see it." She holds out her thin fingers, and I reluctantly put my hand in hers. She takes it up to her mouth and blows hot breath onto the ring. She shakes her head as if it were her own fake. "Sorry, real diamonds don't fog up like that."

I snap my hand from hers as if she burned me. I huff on the diamond Romeo slipped on my finger this morning before heading off to his partner meeting in Newport. All that shine disappears with my breath.

"How do you think I met Peter?" Camille's tone is soft, almost kind. "I was behind the jewelry counter."

"He was picking something out for Mindy?" I say about his

first wife. That's not how he told it. "I thought you met yachting or something."

She shrugs. "How else would I have known to say yes when he asked?"

I don't understand—Romeo has been telling me things were going better with the firm. Adding Jack as a partner and Robin before that had opened up new streams of business.

Good thing, because the whole reason we've been working our asses off since I got knocked up twenty-four years ago is to leave something to our kids. The cars, the big house, the private schools, and the tropical vacations amount to bubkes if he and his partners flatline this place.

Tears start to sting, but it's not the full waterworks. I blink them away right as the saxophone hits the final high notes of the song. The room is silent for a few seconds, and I stare down at the ring, already knowing, on some level, the sparkle was wrong. Too bright. Definitely too big for what we could afford lately.

In any other circumstance, I wouldn't let Camille see my real emotions. But this isn't just about me. She's smart enough to know that much. Her husband is the other majority partner. If I'm getting CZs, then hers are on the way. I stare at her again, the perfect hair and makeup. Shelf boobs and ass even a twenty-year-old stripper would envy.

The truth is she's never looked better. Not even on her wedding day. Maybe she's already got a backup plan.

She sees me staring and smiles a little. That's the funny thing about us and this business. Camille and I have just about nothing in common. Yet our futures, our lives, are tied together with the success or failure of this law firm. At least she doesn't have kids. Lucky skinny bitch.

"Did you at least let me keep the cannoli from LaSalle's?" I ask. "Otherwise, my juice cleanse has been for nothing."

She laughs a little, and we have a moment of peace. My gaze darts around the ballroom, the view of Providence's skyline ahead. The room glows with warm lights and a big Christmas tree in the corner.

I glance down at my new Rolex and wonder if it's a fake too. "They're late," I say about our husbands and the other two partners. "Maybe traffic on the bridge."

She blinks at me like I just switched to Italian.

"They had a big meeting in Newport," I explain. "About the new mall development deal in Washington Park. That's why they left so early this morning."

Absolutely nothing registers on her face for a moment, and then a big show. "Of course, Peter said. I forgot. Crazy day."

That's enough chatting with her until the party next year. Her marriage, her problem. "We should mingle."

I don't feel bad about leaving her standing alone.

Searching for a familiar face, it's clear there are two distinct sides of the law practice. The Italians like Romeo and me. Workers' comp and auto injury. They're the foundation of our business. Sure, people say it's sleazy, until they need that paycheck. Ambulance chasers or back-of-the-phone-book models. Whatever cheap shot they took as we climbed.

Camille's Peter used to work those cases—way, way before she was in the picture or they had these big land-development deals in play. They paid the bills after all. But Peter was always the one who needed to feel better than everyone. Even back when we were all broke. The leased car. The inflated mortgage. The suits on credit cards. The long lunches we couldn't afford at the Blue Grotto to bring in new clients.

So now with his upgraded wife, he has created another side to this firm. I glance at the big mall-deal corporation guys in the corner with Armani suits. It's funny how these new clients mirror Peter and Camille. Everyone is tall and fit and smelling like money, honey.

Speaking of clients, I get a half-hearted wave from Donna Moldova, who looks like she stepped out of a fortune teller machine at the state fair.

Technically, Donna has been Romeo's client for a while, but she's more hippie than the Hill. She's dripping with crystals, from giant slices of pink geodes dangling from her ears to her wrists slathered with stones on bangles. Of course, nestled in her cleavage is her signature necklace that made her a small fortune, sparkling with moonstones.

As I approach, she opens her palms to me as if she's Jesus ready to ascend. "Krystle, your energy is so dark. You're like a black hole."

"Well, merry Christmas to you too."

"No, no, you misunderstand, my angel beauty lovey-love." She takes my chin between her fingers like I'm a child. "Your chakras need to be released. I gave you the name of a wonderful healer. You did not call?"

She has the full mystical accent going now, even though her family has been in the Rhode Island jewelry business for five generations. "Something to look forward to," I say, annoyed that she's even here. I can't remember what business Romeo had with her jewelry company, but this annual dose of her woo-woo-wacko makes me consider finding Camille again.

As if she's read my mind, her eyes narrow. "I see money hasn't given my counter girl any class." She nods at Camille, who's flirting with one of the Armani suits. "Firing her was one of my best decisions. She stole, you know. My jewelry. Just before she stole Peter."

I frown. As much as Camille gets on my nerves, I'd never take her for a thief. Though touché on the Peter point.

I'm saved by someone from the old days. "There you are, sweetie!" Our longtime client screeches as she wraps her frail arms around me. "Mind if I steal her?"

Before Donna can answer, I am saved as the client spins us away and makes the sign of the cross. "Something about that one, yah know."

"Thank you," I say as we head over to the champagne fountain.

"I wanted to tell Romeo I love that new billboard off 95." She adjusts my shoulder pad. "You'll tell him?"

I nod, pretending I will, even though we've fought about it lately. I want him to change up the advertising. If I see one more CALL ROMEO FOR A SWEETHEART DEAL sign, I'll take a swan dive off the Turk's Head Building. He hasn't changed the ad since we opened the doors twenty years ago.

"He's the best lawyer that ever lived, I tell yah," she says. "Romeo Romero makes the Hill proud."

"How's your mother?" I say quickly to change the subject. I pat her hand as she tells me about her mom's rheumatoid arthritis and the nursing home staff that's likely stealing from her.

We built this business with clients from the Hill, but the days of getting the Italian referrals are drying up. It's all new and flashy now. Like 1985 is for the Jetsons, and Romeo and I are about to go the way of the Flintstones.

"There's my oldest. I gotta check on him," I say and kiss her goodbye. "Skip the pizza but get a cannoli."

There is my handsome, dipshit son harassing some woman who should run my aerobics studio. "Rom, this your date?"

He grins. "We're friends, Ma."

For a moment, I wonder if he hired a call girl to come to this party. I mean, she's dressed nice, looks smart, but something about her says…more. "I'm Krystle Romero." I reach out a hand. "This one's mother."

She shakes my hand firmly, and her gaze goes to me, then

him. I can see she's judging me, which means she probably knows my son pretty well. "Nice to meet you. I'm...Tina," she says with a glare at Rom. "I'm a friend of Robin's."

"Why does a lady lawyer like her need a broad like you hanging around?"

"What do you drink, Tina?" I ask, ignoring Rom's comment.

"Champagne," she says.

"Fetch," I say to Rom. "Pardon his manners or lack thereof. But maybe you knew that already?"

She smiles in a way I can't read. "Thank you for having me." Her gaze goes around the party. For a moment, I catch some nerves, but it's gone soon. "Have you seen Robin?"

"She's still with the other three partners at their Newport meeting," I say. "I'm guessing there's traffic over the bridge. I'll introduce you around."

There's that jumpy look again. "I'll wait for Robin."

I take the glass from Rom when he returns. "You didn't put something in it?" I half joke.

"I got my wallet, so no need for that, right, Tina?" he says with a wink.

"Can you not? We're talking. Go find your brothers." I point at my cheek, and he kisses it reluctantly. "Make sure they're not sneaking whiskey again this year."

He gives Tina one long, completely inappropriate look, then leaves.

I sigh and roll my eyes for Tina's benefit but don't feel like apologizing. Rom is my eldest. So he's a dumbass—it is what it is. And I made the oldest mistake in the book. I gave him everything.

"There's Justine," I say. "You know her too?" Tina shakes her head. "Jack's wife. I'll introduce you."

Justine starts making her way toward us, and she looks particularly pretty tonight, if smacking of desperation. I like Justine, even if she's a little skittish. I can tell she's a bear of a mother, and that's something I respect.

I wave at a few more people, and we're getting closer to her. Camille notices me crossing and sees Justine. She begins making her way in our direction. I shoot her a big, "I don't know where the hell they are" gesture, but she keeps coming toward us anyway.

I see Vince, my mom's brother and our family lawyer, with his bushy white hair and bad suit, rushing over. "Where's the phone up here, Krystle?" he says, not greeting me or anything. "Please, hurry."

"Jesus, Uncle Vin." I lead us all toward the back of the room. The phone is on the wall toward the kitchen, and he nearly runs there.

He struggles with the plastic cord, then takes out a piece of paper and dials. He jams the phone to his ear and puts his hand over his other one.

"Have you all heard from Jack?" Justine asks. "I thought he would be here before me."

Camille has joined us, but she doesn't say anything.

"Yes, is this the Coast Guard?" Vince yells into the phone. "I have her here."

I smile at Uncle Vin, wondering if this is some kind of joke. Like maybe Romeo bought me a boat instead of this fake ring for our anniversary today. "What is this, Vin?"

He holds out the phone. "You need to take this, Krystle."

"Hello…" says a man's voice on the phone. I press it to my ear. "Is this Mrs. Romero, wife of Romeo Romero?"

"Yes."

"We've lost contact with your husband's plane."

"His *plane*?" I frown at Justine. "Romeo wasn't on a plane today. He had a meeting in Newport, right here in Rhode Island. He wouldn't take a plane there."

"Mrs. Romero, we have confirmation from the FAA that Mr. Romero, his colleagues, and a pilot all left on a private flight rented by your husband from New York City. We received a mayday distress call. But that's the last we heard. They were scheduled to land at the Providence airport at 6:00 p.m."

"But it's almost 7:00," I say, easily accepting Romeo lied this morning about a meeting in Newport. One more awful fact in this jumble. "He isn't here."

"We'll begin searching immediately," the voice says. "Please, stay close to a phone."

"You'll begin searching?" I say, making eye contact with Justine again. I think of her little boy JJ. I think of my boys. I try to make sense of what this stranger on the phone is getting at. "Searching for where they landed?"

"No, Mrs. Romero, you need to prepare yourself and the others," the voice says. "We're searching for their remains."

JUSTINE

Duck and cover. That's what our teachers drilled into us in the event of a nuclear explosion. Dive under a desk. Crouch in a doorjamb. Hide your face, cover your neck, and try not to breathe.

Some childlike part of me wants to follow these instructions now, though shock thankfully stops me from crawling beneath one of the room's many burgundy tablecloths. The bomb has gone off, not with a flash but with the shrill siren of a woman's scream. It rings in my ears, drowning out all other sounds. Krystle, wife of the firm's cofounder, falls into the arms of her heir apparent. The demure brunette beside her becomes statue-still. Camille, the lady in red, grasps a chair. Her scarlet lips part. Her white teeth clench. Her mouth opens, wailing a name that has no business on her tongue. *Jack.*

Camille's spouse is dead, but she's thinking of Jack, crying the single syllable that I've whispered in private moments and shouted in passion—the name of my love.

Her lover.

How could this have happened? In my mind, I see Jack's crooked smile. Soft lines peek from the corners of his eyes. The picture expands to reveal that his grin isn't for me. He chatted with Camille at the partners' *welcome to the family* meet and greet. I'd caught him in my peripheral vision while holding JJ still. Romeo complimented our son's Mediterranean coloring, and Krystle gave unsolicited advice on raising boys. On the car ride home, I'd asked Jack what he and Camille talked about. Casual party banter, he'd said. He was curious how such a young woman had ended up with his graying colleague, as if the answer wasn't obvious from the title on Peter's business card.

We'd made love that night, hadn't we? The memory of his lips against mine feels so real. I recall the taste of him after that party. The sweetness of whiskey on his tongue. But…no. We'd kissed with our clothes on. JJ was riled up from hours of behaving himself. It took longer than usual to get him to sleep. I passed out on my son's twin mattress.

And Jack? Did he go to bed thinking of her?

My head spins. The room seems to fold in on itself, its corners converging at a central point that is Krystle. Her grief is a black hole, sucking the party guests toward her. A woman pushes past me, swirling in silk, a tornado of fabric. Jewels drip from her ears, neck, wrists, and fingers. Their garish sparkles contrast with the matte black fabric of Krystle's boxy dress. It's as though someone brought a disco ball to a funeral.

Camille attracts her own attention. Men in dark pinstripes and bright ties buzz around her, trying to catch her eye. Her cheeks shine with a sadness that I don't feel, that I won't feel as long as I am in this room surrounded by strangers, transfixed by the blond whose public anguish has stolen my sorrow.

I shouldn't be here. But where can I go? In the eleven months since our move, I've made acquaintances, not friends—certainly no one who could be expected to comfort me during a time like this.

But returning to the house would be wrong. My son is asleep. Waking him with my sobs or, worse, news that his father was in a fatal plane crash would be beyond cruel. It's better that he has one more night of sweet dreams, one more night swaddled in the fiction that he is protected by two loving, doting parents.

What I wouldn't give for a few more hours of believing that I'd created a happy, stable family for my son. I'd never had one. My father left when I was four. My stepfather has always considered me more consequence than kid, a by-product of my mother's brief rebellion from her Jewish roots. It occurs to me now that Hanukkah ended five days ago. I forgot to send gifts.

I gave Jack his present on the last day of the holiday, a Swaine Adeney Brigg attaché case in black to match his wool coat. James Bond used the same brand in the movies. I'd planned to leave the bag wrapped under the tree until Christmas, but Jack had opened up one night about his work stress and the importance of several upcoming meetings that required careful negotiation. I'd hoped that the stylish accessory might give him a confidence boost. Fashion has always done that for me.

A palm lands on my back. It's thick. Male. It should but does not belong to my husband. For a moment, I let myself forget that. I imagine Jack behind me, his broad chest at the back of my head, rising and swelling with his breath. Again, I picture his face: dark-blond hair brushed back to reveal the square forehead that folds like blinds whenever he's concerned or upset. I envision the deep-set blue eyes that once sparkled whenever I entered a room, the smile that always hinted of secrets.

Jack was smart, handsome, cocky. He loved a challenge. Was it the prestige of snagging the senior partner's trophy wife that drew him to Camille? Or was it something else? The blond hair? The creamy complexion? The fact that she looked like the kind of girl an attractive, successful Irish Catholic son of New England might be expected to marry?

"What's going on? Is Jack here?"

There's a hint of a Queens accent in the question. I whirl around to see a man who could be one of Jack's Columbia law buddies. He's about the right age: midthirties with a pale face and dark-brown hair. His clothes fit the bill too—suit straight out of *American Gigolo*, Movado watch. Moreover, he has that *Masters of the Universe* air indicative of Goldman Sachs traders, McKinsey consultants, and Ivy League lawyers. It's apparent in the entitled way he touched my back, as if he knew me and not just my husband.

"There was a plane—"

My throat closes up on the word that was to follow. The man's dark eyes widen. He cups a hand over his thin lips. The Movado's signature solitary diamond flashes from the twelve position. Noticing such details in this moment is callous. But my husband's death is something my brain comprehends without my body, a stab from a knife so sharp that the wound fails to throb despite the blood.

Krystle lobs questions at the older man who led us all over to the phone. *Why were they on a plane? Where were they coming from? Who were they meeting with?*

The answers don't register. I can concentrate on only one thing: Camille.

Mascara trails down her cheeks, cracking her porcelain skin, advertising her anguish. My pain is more possessive. It refuses to be shared. Funny, since the only thing I want to give this woman is pain. I want her wailing in agony—just not over my Jack.

In my peripheral vision, the pretty brunette has broken free of Krystle's orbit. I'd assumed she was the son's girlfriend. If she is, she doesn't seem to feel any responsibility to console him. It looks like she's leaving.

Before I can do the same, the older guy ushers us into an adjoining room, shooing away most of the suits, save for Krystle's son. I realize that I've met the elder man before. He's Vincent

Rossi, the firm's lawyer—or is he the Romeros' personal attorney? I don't remember the guy's exact title. When Jack introduced him at that meet and greet months ago, he'd said, "This is Vince, our guy." He'd quipped afterward that *even lawyers need lawyers,* chuckling at his own joke. Jack always found himself very witty. I'd thought he was funny in the beginning too, before "work" had sapped so much of his energy.

But was it really work? How often was the client in need of urgent attention actually Jack's partner's wife? When he would come home too exhausted to hear what JJ had done during the day, was it because he'd spent hours listening to Camille? When he'd hugged me to his chest and said how much he loved our family—how he wanted to get me pregnant again, maybe this time with a girl—had he been playing a part, pretending to be a loving father and husband so I wouldn't ask too many questions?

Was our life real at all?

This new room looks like a smoking lounge, all black leather chairs and mirrored walls. There's a long humidor, lit to show the cigar brands. A fire burns beneath a framed oil painting of the Turkish guard whose bust gives the Turk's Head Building its name. The scent of burning oak nearly overwhelms the lingering tobacco smoke.

Someone had prepared this room to receive guests. Likely, Jack and the other partners had intended to retire here for their post-party smokes and scotches. Would I have been instructed to rush home and relieve the sitter, I wonder, or invited to stay?

Would Camille have been welcomed back with the boys?

She's sitting atop one of the loungers, elbow propped on a roll arm, head held up by bloodred nails. Her velvet dress spills from the leather seat onto the floor. A diamond tennis bracelet dangles from her delicate wrist. It's the kind of statement piece men give women to stake their claim.

Did her husband give her that, or was it my Jack?

Vince stands in the front of the room. He is adding unnecessary details to the headline we all received earlier. The partners had gone to New York City for some client meetings. They'd chartered a private plane and were all aboard the return trip from Teterboro Airport to T. F. Green in Warwick, fifteen minutes outside Providence. The flight was scheduled to take forty-eight minutes. It was due to land a half hour before the party started. Shortly after takeoff, the plane disappeared from radar. There have been reports of an explosion over the Long Island Sound.

"If something was wrong with the plane, if an engine combusted…" Vince trails off. He doesn't need to reiterate what we already know, what we all knew the moment Krystle told us that the Coast Guard was performing a search. "The firm belongs to you all now." He says this last part on an exhale, as if he can't believe it's true.

"Like hell." Krystle steps toward Vince, pointing at his chest. "Romeo and I built this firm. It belongs to the boys. Romeo Jr. will take over while—"

Vince raises his open palms. "Each partnership stake goes

to the surviving spouse, Krystle. You know that. In the case of Robin, it's whomever her will designates. Once we have the reading, I suppose—"

"Oh, you suppose, do you?" Krystle punctuates the statement with an angry backhand slap at the air. "You suppose the responsibility of running one of Providence's biggest law firms should fall to a stay-at-home mom who doesn't know any of the players and a damn jewelry store clerk who flashed her assets behind the counter to steal—"

"At least I had a paying job," Camille shouts. "Have you ever worked?"

Krystle's hands curl into fists. "I built this firm. My sweat and blood and connections—"

"Your job was raising three boys." Camille's bracelet jangles as she dismissively waves at Krystle's eldest. "And none of them are a testament to your management skills."

Krystle steps forward, fists now aimed at a target. A sick sense of glee bubbles up inside me. I take my own step closer to Camille.

She rises from the couch. But before things go any further, Vince inserts himself into our triangle, breaking the tension. "The rules are clear. You all will have to decide how to move forward—together. There are deals that require attention, one in particular that you'll all need to understand. And, of course, we'll have to notify clients and arrange a public memorial. There should be a formal will reading, and any remaining assets will require transfer. We'll also need to figure out how to keep the place operating while we work out—"

"Enough." Krystle turns like a dog snapping at its tail. For a moment, I think she'll strike Vince instead of Camille. But her arms fall to her sides, unable to carry the weight of all that needs to be done. The burden that now rests on all of us.

Whatever "us" means. We aren't friends. We don't have what it takes to run this firm. Krystle is upset, but she's not wrong about what I'm capable of doing. My business skills have long taken a back seat to raising JJ. I barely understand the fashion and modeling industries anymore, let alone anything about Jack's line of work. Clearly, I didn't know much about how he spent his days.

What I know is abandonment. My dad took off. My mom focused her energies on finding a new man and creating a better nuclear family. My husband was having an affair. What I know are lies. Jack promised to love me forever. He swore to never be like my father. He said he was incapable of turning into the kind of "loser" who leaves his wife and allows his kid to grow up without a dad. Yet there is a woman mourning him before my very eyes because of nights when Jack did just that—when he gave his extra hours to a stranger instead of our son.

My husband would argue differently, I'm sure. But he was a lawyer. What's the truth to a professional liar? It's a blessing that he's not here to plead his case.

Krystle's chin quivers. "Vince, this is all too much right now. Let's focus on the memorial. Right after, we'll get everything sorted out. Rom can help with the day-to-day, but permanent solutions will come later."

"The mall development deal is crucial," Vince continues.

"I'm not asking." Krystle swipes a tear.

The sight of her crying stops the attorney. He says something about picking up this conversation after the funerals. I mumble a few words about the babysitter and back out of the room.

As I leave, my vision clouds. Yet I don't feel sad anymore. What I feel, I realize, is relief. I am free! Free of that room, those women—the other woman. I am even free of Jack. My husband will never again hold me and whisper lies that feel true. He'll never again manipulate me. He won't win any more arguments.

God help me, I'm glad he's dead.

CAMILLE

I follow the funeral procession up the center aisle of the Cathedral of Saints Peter and Paul, and the absurdity hits me. Saint Peter my ass. Not in this town, not when Peter's job was to bring in the big deals and bigger piles of money, even if that meant committing a sin or two to snag clients on the right side of the law.

Otherwise, Romero, Tavani, Kelly, and Calder would continue to cater to, well…not the most *upstanding* members of Providence society. Mobsters to the left of me, gangsters to the right. It's a miracle this place doesn't spontaneously combust.

Through the haze of my funeral veil, I pick out some familiar faces on either side of the aisle. Peter's parents, clutching well-worn rosaries, their mouths moving in silent prayer. His pregnant sister and her deadbeat husband, doing his best to ignore their six squirming kids. Peter's ex-wife, Mindy, blubbering like she didn't spend every day of the past four years telling him how much she hated him. Next to her, Kimberlee catches my eye, and the pity in her expression sends up a fresh surge of tears.

It's been a week. Seven eternal days since the plane lit up the sky and flipped my life upside down. Seven days that have been steeped in shock and grief—the wailing, howling, hair-pulling, soul-crushing kind where my tears have become so constant, I barely even notice them anymore. Kimberlee assumes my tears are for her father, and I haven't bothered to correct her.

The procession dumps us into the front-right pew. The VIP pew. The one dripping in black tulle to indicate it's reserved for us grieving widows. Krystle chooses the spot between me and Justine, and the two of them stare straight ahead, their eyes looking anywhere but my way.

I'm pretty sure they both know.

Father Joseph climbs the steps of the sanctuary, then raises his palms to the heavens. "Brothers and sisters, let us pray."

As one, the congregation rises to their feet.

I stand there in stilettos so stiff my pinky toes are going numb, mentally preparing myself for sixty more minutes of this. Of Father Joseph droning on and on, of Justine's glares and Krystle's icy silence. Of swallowing down my sorrow for a man who wasn't technically mine.

Did Jack know death was coming for him? Did he register the fire before it singed his skin? Did he scream at the coming heat and pressure? I stare at the urn with his name in curly script—fourth one from the left, fourth partner to join the firm—and wonder. Did he feel pain? Regret? In those last, terrifying seconds, did he think of me at all? These are the things that keep me up at night.

"Camille." Krystle hisses my name into sudden silence, and she tugs at a batwing sleeve. "For God's sake. Sit."

I look over my shoulder at the cathedral stuffed with seated bodies, hundreds of eyes watching me with a mixture of compassion and embarrassment.

Look at her up there, poor thing.

Barely married and now a widow.

Such a pretty mess.

I turn away from their faces and collapse back onto the pew.

I told Krystle I didn't want a funeral mass. I told her I'm pretty sure Robin wasn't even Catholic and Peter hadn't set foot in a church since his divorce, after Father Joseph refused to give him Communion.

"Do it to honor Peter," she said. "To honor the four partners, God rest their souls."

She even insisted on a limo, black and stretched a mile long, to cart us here like debutantes going to prom. But this time, I didn't have the energy to fight her. Krystle got her limo and stupid funeral mass, even though there's nothing left for us to bury.

Out of every image that's gone through my mind this past week, I think that one's the worst. When the engines exploded and the plane flew apart, so did the bodies. My beloved Jack, busted into a million pieces by heat and diesel and flying sheets of steel. Carried away on the wind and rained down onto the Long Island Sound. Ashes and dust and fish food.

Which means those four silver urns up there? The ones lovingly engraved and hung with roses and baby's breath, arranged just so across the marble steps?

They're empty. There's nothing inside them but air.

The thought sends up a throaty sob.

Justine flinches at the sound, her body practically vibrating off the wooden pew. I saw her face at the party. I saw the moment the quarter dropped into the slot and she figured out that my tears are not for my husband but hers. She hates me for it, and quite honestly, the feeling is mutual.

I hate her for being his wife, his rightful widow. For being allowed to wail his name while I cry silent, salty tears. For having a house filled with remnants of him—photographs and books and a closet crammed with clothes that still carry his scent, for the rumpled sheets and a mattress with a Jack-size indent. And for Jack Junior, a living, breathing, miniature version of his father, with the same big eyes, that left-cheek dimple and square chin.

And me? Besides my memories, I only have one thing left of my beloved Jack.

Justine can hate me all she wants, but no way in hell am I giving it back.

For me, the saddest part of a funeral has always been the ending—not that I've been to all that many. An eighth-grade classmate back home in Augusta, Georgia, my great-aunt Clarice, a former boss I didn't even like all that much. But as I stand here with Krystle and Justine, watching mourners file out of the church and hurry back to their cars and their lives, I don't want this one to be over, because now what? What the hell am I supposed to do? Kimberlee just left with her wretched mother, and the thought of returning to that big, empty house makes me want to scream.

I take in the dwindling crowd in the vestibule—a couple of clergy members, clusters of men in suits and slicked-back hair, a pretty brunette who can't stop staring from behind her tortoise-shell Vuarnets.

"Did Robin's family come?" Justine asks.

Robin was the only partner still unattached, even though any man would have killed to be with her—and I'm guessing plenty have, but not longer than a night or two. Robin was like a man that way, eternally single.

I shake my head. "Not that I know. I didn't talk to anyone who said they were here for her."

Justine shoots me a look that says she wasn't speaking to me, but when she turns to Krystle, her expression softens into something sympathetic. "That's so sad. I don't know anything about Robin, just that she made partner right before Jack came in. I don't even know where she was from."

Krystle waves at someone, the pretty brunette on her way to

the door. "She was from here. Robin's parents died when she was in law school. Her younger brother is some fancy artist who lives in Paris. He's in the middle of a show at one of the big galleries there. Otherwise, he would have come."

Justine frowns. "How do you know all that?"

"Because I talked to him last week."

"No. I mean, how did you even know she had a brother?"

Justine's question might sound strange to an outsider, but it didn't take more than a couple of conversations with Robin to know how much she valued her privacy. While she could charm everyone's socks off at parties, her flirty, friendly banter revealed exactly nothing about herself. Robin never talked about anything personal.

Krystle shrugs. "I know a lot of stuff. Oh, hell. Rom!" She hustles across the vestibule, trying to catch her oldest son before he chases the pretty brunette out the door.

I turn back to Justine, but she's walking away too.

Yep. She definitely knows.

From behind, a warm hand taps me on the bicep. "Excuse me. Camille Tavani?"

I nod, and he extends a hand; the old me would have spotted this guy hours ago. His suit says rich and powerful but not in a mobster way—the cut is too corporate, the fabric too understated. He's young but not too young, judging by the faint lines carved into his high forehead. Before Jack, I would have been fluffing my hair and batting my lashes for this guy. Now he barely makes a blip.

"My name's Martin Ellis. I work with Peter—I mean, I

worked with him on the mall development deal." He says it with just the right amount of sorrow, and he gives my hand a sympathetic squeeze. "I'm so sorry for your loss. Peter was a great guy and a brilliant attorney."

A brilliant attorney, sure, but a great guy? Debatable.

Still, my ears perked at the words "mall development." That deal was—and still is, according to Vince—our golden ticket, a multimillion-dollar development that will set us up for life or break us if it doesn't go through. I try not to think too hard about the second possibility.

"Thank you. For coming too. I'm sure Peter would have appreciated it."

Martin grins, revealing two rows of perfectly straight teeth. "No, he wouldn't. Peter would have asked why the hell I was playing hooky when I should be back at the office, getting this deal lined up."

I can't help but smile. "That does sound more like him, actually."

"I'm really going to miss working together. He had such an eagle eye when it came to contracts. Speaking of, did Peter say anything to you about the mall deal? Right before the...well, *you* know, he mentioned stumbling on a little hiccup, but he never got a chance to tell me what it was."

"I'm sorry. Peter and I didn't talk about work." The truth is, these past few months, we didn't talk about much of anything at all. But now I'm curious.

"What about papers? Did you happen to find any lying around?"

"I hardly ever go in his office, but I can take a little look later tonight. Why? Is something wrong?"

"No, no. Nothing like that. As far as I'm concerned, we are still full speed ahead. But the more I know, the better I can put out any potential fires before they spark." He slides a business card from his inside suit pocket and holds it in the air between us. "If you find anything that concerns the Terminal Road property, do me a favor and give me a call, will you?"

I pluck the card from his fingers, my acrylics bumping up against the embossed text. Martin here isn't just any old business-man. He's the owner and CEO of Ellis Development Corp., one of the largest commercial developers in the area.

It's why I give him my most charming smile. "Absolutely. If I come across anything, I'll call you that very second."

He thanks me and we say our goodbyes, and in a cloud of Drakkar Noir, he's gone.

So is everybody else. Sometime while the two of us were chatting, the vestibule emptied out. I grab my fur from an office off the hall and go in search of Krystle and Justine.

I find Krystle outside on the church steps, talking to a man I've never seen before, but I know exactly who he is. Slicked-back hair, pinky ring, silk pocket scarf. This guy has the mobster look down pat.

And I realize they're not exactly talking. They're arguing.

The man stabs a finger at Krystle's nose, his breath curling white wisps in the air. "...know what's good for you, you'll get that money."

Krystle pulls her fur tighter, gathering it in fistfuls under her neck. "I already told you, I don't *have* the money. It burned up in the plane."

"That's a real shame, but it doesn't change the fact you owe four million clams."

Despite the icy air, my skin goes hot. Krystle owes a mobster four million dollars?

No—that's not right either. The four partners were the only passengers on that plane, so whatever money they were carrying likely belonged to the firm. But four million dollars? Why would they be carrying around that much cash?

"I—I don't have that kind of money." Krystle's gaze flits over mine, and her eyes flash "danger," but she doesn't otherwise acknowledge me. The man hasn't noticed me yet, and she doesn't give him any reason to. He takes a threatening step forward, and Krystle totters back on her heels. "*Now.* I don't have the cash *now.* But Romeo had life insurance, and I'll find out what else there is today at the will reading. I can get you that money. I'm just going to need some time. Like I said, in another week or two, I'll have a better handle on things."

The mobster shoves up his sleeve to check his watch, a gold monstrosity that covers half his wrist. "The clock is ticking." A black Lincoln slides to the curb, and he hightails it across the sidewalk, pausing at the passenger door. "He'll give you through the holidays, because you're in mourning and he's a nice guy. But come January first, you better have a bag full of dough." He yanks open the door and falls inside, and with a gun of the motor, the car heads out of the lot.

Krystle looks at me, and something passes quicksilver between us. Shock that the mobster would confront her here, at her husband's funeral. Fury that he left her with a four-million-dollar hole to fill. Fear of what will happen if she can't pay. I think of that big CZ on her finger, and my heart gives an ominous thud. At the same time, I feel a stab of something it takes me a moment to place: solidarity.

Krystle is a widow too. Our husbands went down in the same plane. They left us with the same responsibilities, whether we want to accept them or not. Their deaths put us solidly on the same sad team. Justine too, dammit. She's one of us.

I don't realize she's behind me until her voice calls out over my shoulder. "Who was that guy? What's going on?"

Another question that wasn't for me, but I whirl around and give her the answer. "Whatever it is, it doesn't look good for any of us."

MEREDITH

My temples throb harder as the elevator rises. I lean my head back against the paneled wall and shut my eyes for a second, holding Robin's leather portfolio tight against my chest.

Going to the funeral this morning was a mistake. Going sober was an even bigger one. I thought it might give me closure. Instead, the whole thing felt like a slap in the face. Especially seeing the three of them, sitting there in that black-draped front pew, accepting condolences while I lurked in the back of the church like a criminal casing the joint.

The past week is a blur—except for the night when I reached the bottom of the crystal decanters in Robin's liquor cabinet, and Frankie came through with enough cheap vodka from the club to keep me sedated through Christmas. She was nice enough not to give me any shit about my drunken wallowing, but she did make me turn off the television.

I knew it was pointless, torturing myself with all that local news coverage. They don't know anything more than they did the day it happened, so they keep repeating the same awful talking points: no bodies, no answers. And every time they showed Robin's picture, that professional headshot with her pomade-smoothed hair and Mona Lisa smile, it felt like I'd lost her all over again.

I step out of the elevator and into the offices of Romero, Tavani, Kelly, and Calder. There are still remnants from the holidays littering the foyer, wilted poinsettias and dying evergreens. All the lights are off, except the ones in the main conference room. Through the open double doors, I see them: Krystle, Camille, and Justine. The women who, unlike me, can legally call themselves widows.

They still don't know who I am. Well, enough is enough. Today, I'm going to tell them. They might not accept me as one of them. They might even think I'm a liar. But they won't be able to deny what's mine.

Robin made sure of that.

Vince Rossi is there too, hovering over Krystle's shoulder. They're at the head of the table, under a larger-than-life portrait of the firm's founding partners. Camille and Justine sit on opposite sides, staring each other down like a couple in the midst of a messy divorce settlement.

Robin had her suspicions for months about Jack and Camille. She loved collecting other people's secrets, filing them away for future use. By the time I figured that out, I'd already told her far too many of my own.

The women are all still wearing their funeral clothes, but Camille has piled on some extra makeup to cover up her tear-swollen eyes. I straighten my blazer—borrowed from Robin's closet, black silk with a sharp leather lapel—then tuck the portfolio under my arm. Ready or not, I can't put this off any longer.

But just as I'm about to walk through the conference room door, someone rushes up behind me.

"Tina?"

Rom Romero punctuates my stage name with a harsh sniff; at least he got all the powder in his nose this time. I didn't put it together until the Christmas party, but to think, all those times I complained about my handsy cokehead regular and Robin groused about her boss's idiot son, we were talking about the same man.

"What the hell are you doing here?" he asks. "Were you at the church too? I thought I saw—"

"Rom, get in here," Krystle calls from inside the conference room. "We don't have all day."

Rom flushes red with embarrassment—or maybe that's just the coke kicking in. "Sorry, Mom, I was just—"

I slip into the room behind him. Krystle's already out of her chair, striding toward us. None of those friendly party-hostess airs this time around; she's all business.

"I'm sorry, sweetheart. But this meeting is for family only."

It's now or never. I can slink off into the shadows or stand my ground and claim what's rightfully mine. Robin's voice echoes in my head—the words she whispered in my ear as I signed my name right underneath hers, her engraved fountain pen heavy in my hand.

I want you to have everything, darling.

"Actually," I say, "I am family."

They're all staring at me now. I'm used to being stared at in my line of work, but not like this. I run my thumb over the corner of the portfolio, where Robin's initials are embossed in gold, and try to imagine her here with me. Standing at my side, her hand on the small of my back.

Don't let them see you sweat.

"What's your name, dear?" Vince asks.

"Meredith."

"Give me a break." Rom jabs his thumb in my direction. "Her name's Tina, and she's a fucking stripper at the Wolf Den."

"Watch your mouth, young man," Krystle says.

"Mom, I'm telling you. She's a stripper. There's no way she's—"

"My name is Meredith Everett." I stand up taller, glaring back. "And yes, I am a 'fucking stripper.' But I'm also Robin Calder's partner."

Vince arches one thin gray eyebrow. "I wasn't aware Ms. Calder had any other business partnerships."

"Not a *business* partner," Justine says—under her breath but loud enough for everyone to hear. She's the only one who doesn't seem the least bit shocked by my revelation.

Vince looks like he might have a stroke. "Oh," he says, sinking into the nearest available chair. "I see."

"This should explain everything." I slide the portfolio across the table to Vince. He flips through the documents inside, quickly at first, then again more deliberately, like he's looking for flaws, signs of fraud. But I know it's in order: Robin's life insurance policies, her last will and testament, a durable power of attorney, all notarized and all naming me as her next of kin. I might not officially be her widow, but she made certain that, in the eyes of the law, we were everything else to each other.

"Well, Ms. Everett." Vince clears his throat. He can't look me in the eye, but he motions for me to take a seat. "I suppose you should join us."

"This is ridiculous," Rom says. "How do you know she didn't forge all that shit? I knew Robin, and I think I would have noticed if she was a—"

"Can we please just get this over with?" Justine says, cutting him off. "It's been a long day, and I need to get back to my son."

"Yes, of course," Vince says.

Rom looks like he wants to say something else, but one sharp look from Krystle shuts him up. He doesn't sit beside her at the head of the table, opting to stay standing, leaning against the wall next to the portrait of his father. The resemblance is clear, but

Romeo Senior looks a lot warmer than his firstborn, a twinkle in his eye instead of Rom's reptilian gleam.

I slide into the chair beside Justine's, and she gives me a small, weary smile. She's even more stunning up close, one of those natural beauties with an inner glow even grief-stricken exhaustion can't dim. What the hell was Jack Kelly thinking, cheating on a woman like this?

Vince unclasps a battered leather briefcase and takes out a stack of folders. The wills of the other dead partners, I assume—much skinnier than the portfolio of paperwork I brought. Must be nice to need so little documentation to validate your relationship.

"Obviously," Vince says, "you're each the sole heirs to your late spouses' estates. However…" He trails off, looking queasy again.

Krystle rolls her eyes. "Just spit it out, Uncle Vin."

"Quite a few assets are tied up in the Ellis Development deal."

"The *firm's* assets," Justine says.

"Jack didn't tell you?" Vince takes in the blank looks around the table and sighs. "I thought they would all have discussed it, given the amount of money…well, never mind. I suppose it's too late now. Bottom line, they needed this deal, and the major players wanted everyone to have some skin in the game. The firm didn't have the resources on hand to get the deal underway fast, so the partners invested their personal assets. Romeo, Peter, Jack, and Robin contributed about a million dollars—each."

All the air leaves my lungs. I knew Robin was rich—no mortgage on her townhome, a new BMW every other year, a closet full of designer clothes. But a million dollars in one deal? That must have drained her bank account to the last dime.

I glance around at the others, who seem to be coming to similar revelations. Camille's lacquered mouth is fixed in an O of shock, fury roiling behind her eyes. Justine sets her jaw like she's been bracing herself for this—another betrayal.

Krystle doesn't seem as surprised as the other two, but if anything, she's even more pissed. She keeps tapping that rock on her finger against the table like she's trying to shatter it. "Seems like an awfully big investment," she says as if struggling to keep her cool. "Even for a major real estate venture like this. Where was all that cash going anyway?"

Vince crosses his arms. "I didn't ask. I'd suggest you don't either."

"Well, Sal's guys are asking." She slams her hand on the table. "They threatened us outside the church. They said we have a few freaking days left to pay back the full four million."

"Wait, I'm sorry." I stare across the table at them. "Sal's guys—you owe four million dollars to Salvatore Ponterelli?"

"No, sweetie," Krystle says. "*We* owe four million dollars to Salvatore Ponterelli."

"They borrowed from some low-life gangster to make the mall deal happen?" Camille says with wide eyes.

"Sal isn't just 'some gangster.' He runs half of Providence,"

Krystle says. "He's got his hand in plenty of legitimate businesses. Real estate, garbage collection, entertainment."

That last one Krystle says with a loaded glance at me. The Wolf Den is one of the Ponterelli family's many local businesses, and Sal keeps an office in the back. None of the dancers are allowed to set foot in there (unless he invites us—personally) but I've heard the rumors. And, occasionally, the screams. The security guys at the club may be easily subdued guard dogs, but Sal? That man's called "the Wolf" for good reason.

Krystle turns to her son. "You told me the cash was on the plane when it went down. You're sure?"

Rom nods, looking uncharacteristically solemn. "I saw Dad before he left that morning. He had it with him, in a suitcase."

Justine presses her fingers between her eyebrows. "They were carrying around four million dollars in a *suitcase*? In New York City? Why would they do that?"

Krystle stares at her like she's simple. "Salvatore Lupo Ponterelli only deals in green."

"Why should we take his word for it that the four million is his?" Justine says. "Maybe he's lying. Trying to shake us down."

"I'm not saying there's anything that'll hold up in a court of law," Vince says. "But guys like Sal don't need to take you to court to get what's theirs. Plenty of his guys were close with the firm, with Romeo. He's not making this up."

Justine shakes her head. "Jack wouldn't have anything to do

with those people. I guess I can see him investing in a promising development, but he wouldn't owe a gangster a dime."

"Peter was smarter than that," Camille says. "No way."

Krystle pointedly looks from Justine to Camille. "Well, maybe you didn't know your husbands as well as you thought." She turns her attention to me. "You still want to inherit everything from your lesbian lover? This is what you get in a *real* marriage, honey: the good, the bad, and the ugly."

I'm not at the club. I don't have to smile and play nice and hustle for tips. Fuck this. Fuck *them*. Camille and Justine aren't laying into me like Krystle is, but they sure aren't lifting a pretty finger to help me out either.

I stand up, bumping my chair back so hard it almost tumbles to the carpet. "You don't want me involved, fine. You work this out among yourselves, and if there's anything left over, send me my cut. I think you know the address."

Krystle stands too, leaning over the table like she wants to lunge at me, claws out. "This is Robin's fault more than anyone's. She's the one who put together this deal in the first place. My Romeo told me so. From the moment Jack brought Martin Ellis in as a client, Robin had her hooks in him about that mall."

One night a few months back, Robin came home in a flurry of excitement, smelling like cigars and expensive scotch, and told me she'd just made the deal of a lifetime. *You can finally quit the club. I'll take care of you, I promise.*

She never mentioned investing her own money, let alone a million. Though, to be fair, we were too busy celebrating to talk much after that.

"What about insurance money?" Camille asks. "They had life insurance through the firm, right?"

Vince nods. "Yes, and you're all named as beneficiaries."

"So we could use that money?" Justine asks. "Until the deal goes through?"

"I'm afraid it's not that simple. The insurance company can't release the funds until they've concluded their investigation."

Rom scowls. "Investigation? Of what? It was an accident. The plane malfunctioned or something."

"The investigators haven't ruled anything out at this point."

"If it wasn't an accident, then it must have been this Ponterelli." Justine glances around the table for confirmation, her gorgeous eyes growing enormous with fear. "Right? Who else would do something like this?"

Krystle shakes her head. "Not a chance. Sal and Romeo go way back. Besides, why would he blow up his own money?"

"He might not have known it was on the plane," Camille points out.

"How do *we* know the money was really on the plane?" I ask.

Rom opens his mouth to defend himself, but his mother beats him to it. "You calling my son a liar?"

That's probably the nicest thing I'd ever call her son.

Camille's big blue eyes are brimming with mascara-wrecking

tears again. "What the hell are we supposed to do? They can't just leave us to fend for ourselves with *nothing*."

"*I'm* the one with a young child to raise," Justine mutters. "I'm sure you'll still have plenty to spend at Filene's Basement or wherever you shop."

Now Camille's the one who seems to be on the verge of clambering across the conference table. Justine folds her arms and stares back, daring her to try it.

Krystle shoots them both a warning look, and it's enough to keep them in their chairs—for now. But who died and made her the boss around here? Not Romeo Romero Senior, that's for damn sure. Robin told me what a completely useless asshole he'd become: head of the firm in name only, taking all the glory and none of the responsibility while the rest of them did the real work.

"The best thing for all of us to do for now," Vince says, "is stay calm. And stay close by."

"How long do investigations like this usually take, Uncle Vin?" Krystle asks.

"It depends on what they find. Complicated insurance investigations can take months. Years, even. In any case, I'd strongly advise you all to remain in Providence until this is settled."

Rom's face turns even redder than before. "They can't seriously think *we* had anything to do with what happened."

"As I've said." Vince clears his throat. "They haven't ruled anything out. Or anyone. You'll probably hear from the police or even the FBI. It'll take time, but be prepared."

The temperature in the room seems to drop as his statement sinks in. The four of us thought we'd leave here today rich—or at least taken care of for the time being. But until they figure out exactly what happened on that plane, we're all destitute.

Even worse: we're in this together.

KRYSTLE

Would I rather swallow the CZ on my wedding ring finger with a stick of dynamite than get in this limo with these three broads? Yeah, no shit, Sherlock.

"Come on, girls. This might be the last time we're in one of these for a while," I call to the three women as the rented limo pulls up.

"Can we talk later?" Camille whines for the third time as another blast of bitter wind whips around the Turk's Head Building.

Instead of answering, I hold the limo door open with my ass and pull my fur tight against my neck. The gesture reminds me of Sal's capo shoving his finger in my face about the four million he says we owe him. After my Romeo's memorial on the steps of the church, for chrissakes. The nerve.

In they go, the ladies in black, one, two, three. I drop into the seat by the door.

"My house, Franco," I call out to the man who has been driving firm clients since we opened, though usually in the company town car. "Some privacy, please."

The window separating our two seats from his goes up slowly. No one is making eye contact. We're alone together for the first time in, well, ever.

We remain silent as the car pulls off the curb and begins heading toward College Hill.

"I really need to get back to JJ," Justine says as the champagne glasses next to her tinkle. I spot the magnum of Dom calling to me like a lighthouse in the fog.

"That cold enough to drink?" I ask Justine, who's sitting next to the booze compartment.

"Today we said goodbye to our husbands, learned that they might have been murdered, and realized we owe millions to the mob," she says in her soft but still judgy voice. "Do you really think champagne's appropriate?"

Apparently, grief has given this one a backbone. "I'm not celebrating," I say with a dismissive wave. "I need a drink."

"Pop it open. Pour me one too," Camille says, staring out the window. Her leg is crossed, so we're seeing a lot of thigh in her funeral dress. I shake my head at her having a slit like that in church. Second wives, I guess. Saying goodbye with the reason he ever said hello.

"You want to do the honors?" I say to Meredith. "Bottle service, right? Area of expertise?"

Her eyes flash the *go fuck yourself* I deserve, but she scoots closer to Justine, who hands her the bottle. She pops it in seconds, pretty much making my point. Justine hands her a glass, then another.

There's a moment of hesitation, but then Justine picks up the other two glasses. I wink at her because it's about time we stop pretending we're fine. We've never been further from it.

I take a sip and the others follow. The fizzy bubbles slide down my throat too easily. I close my eyes and tip the whole thing back. My head swims for a moment, and I can almost imagine Romeo next to me. Him and Uncle Vin yelling about something as I sip my drink and try not to laugh.

But when I open my eyes, it's just the four of us in our funeral dresses, and no one is laughing.

"I'll take a refill," says Camille.

Meredith pours refills all around. "Good thing it's a magnum."

Camille takes a long drink. "Not every day I get accused of killing my husband by blowing up a plane."

"They're trying to scare us," I snap, angry at how Uncle Vin delivered the news. "None of us has a reason to kill our husbands. At least not like that."

"What, poison under the sink is reasonable?" Camille says.

I shrug. "Wait until you've been married twenty-plus years. Then we'll talk."

Justine smooths her dress, not looking up. "They don't have

evidence that it was sabotage. You said the mob wouldn't have done this with their money on board. It has to be a terrible accident."

"Here's hoping." I tip my glass. "But that doesn't give us any slack with Sal's muscle."

"The mob money is definitely a *you* problem to fix," Camille says with a slight slur. I'm sure she hasn't eaten in days, which means one drink is like three, so she's at six.

I'd guess the same for Justine too, who is uncharacteristically chatty. "Jack told me Romeo had a whole list of 'guys from the hill' he'd hire to help with issues for clients. Now I get what he means."

"Excuse me." I put my hand to my chest in disgust. "You know, just because I'm a proud Italian American does not give you the right to assume I have Mafia connections. We're not all wise guys."

"Wasn't your father, like, a capo in the mob?" Meredith asks coolly over her glass. "Rom brags about it all the time. Says his uncles are connected too."

Well, leave it to my dipshit son. I let my outrage deflate. "Let's not split hairs. Your significant others signed up for this pony ride. Like it or not, your ticket is punched, and your ass is in the same saddle."

"I don't even know why I'm here," Justine mutters. "If the money burned up on the plane, that's it. We can't give what we don't have."

"You think that excuse ever works?" I say with a laugh. "People don't survive owing the mob that kind of cash. We *all* have to come up with our share somehow."

"Let's go to the police," Justine offers. "Tell them what's happening."

Meredith shakes her head firmly. "We don't want them involved. Not until we know the parameters of this mall deal and what the payment to Sal was really for."

"We didn't have anything to do with it," Justine tries again.

"The police could get the FBI involved," Meredith says. "Then we're talking freezing assets and taking property. Truly ruining our lives."

"They'd fuck us every which way to Sunday," I say more forcefully to Justine, who flinches. "We have to figure this out on our own."

"Then the mall deal has to happen," Camille says with confidence.

"You got a suggestion?" I snap.

She leans back to reveal even more aerobicized thigh. "I can call up Martin Ellis, who's leading the mall project, and explain the situation. He gave me his card. I'm sure I can work something out."

"Oh, I bet you can," I say. "What does he want besides the obvious?"

"Oh please. I mean maybe he can get us a loan or an advance," she says. "Even I know what I got ain't worth four million."

"Obviously," Justine murmurs. "I just can't believe that Jack would have gotten himself involved with the mob. He brought in corporate clients like Ellis."

That stuck-up attitude zings me. "If we've learned anything in the past week, it's that you never know anyone. Especially who you're sleeping with."

Justine shoots Camille a look that could peel the acrylic right off those red nails.

"You got something to say to me?" Camille pokes one of those nails at Justine, whose face blazes with a similar color.

"I have more important things to worry about," Justine says. "Like my son."

"I don't need to be involved either," Meredith says. "When the firm is sold and the insurance money comes through, we can pay back the million each. I'll take my cut of whatever is left, if anything. You can leave me out of the rest."

I glance at Camille, who mirrors my outrage. "You think you can just strip your way into our firm and not lift a finger before cashing out?"

"You don't know anything about me or my relationship," Meredith says, finally dropping some of her cool. "As I understood it, my…Robin was the only partner who was bringing real money into this firm. And this mall deal was going to be huge."

I lean forward, a mile past tired of her attitude. "So you thought Robin was going to make you rich with this deal. Huh…"

"What are you implying?"

"You signed your papers. You knew Robin's share of the firm would be coming to you. Maybe you were sick of being a secret lesbian lover. Maybe one of those shady men at the Wolf Den offered to help get you rich. Who knows what he'd do for the lady grinding on his Johnson and Wales?"

"Like your son?" She smirks at me.

I cross my arms and smirk right back. "Like any guy there who knows how to get a job done."

"You've got a lot of nerve, throwing accusations around."

"Oh, accusations, huh?" I say, not able to stop myself. "You learn that word for the SAT to stripper school? Or the scissor sister academy?"

"Screw you, Krystle. Robin took care of me because she loved me. We were happy and had a future planned. Trips to Paris. Shopping on Rodeo Drive. Fast cars and fun together. Sorry if that's not your relationship. Sorry if all you had was one Christmas party a year to look forward to."

"I helped Romeo build this firm for the past twenty years." I scoot forward in my seat. "You think you deserve as much as me after this mall deal goes through? Any of you think you do?"

"The only reason the firm still *exists* is because of my husband," Camille yells. "Peter was the one who brought in the clients shittin' in high cotton."

"What the hell does that mean?" I say, grossed out before I even know.

"It means the mall deal was gonna save our asses, sister."

Camille flips her hair over one shoulder. "The only reason we're gettin' anything is because of my husband bringing the property owner to the table and setting the firm up with Ellis Corp."

"Actually, *my husband*, Jack, was the one who brought in Ellis Corp. to begin with," Justine snaps. "He's worked with Martin for years."

"Robin had as much to do with it as any of them," Meredith says, getting closer to me. "Maybe even more. You're not getting my cut just because I have more important things to do with my time than pick out cannoli."

"You're gonna wish you only had cannoli to worry about," I shriek. "If we can't get the insurance companies to pay up, we're dead!"

Camille huffs. "But the mall deal—"

"Gag me with your *shittin' in high cotton*. We're up shit creek without a paddle!" I'm yelling, but I can't stop. "You heard my uncle Vin. The mall deal will take time to close, if it goes through at all. The mob wants its money by January first. We need assets. Refinance our houses. Fast. Whatever it takes!"

Camille shakes her head. "Take a chill pill, Krystle. There's plenty to worry about without going hysterical."

"Missed nail appointments?"

"Actually, those insurance creeps not paying out until they clear our names," Camille says.

Justine's hand holding the glass is trembling. "Worried they'll figure out your tears weren't for *your* husband?"

"Maybe they noticed you didn't even have any tears for yours," Camille says.

I can almost hear the snap inside Justine. She rears back with her quarter-full glass of champagne and throws it directly into Camille's face.

"You bitter bitch," Camille screams and wipes at the bubbles dripping down her face and onto her dress and fur. She looks to me for help. "Can you believe she did that?"

"Let's be honest. If you were screwing Romeo, I'd have given you the bottle across the face instead of the drink."

"Please!" Camile rolls her eyes. "There wasn't a snowball's chance in hell of that happening."

"On both sides, I assure you," I say. "But let's put the cards on the table. Were you boinking Jack?"

Camille sucks in a deep, shocked breath. "No, we were not *boinking*."

"You are such a liar!" Justine yells.

"Fine! You want the truth, Justine?" Camille grabs a tissue and dabs her face. Then she tosses off her fur coat. Her fake boobs heave as she leans into Justine's face. "We didn't boink. We made *love*. A lot. Everywhere. All the time. And it wasn't going to stop anytime soon. So when that plane went down, I lost my husband *and* the man I loved."

Justine is grinning like a maniac, and the crazy radiates from her eyes, causing us all to lean back.

"Easy, girl," Meredith murmurs. "She's not worth it."

"I know she's not," Justine says slowly. "That's why you were a dirty secret, Camille. Jack was using you. Then he was going to toss you out like the trash you are."

"That so?" Camille wipes droplets onto the carpet before she grabs the bottle and pours what's left into her glass. "He said he once thought you were a diamond, but you lost all your shine. We laughed about it. No sparkle. No heat. Just dull disappointment."

Justine gasps as if the words hit a nerve. She grabs Camille's refilled glass and throws it right in her face.

"Are you kidding me?" Camille screams, then rears back and slaps Justine across the face.

"Hey now," Meredith says as she reaches over to the bucket and gives wincing Justine a piece of ice for her red cheek. "You deserved that, Camille, and you know it."

"Oh, I did, did I?" Camille grabs Meredith's glass and tosses what's left at her.

Justine lunges toward Camille and rips the mourning veil straight off her face. "You were married! He was married! Does that mean nothing to you?"

Camille slaps her again, but Justine doesn't flinch as she lunges. She starts shaking Camille like a rag doll. I try to separate them but am quickly thrown back. "Are you going to do something?" I call to Meredith.

"Camille deserves it," Meredith yells. "And she's not the only one."

"Excuse me?"

"You're not the boss here, Krystle. Even if it's been decades and decades of getting your way."

"Oh, I'm getting my way." I jam my finger in her face. "You are not going to just shake your stripper ass around here to get whatever you want. I built this firm. It's for my sons."

Meredith laughs and takes out her earrings. "Then it's as good as gone anyway, with Rom driving what's left into the ground."

"I'll drive you into the ground, you twat!"

The car pulls over, but it barely registers as everything goes red. On some level, I know this isn't Meredith's fault. But on another level, I just don't care.

With a primal scream, I launch at Meredith. She's young and quick, damn her, and goes for the door, half rolling and crawling out onto the curb.

Justine is also yelling, and Camille is trying to escape. They tumble onto the curb as Meredith army-crawls out of the way.

"You're not going anywhere, stripper tits!" I scramble out toward Meredith and fall hard, hitting my shoulder on the frozen-over lawn.

Camille is screaming about Justine having a clump of her hair as I reach Meredith to shove her face into the dirt.

"Guess they're roughin' each other up so we don't gotta," says a man's voice above us.

We freeze in all our disheveled glory, gasping, scraped up, and smacked around. Not to mention a big clump of blond hair in Justine's hand. We look up at two big beefy guys with guns.

"Arti?" I say, shocked to see one of Sal's goons on my lawn. I try to keep up with everything happening: someone trying to break into Rom's Camaro in the driveway, a guy carrying my TV, another guy with an armful of my best furs, and another one putting our eight-track player in a van.

"Hi, Mrs. Romero," Arti says dully. "Sorry."

"You're sorry…for ransacking my house? Stealing my car?"

"No. Sorry for this." Arti steps on my hand with his heel.

The pain is sharp and I scream, but I know not to pull and make it worse. He reaches down and plucks my wedding ring off, then lifts his foot.

"Damn it," I hiss, curling my hand into my chest. "In the old days, they didn't hurt innocent women."

"Innocent?" says the goon next to him. "If some broad owes four million clams, they probably did something."

Camille pulls me toward her. "Let me see." She fumbles with my fingers that won't straighten. "You jerk. That ring's worthless anyway."

Arti frowns as if maybe she's trying to trick him.

I elbow her and make a face for her to *shut up*.

"That's the last of it," the guy with the furs yells. "No stacks of cash yet, that's for sure."

"You idiots," Camille says with a slur. "The cash burned up in the plane."

She blows a raspberry at me. We gotta get this girl some food.

"Even if it did blow up, it don't cancel what you owe," the other goon says and flashes oddly sharp-looking teeth to match his tiny beady eyes. "We'll get that four million. One way or the other. Sal wants it by the first of the month."

Justine grabs Meredith's arm. "We don't have anything. We can't sell our homes that fast, or—"

"We got orders to search here," Arti says in his monotone voice. "You gals will be gettin' your visits soon enough. Then we move on to plan B."

I am too scared to ask about plan B. Tears sting my eyes because my boys will be home any minute. I sit up, pulling my coat tight with my nonthrobbing hand. "How much longer are you going to be in my house, Arti? I don't want my boys to see."

The other guy gets in my face. "Boss says the money is here. It'll take as long as it takes. You keep slowing us down, your boys are walking *smack* into the same trouble as you. Your call, Mrs. Romero."

JUSTINE

I recognize the sedan in my rearview. The same black Chrysler Imperial was a couple of cars behind me on the interstate. Its driver must have taken my exit because the long hood is nosing through the crosswalk that I rumbled over moments before. The vehicle is traveling too fast for a residential neighborhood, whizzing past the row of clapboard homes previously in my passenger window.

My heartbeat speeds up, urging me to step on the gas. A glance at JJ steadies me. He sits in the back seat, the belt pressed against his neck, primed to choke him should I stop short. My father-in-law insisted on removing the booster so that both his wife and I could ride beside their grandson while he drove to Jack's funeral—the real one at Saint Sebastian's, not that monstrosity of a memorial service that Krystle planned for all the firm's mobster clients to pay their respects. For all I know, one of those *clients* killed my husband.

One of those clients is driving the Imperial on my tail.

I slow down before swinging left onto Broad Street, but I don't put on my blinker. Refusing to advertise the turn fails to confuse my stalker. The car follows suit, closing the gap between us. For the first time, I see the driver. Fair skin. Sunglasses. Horseshoe mustache. His receding hair is slicked back, a style that I once associated with stockbrokers but now consider an indicator of a very different vocation.

A traffic signal flips yellow several yards in front of me. Do I slow down or blow through the light?

I scan for oncoming cars. There aren't many vehicles on the road, though there are people. Some young men are hanging out beside a three-story brick building. Gold chains dangle over their leather jackets. Crimson Starter caps adorn their heads. Would they help?

This man in the Imperial is coming for me, the same way those mobsters came for Krystle three days earlier. Maybe the same way they came for our husbands. I haven't had a house call yet. This Sal guy could have decided that confronting me here was better. People disappear in neighborhoods like this more easily.

Red and blue lights suddenly flash from the dash of a brown Crown Victoria. A man emerges from the unmarked car. Though he's not in uniform, the way he stands as he confronts the young guys—his hands on his hips and fingers near the pockets of his wool peacoat—suggests he's law enforcement.

Before the traffic signal can change, I pull to the side of the road, put my car in park, and pray that the police officer's presence will spook my stalker.

The Imperial reduces speed as it approaches. Its driver turns his head. His glasses are off. Blue eyes glare beneath heavy brows. The plainclothes officer turns his attention from the young men to the slowing vehicle.

Seconds seemingly stretch into hours as I clench the steering wheel and silently pray for the car to move on. All the mob can get from me now is blood. Jack's million-dollar debt must have blown up on the plane. On Krystle's orders, I turned my house upside down and, not surprisingly, didn't find more than pocket change in the couch cushions. Krystle said the others reported similar stories after searching their own homes. The only money I have is tied up in our home's down payment. To make Sal's deadline, I'd need to list my place at a huge loss, which would surely end with me owing the bank money. And neither my folks nor Jack's parents have that kind of cash—not that either would give it to me if they did.

The light changes. Tires screech. The Imperial drives on.

My vision blurs. I blink at the car's ceiling, a desperate attempt to again plug the dam that has threatened to burst since hearing of Jack's death ten days ago. But I'm all out of emotional spackle. Fear has stolen my ability to focus on what's next. I used up the last of my anger throwing champagne in Camille's overdone face.

Her words wounded as only the truth can. Jack always said that I was a diamond in the rough: a beauty from the outer boroughs, made multifaceted by a lifetime of cuts. When Jack met me, I was at my showiest, flaunting my looks, my charm, and my performing chops in hopes of convincing some rocker or director to cast me in a music video and give me my "big break." The flaw in my strategy was that those guys didn't want a diamond; they wanted white rock and easy lays. They all acted like addicts, insisting on sampling *the goods* before making an investment. I wanted to sell my talent, not my body.

Jack used to say that he fell in love with all of me. Thanks to Camille, I know he fell out of love because I gave my all to my son. JJ made me forget my ambitions. From the moment I had him, all I wanted to do was provide the affection and stability that I'd longed for as a child. I became JJ's, and I lost Jack.

The tears come with a series of gasps, moans, and pleas to a silent God whom I've been told to trust this week. There is no one else to comfort me. My mother is in South Florida at my stepfather's parents' place with my thirteen-year-old half sister and my fifteen-year-old stepsister. She wanted to come to Jack's funeral—or so she said—but the tickets from New York to Miami were already so expensive, and she couldn't exactly leave her husband with two teenagers *plus* his elderly parents. Moreover, how many more holidays would they have with Bubbeh and Zaydeh? I understood, didn't I?

I understand. I'm alone in this. There's no one to help offset my million-dollar share of the firm's debt. No loved one will take me in once I'm destitute.

The closest person I have to a friend is Meredith, a woman I've known all of three days who was apparently the much-loved significant other of my deceased husband's similarly dead colleague. She was the only person willing to back me up in my first physical fight since grade school.

"Momma?" JJ calls from the back seat. His voice is squeaky. Uncertain. I'm scaring my son.

"Come on, honey." I keep my voice bright. "The library is right around the corner."

I catch JJ's doubtful expression. Even he can tell that I shouldn't be outside the house in this state, but I've already driven across the city. His Christmas was filled with presents from Jack's parents and grandiose tales about when his father was a boy. I wanted him to have a day of simply being a three-year-old without the burden of making adults happy with his willingness to listen to an endless story or play with some toy that his dad had once loved. I wanted us to make some more good memories—just in case.

"Come on. Maybe we'll see Denise and Robbie."

I wipe my face with my jacket sleeve and then open the door. Wind attacks my damp cheeks, adding a fresh sting to the yellow swath where Camille slapped me. Fighting her was my last-ditch effort to restrain my tears, to explode with anger rather than give way to despair and terror.

JJ unbuckles with too little effort. He's opening the door

before I can walk around to the other side. I imagine the Imperial driver materializing, grabbing my son around his torso.

"Don't get out of the car!"

"But I see her," JJ shouts back.

I don't understand what my son means until I'm in front of the open passenger door. Feet away, Raquel pushes a green and white umbrella stroller. Denise sits beneath the canopy, nearly swallowed by a red and black flannel blanket.

JJ beelines for the stroller. "Hi. It's me!"

I give Raquel a sheepish smile as I shut JJ's door. "Hi, Raquel. How is Robbie?"

Raquel grimaces. "He's been in and out of the hospital for different scans. Doctors think it might be neuroblastoma."

I'm not familiar with the disease. Whatever it is, it kills young children. Innocent children like my son. Like Denise.

I consider the child in the stroller, the cloudy eye beside her big, brown one, blinded by the illness necessitating the chemo, the bright-green hat covering what I know is a balding head. The world is too cruel. My husband is dead, likely murdered; his life insurance won't pay until it proves that I didn't kill him; the mob is threatening me for money I don't have; and the woman in front of me has it so much worse.

"I'm so sorry to hear that." My throat closes up on the last word. The tears return full force, dribbling down my cheeks and dangling off my chin. I feel JJ tense against me, unsure of whether I need a hug or for him to stand on his own.

"Maybe it will be something else."

Though I hear Raquel, I don't see her. My eyes are shut tight, trying in vain to control the waterworks.

"I'm sorry. It's—" My voice breaks a second time. I tilt my head back and exhale. Puffs of condensation advertise my sobs.

"My daddy is dead."

JJ's statement snaps me from my own sadness, forcing me back into mom mode.

"His plane fell out of the sky," he continues, echoing what I told him ten days earlier. "My dad loves me, but he not come back."

Raquel's jaw drops. She tilts her head to the side and stares, seeking confirmation that JJ is telling the truth and not repeating the plot of some awful animated movie.

"It happened before Christmas," I say.

She pats my arm. Even through my thick wool coat, I can feel the warmth of her touch. It makes me want to cry more. "That crash on the news? With the four lawyers?"

I retract my lips as I nod. They feel rough and cracked, sliced by the icy air. It can't be good to keep standing out here.

"My apartment's in this complex." Raquel points to the multistory housing development. "Do you want to come up for tea or coffee or something?"

———

Raquel talks as she leads the way. She's lived in Providence her whole life but has been in this development only since she had Denise. Her stay in "the projects" was supposed to be temporary. She'd had a cousin who could have hired her as a store manager, a considerable upgrade from serving Brown students cafeteria food. Unfortunately, her daughter grew ill, and she realized the extra cash couldn't compete with the university's healthcare plan.

As she chats, I scan for the Imperial driver. Neither the car nor the man seems to be anywhere nearby. The trees aren't thick enough to hide behind, only shivering saplings clinging to life from sidewalk cutouts. On the opposite side of the development is an empty dirt lot, perhaps the size of several football fields. Chain-link fencing surrounds the entire area. Just behind the barrier sit rows of excavators, their giant yellow claws hovering above the ground. Beyond that I can make out a sliver of sparkling Providence River.

Raquel notices my attention to the construction site. "This land was all owned by the Ponterelli family, you know. In the late '60s, Salvatore Ponterelli Senior donated part of it to the city, which then built all this Section 8 housing. His son just gave the rest of it away for a dollar so that someone could build a mall. He was here doing a big press conference about it a couple of weeks ago."

A metal sign is affixed to the fence. It's mostly a logo: a big E cut out of the shadow of high-rise buildings. Beside the main letter is the firm's full name: Ellis Corp.

My breath catches in my throat. This is the site Vince was

talking about, the one on which Jack mortgaged our entire financial future. Is this what my life is riding on? A dirt field?

Raquel resumes pushing the stroller. "It will bring jobs to the city. God knows folks around here need them. You know I've disliked Italians since Christopher Columbus, but Ponterelli's a damn saint, helping folks out, if you ask me." She stops. "Here we are."

Keys jangle. There is a screech of metal against metal as Raquel opens the massive security door. I put JJ down as we enter, letting him walk now that we're in the safety of a building. Ponterelli's Imperial driver couldn't get in here.

Still, I glance over my shoulder as we follow Raquel down a tight hallway that smells of cooking oils and allspice. She stops at apartment 1D and again fiddles with her keys. The new door opens, revealing a bright light and little else. She passes through with Denise, urging me to make myself at home.

Inside is warm, nearly hot. I remove JJ's jacket as I take in the surroundings. A maroon love seat faces two windows partially blocked by a knee-high entertainment center. I strain to see through the visible glass. Cars pass outside, but I don't spy the Imperial.

"In our house, the Christmas decorations stay up till after New Year's."

Raquel thinks I'm staring at her tree. It's squeezed between the table and the hutch, standing slightly taller than my son. Red baubles and snowflake cutouts decorate its branches. At the top, in place of the star, is a framed photo of Denise's smiling face.

"It's nice." I catch Denise's eye as I pull off my coat. "The angel at the top is very beautiful."

Raquel frees her daughter from multiple quilts and a jacket. "Nissie, why don't you show JJ your stuffed animals and cars while I get y'all some water?"

Raquel ducks into the kitchen. I follow, offering an extra pair of hands to deliver the drinks.

"Girl, I told you I serve food all day." She laughs. "A couple of waters is nothing."

She opens a cupboard full of dinner glasses. As she turns on the faucet, I notice that her fridge is decorated with fruit magnets. Someone, probably Denise, has arranged them in a heart shape.

"You're being so kind to let me come over on the spur of the moment like this. I don't want to be any trouble." *Or bring any trouble with me,* I think.

Raquel passes me the giant glasses. "Okay, fine. Give these to the kids then."

The liquid inside is foggy. My face must be twisted in some distrustful expression because Raquel's smile turns down at the corners.

"Newish construction but old pipes, according to the super. Lots of air gets in there. It settles."

"It's great. Thank you."

I find JJ and Denise back in the main room, along with a small army of stuffed dogs. Denise is explaining the relationships between all the animals. Some are cousins. Some are brothers. Some are friends the canines call cousins. JJ takes it all in, nodding along as he makes one puppy hop toward another.

I peer through the window at the street before handing them each a glass. Denise sips hers. My son downs his like he's been hiking the Sahara. His ears are flushed. I might have bundled him in too much clothing earlier. He has his father's Nordic genes. He probably doesn't get as chilly as I do.

JJ hands the glass back. "It's hot in here."

Raquel must hear him in the other room because she immediately starts explaining. "My apartment is closest to the boiler room, so it's always really warm in winter. Denise likes it that way. But I can open a window."

"No need." My son, I realize, may be as particular and spoiled as his mother. "I'll just grab him another drink."

When I reenter the kitchen, the kettle is on, and Raquel already has a water glass ready for me. I bring it out to JJ in the living room while my hostess extols the merits of tea over coffee. She switched last year after reading that too much caffeine can fry the nerves. Black tea is her favorite. But she's getting into green.

Raquel shares all this as she prepares our drinks, performing like an actor on the Home Shopping Club. I don't think she is trying to sell me on tea as much as she's trying to be distracting, filling the silence so that I won't feel the need to discuss my husband or his death or whatever else she's seen about the accident on the news.

"Studies say caffeine can lower the risk of some cancers though."

Raquel slips in the comment as we sip our Earl Greys. The liquid is warm. Sweet. It would be calming if I weren't on alert.

"So maybe I should go back to Folgers," Raquel continues.

My throat tightens. "How is Denise's prognosis?"

Raquel offers a brave smile. "We're fighting." She casts a hopeful look at her daughter. "We're going to kick cancer's butt, right?"

As Denise repeats the words, tears well in my eyes. They disappear as I catch the view out the window. A black Imperial has parked outside.

I try to convince myself that it might not be the same one as I thank Raquel and gather our coats. Imperials aren't uncommon. But as long as I'm not certain, I can't stay here. Raquel has enough struggles as it is.

"JJ should go down for a nap. He always sleeps in the car," I explain, shoving one of my son's gloved hands into his jacket.

"Your son is a very sweet boy. It's hard to have playdates sometimes when you have a…" She trails off, glancing back at her daughter. "People are afraid it's catching or something."

I assure my new friend that JJ and I would love to do this again. We exchange telephone numbers, and I suggest my house for a future playdate, even promising to pick them up. I don't explain that my offer is contingent on the mob *not* ransacking my home like they did Krystle's—or doing worse.

I refuse to allow JJ to walk as I scoop him in my arms and start toward the Mercedes. Despite me carrying him, we can't move fast enough. He's a solid kid at thirty-four pounds, and it's difficult to see around the large jacket hood covering his head. I strain my neck left, then right, desperate to confirm that the Imperial driver isn't waiting for us.

The street is silent as I walk. Only my footsteps crunch on the sidewalk salt as I round the corner to my parked car. I set JJ down by the passenger door. The guys from earlier are gone. Hopefully, my stalker left too. Maybe it was another kind of Chrysler that I saw outside the window.

"Aren't you Jack's wife?"

The voice isn't deep or threatening, more midtoned and gravely, like car tires running over a rough road. Still, I know who it is before I look up. I figure I'll see his horseshoe mustache draped beside a terse mouth. Already, I can feel the heat of his stare.

I grab for JJ's hand, but it's beyond my reach. The Imperial driver is standing almost between my son and me. Even a few feet away, he towers over me.

He steps forward, further cutting me off from my child. "I don't forget a face, especially not a face like yours."

The words could be flattery, but his tone is not complimentary. It's flat. Clinical.

"Not really black or white," he continues. "It's striking. Easy to spot."

He smiles, wide enough to flash his top teeth, like a dog baring its incisors.

I step toward my son, sliding through the narrow space that the stranger has left between him and the car.

"Have we met?" I deliberately play the ignorant spouse, buying time and hoping the cop will reappear.

"Not exactly. Why are you here?"

"What do you mean?"

"Why are you all the way out here?" His voice darkens, emphasizing that his question is not rhetorical.

"I read at the library sometimes."

"The library isn't around the corner."

"I met a friend at the library. We came to visit today."

"A friend. In the projects." He nods in a way that I've watched parents do when they can't understand what their kids are saying—or when they don't believe them. The man crouches, bringing his head level with my son's. "Is that right, JJ?"

He knows my kid's name. Worse, he knows my kid's nickname.

JJ reaches for me. "We saw Nissie and her mom."

The mobster straightens. In one swift move, I grab JJ's hand and pull him toward me. I drape both my arms around his chest, fashioning a protective vest of limbs. "What do you want?"

"Jack had something belonging to an associate of mine. I

need it back. Jack was a smart guy—he would have put this in a safe place. Where's safer than home with your family?"

The threat is not subtle. This man can make my home unsafe. He can hurt my family.

"My husband never brought work home. Whatever he had was lost on the plane."

"I don't think so." He looks down at JJ. "Maybe you can help me look, bud. It would be nice to have a man in the house again, right?"

"I'll look. Please, I'll look." My voice is high and loud, begging for attention. I need him focused on me, not my child. "Just tell me what I'm looking for. I'll get it. I just don't know what you want."

"I'm not sure that's true." The man checks up and down the street, considering his surroundings. When he again looks at me, the fire has left his eyes. What I see now is ice. Cold. Frozen. Dead. He licks his top lip. "The next time I come see you, you'll have what I need. Or I'll search myself. And you might not like the way I go looking for things."

CAMILLE

Martin Ellis is already seated at the bar at Hemenway's when I push through the heavy glass door. Of course he is. Nursing a martini and checking that fancy watch of his, wondering what's taking me so long. I've only been playing this game forever. I know all the tricks, and trick number one is to keep your date waiting.

Not that this is a date. This is business. We all have our marching orders, and now I'm here on a mall-sized mission. Funny how those bitches screeched and hollered at me for pursuing Jack, then in the same breath begged me to turn my feminine wiles on Martin. This is why I don't have girlfriends.

The bleached blond behind the hostess stand opens her mouth to greet me, but the maître d' silences her with a swift hand. "Mrs. Tavani, welcome. Please, allow me." He rushes over, and I shrug out of my fur, cradling it like a giant fox over an arm. "Will you be dining with us this evening?"

"Not tonight, I'm afraid. I'm just meeting someone for a quick drink. Business, not pleasure, as I'm sure you can imagine."

I say it with the appropriate amount of melancholy. Hemenway's has only been open for a few months, but already it's Providence's latest "it" spot, and Max here was pilfered from Capriccio across the river. He knows everybody in town, and he knows me from back when I was selling overpriced jewelry to married men who would occasionally take me there for dinner. Anyone who doesn't spy me bellying up to the bar themselves will hear about it soon enough.

He gives a solemn nod. "I can't imagine how devastating this time must be for you and Miss Kimberlee. You both have my sincerest condolences."

This guy has no idea. Peter and Jack were gone in one brutal boom, my husband and my lover both obliterated into dust, and now the mob is coming after me. Devastating? More like terrifying.

I thank him and head into the happy-hour crowd, a sea of men in dark suits. Pinstriped, double breasted, three pieced, and notched lapeled. Scattered clusters of big shots buying low and selling high in between chain-smoking Marlboros. They pause their negotiations to give me an appreciative leer as I pass, taking in my slinky blouse and sparkly skirt slit up to there, plus the highest, pointiest heels in my closet. These men may be dressed for business, but I am dressed to kill, stalking ever closer to my prey.

Martin stands, taking me in from head to toe. "I hope you don't take this the wrong way, Camille, but *wow*."

Any other day, any other circumstance, the compliment coupled with this man's Colgate smile might make me go tingly. But not today.

Focus, Camille. Keep your eye on the prize.

"Now why on earth would I take that the wrong way?"

"Because women these days, especially smart, capable women like you, don't like to be objectified."

I laugh. "Martin Ellis, are you calling me a feminist?"

"Well, I don't know. *Are* you?"

"Honey, I'm from the south. There are no feminists down there—or if there are, they'd never admit it out loud. It's like being a Democrat or a lesbian. Better just to keep those kinds of thoughts to yourself." I press a finger to my pursed and glossy lips.

The bartender appears with two vodka martinis, extra dirty. Peter's drink. The thought plays through my head, but I shove it away. This is no time for morbid thoughts, not with so much on the line. And besides, it's Peter's fault that I'm here in the first place. What the hell was he thinking, taking on a million-dollar debt to the mob? The *mob*. Good thing he's not here, because I'd strangle him.

I clink my glass against Martin's and take a long, grateful sip. The vodka hits my belly with a burst of welcome heat.

"So. How are you holding up?"

"I'm good." No, that's not right. I shake my head. "I'm okay.

To tell you the truth, it's been a really long, really crappy week. Do you know how much there is to do when a person dies? Planning the funeral. Cleaning out closets. Dealing with family and all the legalities. It's kind of exhausting, really."

"I'm sorry. On top of the grief and shock, it must be very difficult."

I wave a hand through the air. "It's fine. Well, it's not fine, but I will be. Eventually. I'm just glad to be out of the house, to be honest."

A place that without Peter and Kimberlee is too big, too quiet, and spooky. And every time I do hear a noise, I imagine it's those two mobsters coming to clean me out like they did Krystle, and then I wonder why they haven't yet. Regardless, that's why my best jewelry is hidden in a shoebox under the floorboards.

"And Peter's daughter? What's her name again?"

"Kimberlee, with two e's. She's a mess. It doesn't help that her mother is an even bigger one. Between you and me, that woman could use some counseling. Kimberlee has been staying with her since the crash, but I tell you what, this evil stepmother isn't looking so awful now, is she?"

Martin gives me another once-over, a slow, admiring eyeful from top to toe. "I don't think you look awful. In fact, I'm pretty sure you've never looked awful, *ever*, in all your life."

For the first time since the crash, I feel like the old me. A woman who seduces millionaires in bars, not the sudden widow running from the mob and a moody teenager who hates me almost as much as she needs me to parent her. I don't want to talk about money and the stupid mall. I want to sit here, downing martinis and basking in Martin's glow. My body goes warm, loose.

And so, apparently, does my tongue. "So speaking of lesbians…"

Martin sits up a little straighter. He wasn't expecting the change of subject, but his sly grin says that he welcomes it. I drain my glass, and he signals the bartender for a refill.

"Okay, so maybe *I* was the one speaking of lesbians, but that's because—"

"You *are* one?" His expression is so boyishly hopeful that I laugh and swat him on the arm. He could at least *pretend* he's not fantasizing about a threesome with a grieving widow.

"No, silly, but Robin was. Did you know that? Robin Calder was a big ol' lesbo. She loved the ladies. One lady in particular."

"I am intrigued. Tell me more. And don't spare me any details."

"Look at you, getting all hot and bothered at the thought of some girl-on-girl action."

Martin lifts his hands, a guilty-as-charged gesture. "Doesn't every man?"

I smile, not because the role demands but because part of me is actually enjoying this. It occurs to me I might be a little drunk. That first martini went down in record time, and now here comes another one, sliding across the bar and into my hand. Nights with

Jack always started like this, with drinks and innuendo and flirtatious banter, a fun, drunken slow dance that always led toward an inevitable finale: mind-blowing sex somewhere naughty—an abandoned hallway, the back seat of a car, an elevator stopped between floors, the alarm wailing. I think of him, and I feel a woeful ache.

"What's wrong?"

I shake it off, waving an arm in a *silly me* gesture. "I'm fine. It's just…" I shove up a peppy smile, returning my focus to the reason I'm here. "Vince filled us in on the firm's involvement in the mall deal, and I could use a little advice. And I'm asking you, because of all the smart, successful businessmen I know, you were the first person who popped into my head."

Martin lights up with pleasure, and it really is that easy. Peter liked to be buttered up like this too. So did Jack. So does every man on the planet. Bombard him with compliments, lay them on thick, and the next thing you know, he's forking over his credit cards.

I fiddle with a button on my blouse. "Vince says the partners were investing a million dollars apiece. Four million total, and in return, they'd get a major stake in the deal."

Martin gives a low *hmm*, one I take as an affirmative. His gaze dips to my hand and lingers.

"Vince didn't tell us the details or what we get in return, but we've had a little encounter with some folks wondering where their money is, and these fellas work for Salvatore Ponterelli." I watch Martin's face at the name, but he doesn't so much as blink. "So it seems to me that four million was some kind of payment to grease the wheels of this mall deal somehow, and it was to be delivered under the table, real sneaky like… Am I warm?"

He smiles. "Sweetheart, you are nice and toasty."

Bull's-eye. So Martin is aware of the off-books deal with the mob. I'm not sure exactly what that means for the mall just yet, but he knows. I file it away to think about later.

"But as it turns out, the other ladies and I…" I glance at the scattered groups of people around us, but the bar is emptying out, spilling into the dining room, where the dinner rush is in full swing. Still, I lower my voice. "We have a little bitty problem. That four million dollars is gone, Martin. The money burned up in the plane."

His eyes narrow just a tad, but otherwise, his expression doesn't change. "That problem seems a great deal larger than little bitty."

"Well, it's little bitty because it's *temporary.* The partners' life insurance payout will cover it, but it'll be a little while before that money comes through, and what about in the meantime? No one wants this mall deal to fall apart. Isn't four million a drop in the bucket compared to the total costs? I'd imagine the investment is at least a hundred million."

"A few hundred, yes."

"So now what? What should we do now?"

The *we* is intentional, as is the hand I drape over his wrist. He doesn't move or pull away, and he holds my gaze and I hold his.

I know what we need—a floater loan from Ellis Development. He wants this deal as much as we want the mob off our backs. But even when neatly teed up, solutions work better when the man suggests them.

After an eternity, Martin sighs. "I'm not going to lie, Camille. When you called, I really was hoping it was because you found that report."

Not exactly an answer, but I'm careful to keep my expression cheery. I pull my hand away, reaching for my drink instead. "You never told me I was looking for a report. What kind of report?"

"One on Vista Corp. letterhead and embossed with a notary seal. I've not seen it yet, and I can't do a deal without the necessary due diligence. I need the original report before anything moves forward."

"Why not call up the folks at Vista Corp. then? I bet they can make you another one."

"If you can get a hold of them, have at it. As it is, I've left them messages all over town, and every day we're delayed is costing me money. I was really hoping to skip a few steps by coming to you."

"Well, it's not in Peter's office, that's for sure. I'll have you know, I tore that place apart, and nothing."

"What about Jack?"

He says it casually enough, while reaching down the bar for a bowl of peanuts, but the question still startles me. The alcohol has slowed me down some, ripped the poker face right off my expression. I'm shocked, and Martin knows it.

"What *about* Jack?"

"Come on, Camille. I'm not the only one who heard the rumors, and in my experience, where there's smoke, there's fire. And both Peter and Jack worked with Vista Corp., so…" He drops a handful of nuts in his mouth, chewing them thoroughly.

Was our affair really that obvious? I think of that champagne facial Justine gave me in the limo, the ridiculous catfight that landed us on Krystle's frozen lawn. I'm pretty sure she didn't know until after the crash.

But I'm not drunk enough to miss the bigger picture. This report is important, and it explains why he approached *me* at the church and not Justine. He probably figured two birds with one stone. He'd be crossing both partners off his list by asking me.

And that's when it hits me. That piece of Jack I have at home, the one tucked in the crawl space behind my bed? The one that doesn't belong to me but there's no way in hell I am ever giving back?

It's his briefcase.

He left it in my car, the night before he boarded a plane that blew him and three of his partners into a million pieces. If that report is anywhere, it'll be there, tucked between a pile of folders and that stack of Polaroids I gave him.

Of me.

Nude.

My smile is as naughty as it is charming. "If I could get my hands on that report, how much would it be worth to you?"

MEREDITH

With every dollar bill I pick up off the stage floor, I think of how many more I'll need to pay off the debt.

Robin's debt.

I should probably have taken a few more days off work. But strippers don't get bereavement leave. I was worried I'd lose my spot on the schedule, and I guess I really do need the fucking money.

I checked Robin's bank accounts after that disaster of a meeting at the law firm, and sure enough, the sum total left is less than I have tucked away in my underwear drawer. A part of me always knew she was too good to be true. The gifts, the promises she made me, the way she talked about our future together like it was a sure thing. I know better than to believe in sure things, but I decided to enjoy it while it lasted. If she left me one day, fine. I'd survive.

But I sure as hell never imagined she'd leave me like *this*. She screwed me, and then she screwed me over.

The club is dead tonight, which is the only reason I can get away with being this lifeless. I pivot clumsily around the pole, not even trying to keep time with the bouncy electronic beat of "Everything She Wants" by Wham!, and my hands keep slipping on the body lotion the last dancer left behind. My only audience is a scuzzy-looking dude who seems to have bellied up to the stage just so he'd have a place to set his beer and cheese fries.

It's always like this in the doldrums between Christmas and New Year's, when most of our regulars take time off to pretend to love their wives and girlfriends. The sad sacks with no one in their lives are the only customers left.

The DJ fades into a song that's a better match for my mood: "Every Breath You Take" by the Police. For all I know, Ponterelli does have his guys watching every move I make now. I'm used to the club's security protecting me, but he could just as soon set them on my tail.

Don't think about it. Just keep dancing. I strip out of my black string bikini top, grinding against the pole like I'm trying to get it off. The second song of my stage set over, I gather up my meager tips and stick them in my garter. You know it's a bad night if all the bills will fit in your garter. French Fry Guy is still sitting there, licking grease off his knobby fingers. He's not even looking at me anymore, but he's my only prospect at the moment. Time to turn on the charm.

I perch on the edge of the stage, parting my legs just enough to give him a sneak preview. This isn't my usual technique. Every girl at the club has her thing: there are the bubbly, girl-next-door types; the vampy seductresses; the barely alert, drugged-out bimbos. My thing has always been to stay aloof, so when a guy gets my attention, he feels like he's accomplished something. Like he's special. Robin told me once that my stripper persona reminded her of a cat she had as a little girl: always slinking around, rubbing against people's legs, but you never knew if it was going to purr or claw.

Some men like that. Robin sure did. This guy seems like he'll require a harder sell.

"Hey there, handsome," I say. "You here all by your lonesome tonight?"

He blinks at me—slow. That can't be his first beer. Probably not his second either. "You're lookin' lonesome too, baby girl."

I laugh, and even over the thumping beat of the Madonna song the DJ's spinning now, I can hear how hollow it sounds. "Well, I won't be lonesome if you keep me company."

He stands up, brushing a finger over my kneecap. But that's not why I want to punch him in the nose. It's the look on the guy's face, that slightly pitying expression, as he stares at me and slurs, "What's goin' on behind those sad eyes, darling?"

Darling. His voice echoes, rattling around my mind, repeating and distorting and blending with Robin's.

I love you, darling. I'll see you soon, darling.

The guy doesn't register my state of distress and distraction. He gets even closer, so I can smell the fake cheese and cheap beer on his breath. "So how 'bout we—"

"Absolutely not!"

My thoughts exactly, but not my voice. It's some middle-aged woman, shouting at a security guard over by the bar. I squint through the mood lighting to see what the trouble is.

Krystle Romero. What the hell is *she* doing here?

"Ma'am," the guard says, and Krystle visibly bristles. "Maybe if you came back at—"

"We will *not* come back later." Krystle gets up in the guy's face, jabbing her finger into his chest. He stands there, immovable as the brick wall behind him, staring down at her. Krystle's idiot son is there too, but he's making a smart decision for once and staying out of it.

"Excuse me a sec," I tell my potential patron. One of the other girls will have swooped in to claim him by the time I get back, but whatever; I couldn't squeeze much from him anyway.

I cross the floor toward Krystle and Rom. Frankie's behind the bar, polishing one of the always-cloudy glasses, and she tracks me with her eyes.

"Mrs. Romero," I say to get Krystle's attention. "I can't believe this was your plan."

I called Krystle earlier when Sal got to the office, per her pointed instructions. But I didn't think she was planning to confront him here of all places.

She takes in my work attire—or lack thereof—with equal forces of disgust and jealousy battling on her face. "Don't worry," she says. "*I'll* take care of this."

"You know this broad?" the security guy asks me.

"Unfortunately. You better watch out. She's stronger than she looks."

Krystle glares like she's considering grabbing me again. I'd like to see her try in this joint. She seems to think better of it, though, and turns her wrath on the guard again.

"That's right. I don't have time for this. I'm not leaving until I talk to Sal."

The security guy sighs. "Fine, come with me. But don't say I didn't warn you."

Krystle starts to follow him toward the back office but turns to get in my face. "You better go through your girlfriend's house tonight and report back to me right away. You're the only one who hasn't."

"You got it, Napoleon," I say as she starts to follow the security guy again.

Rom snorts and scurries after her, but the guard puts his hand up. "Just your ma, Junior. You wait here."

"I'll be right back," Krystle tells Rom. "Don't do anything I wouldn't do."

I turn to Rom as soon as she's out of earshot. "You brought your mommy to the strip club? Really?"

"It wasn't my idea, believe me." Rom looks as slimy as ever, but his eyes are a little clearer than usual—he's sober, I realize. Maybe the first time I've ever seen him in an unaltered state. I guess owing a million to the mob will do that to you.

Rom sweeps his eyes around the club, upper lip curling into a sneer. "I can't believe Robin let you keep working in this joint. No girl of mine would ever—"

"Robin didn't *let* me do anything. And when was the last time you had a girl you didn't have to pay in advance, Romeo?"

He gives me a nasty smile. "How about a dance while I wait?"

"Sorry, I don't take pocket change."

He's wearing the same suit he had on the day of the funeral—maybe Ponterelli's goons ransacked his bachelor pad too. The wrinkles in the black fabric make it look even shoddier than usual. Rom likes to pretend he's a high roller, but I've spent enough time with my bare skin touching his pants to know just how cheap they are.

I can't afford to be too smug though. It's only a matter of time before they bust into Robin's town house too. I could sell the place, I suppose. That might get me a little closer to paying off Ponterelli. But no matter how pissed I am at Robin right now, no matter how betrayed I feel, I'm not ready to let her go.

Selling the house would mean losing the last place I ever saw her. The bedroom where she made me scream her name until my throat was raw, the kitchen where she cooked me pancakes from scratch wearing an undone tie and nothing else, patterned silk falling between her perfect breasts. I don't know how much the house is worth, but those memories? They're priceless.

"Hey, Tina. This guy bothering you?"

It's not one of the guards coming to my aid this time but Frankie. She's tiny—a couple of inches shorter than me even when I'm not in my platform heels—but there's something intimidating about her. You can tell she knows how to throw down.

"He's trying," I say. "But I'm fine, thanks."

Rom turns his leer on Frankie. "This another one of your close, personal friends, Meredith?"

If Frankie's surprised that this jagoff knows my real name, she doesn't show it. Without even blinking, she loops her arm around my waist and pulls me against her side. I'd smack the shit out of a guy for this, but when Frankie does it, it feels good. My first bit of physical contact since Robin died, unless you count Krystle smashing my face into the dirt outside her tacky-ass mansion.

"Wouldn't you like to know?" Frankie says.

She goes up on her tiptoes and kisses me—on the jaw, leaving a lipstick print like she did on that cocktail glass. I know she's just doing this to fuck with Rom, but it sends a shiver down my spine all the same. And now all the eyes in the place are staring our way, probably wondering what we'd charge for a private show.

The security guy who left with Krystle reappears from the back and waves Rom over. "Guess I'm invited after all," he says, not sounding happy about it.

"Good luck," I call after Rom. "Hope Sal's in a forgiving mood tonight, *Junior*."

"He knows your name," Frankie says after Rom disappears behind the swinging black door. "Are you two—"

"*No*. Definitely not. He's Robin's boss's son. That woman with him, that's one of the other widows. Krystle."

"And she came here to meet with Mr. Ponterelli? About what?"

"This deal the firm was putting together. It's all a mess, with the partners dying suddenly and—" I shake my head. "Sorry. You don't want to hear all this boring estate crap. I should be getting back to work anyhow."

"How well do you know him?" Frankie asks.

"Who? Rom?"

"Mr. Ponterelli. You called him 'Sal.'"

"He has all the dancers call him Sal." I shrug. "Says it makes the club feel more like a family."

"So you're not going to his New Year's Eve party tomorrow night?"

Fuck. With everything going on, I'd completely forgotten about that. I forgot tomorrow night even *was* New Year's Eve. I'm sure one of the other girls would be happy to cover for me. But the money… More than ever, I could really use that kind of money.

"I'm not sure yet," I tell Frankie. "Why?"

"I was wondering if they needed any more bartenders. From what I've heard, Mr. Ponterelli knows all of Providence's biggest tippers. But you have to be personally invited, right?"

"Yeah, something like that. Look, I don't know if it's really your scene. Sal's parties can get pretty wild."

Frankie grins. "So you *have* been to one before."

More than one. Salvatore Ponterelli throws these parties at his mansion every month. I worked all twelve last year, and those dozen nights made up over half my annual income. Not that I told the IRS that—or Robin, for that matter. She had some reservations about my work, but if she'd found out what I did at those parties…well, let's just say she wouldn't have been happy. Maybe it's for the best that she died not knowing.

"I was working," I say. "Sal likes having some of us girls on hand, as entertainment."

"Stripping?" Frankie asks.

"Sure. Hey, listen, I should be getting—"

"Back to work, yeah, I know. Let me know if you get thirsty."

My heart pounds as I watch her head back toward the bar. I do *not* need this right now. A rebound would be one thing, but with a coworker? I'm smarter than that. I have to be.

I make a beeline for one of the guys who was staring extra hard at us and give him my most lucrative smile. "Want a dance, baby?"

"Can your friend join us?" he asks.

"She's busy." I straddle him and toss my hair so he gets a whiff of the honey-sweet perfume I sprayed into the strands. "But I'm all yours."

As I writhe against him and he rains wrinkled bills on the

floor around us, I'm miles away. But finally, my mind's on something other than Robin.

Sal's parties—they're legendary. Anything goes, and everyone sets their own boundaries. But boundaries have a way of shifting when there's that much cash involved. When you already take your clothes off and dry hump strangers for a shower of Washingtons, what might you be willing to do when they're tossing Franklins instead? That's what I ask myself every time I set foot inside the Ponterelli mansion.

And every time I walk out the door, I promise myself: that was the last time.

KRYSTLE

"You know, I never liked you since you banged my older sister," I say to Sal Ponterelli in a decently decorated office at the back of his strip club.

"Which sister?"

"All of 'em, probably. They always had a thing for guys like you."

"Like me?" Sal leans back at his big desk and puts his hands behind his head. He hasn't given that amused smirk a break since I marched in the door. "Handsome as the devil, you mean?"

"No," I say flatly.

I stick out my chest through the unbuttoned fur coat that I managed to keep in the ransack. I wore my lowest-cut dress that's a little off the shoulder. It's black, of course, and I hoped the white polka dots and big belt would shrink me in all the right places.

Romeo loved this outfit, and for a moment, I waver. His loss is always on the edge of my mind, ready to slice right down to my heart. Then just as quickly, I'm mad, standing here cleaning up his mess.

I focus back on Sal, which is no hardship. He *is* handsome as the devil, with that slicked-back black hair and light-brown eyes that don't miss a thing. And always with the easy smile.

My dad worked for his dad, who ran most of the organized crime on the Hill for decades. Since Mr. Ponterelli Senior's passing, rest in peace, Sal, as his only son, has kept things going. But he cares a bit more about his image than his old man did. Good suits, thousand-watt smile, and big muscular shoulders that seem less about dumping bodies than filling out suits for photo ops and ogling. He's on the local news every Thanksgiving, handing out pumpkin ravioli and turkeys to families in the projects.

I toss my poofy red hair, wishing it was glossy like Meredith's or blond like Camille's or curly like Justine's. "Can we get back to why I'm here?"

"You gonna take off your coat?" he says, as if my next stop is toward the pole.

"You gonna ask to take it?"

He gives me a big laugh for that one. "May I take your coat, *Mrs. Romero*?"

I get that annoying ripple in my gut at the way he says my name. It happened when we were young, though he'd call me Krissie, and I'd nearly hit the roof. Sal would laugh his tight ass off as he left to seduce one of my sisters. I told myself I didn't care. I'd take smart and dumpy over pretty and stuck on the Hill all day long.

Sal slowly takes my coat, brushing his warm fingers along my neck and shoulders. I know he's not really flirting. I've heard "at least she's smart" and "thank God she found Romeo" enough times to know the score.

Handsome guys like Sal think they're saints for flirting with the ugly sister.

"Enough with this. I'm in mourning."

He shakes his head slowly as he hangs up my coat. "Romeo never deserved you. Smart and ambitious, even a dunce like him could be successful with you bossing him around. I never figured why you married him."

"I doubt you gave it much thought until this second. I'm not smart, Sal. Otherwise, I wouldn't be at your tit club begging for more time."

He cracks his neck to one side. "With this much money… my hands are tied."

"I've talked to every bank," I say, only recounting a small part of the humiliations of the past few days since the memorial. Abruptly ended phone calls, if they were ever returned at all. Doors literally slammed in my face. "Each of us are wiped out with this payment to you. We've gone through every piece of paper looking for assets. I can't get cash advances or a new mortgage. Even if I could, that's not a dent. We are maxed out and underwater."

"You don't understand. You're not just leaving me high and dry," Sal returns, staring down to tower over me. "This money is already late. Real, real, late."

"What?" I wrinkle my nose. I'd kill Romeo if he wasn't already dead.

"I gave you until New Year's Eve as a personal favor. You can't imagine what the guys are saying about that gift." He takes my chin lightly into his hand to tip my head back, almost like a kiss, but it feels like a punch. "Four million tomorrow night, or things go a way neither of us wants. You know how this works, honey."

I'm not getting anywhere. "Speaking of how things work, where's the code to leave women and children out of it? On the day of Romeo's memorial, you raid my place and take my wedding ring."

"Got your attention."

That's an understatement. "Why? You think I'm not scared? I'm fucking terrified."

"That's 'cause you are smart. You should be terrified of me."

I hold up my hand. "Well, Arti didn't have to almost break my finger to prove it."

He cocks his head to the side and takes my injured fingers into his. He runs his thumb over the bruised knuckle. His jawbones click like a snake's rattle. "Arti did this?"

"Yeah. New shoes, I think. Heel really dug in."

Sal traces his thumb along an injured finger. "I'll make him eat those damn shoes."

"Thank you." I find the courage to ask softly, "Does that mean you'll give me an extension? Please, I'm begging you."

"On your knees?"

I stare hard at him to figure out how serious he is. *Would I?* A flush starts up my neck, and I press my hand on my waist where my belt is now squeezing.

"Jesus, Mom, are you going to let this guy speak to you like that?" Rom yells from the corner.

"The adults are talking," I shout, not even turning around. "You had to bring him in here?" I say to Sal.

"Romeo Junior is part of your solution." Sal strides over to the door and bangs it once, loudly. Arti, that bigfooted jerk, slinks inside. "First, let's fix this. Arti. Apologize. And give Mrs. Romero your shoe."

I start to protest, but Arti quickly does as he's told, and I'm clutching the shoe that nearly snapped off my finger.

"I'm sorry, Mrs. Romero," Arti says in that deep Eeyore voice.

"Put your hand on the desk," Sal says to him, that amusement back in his eyes. "Your move, Mrs. Romero."

I'm not missing this opportunity, so I get in Arti's face. "Your mother would be ashamed of you, God rest her soul. I'm a widow with three boys to take care of, and you cleaned me out of everything. What the hell are you going to do with a fondue set?" Before he can answer, I slam the shoe down on his fingers.

He barely reacts but dully says, "Ow."

I see red again, a whole tunnel of it, and I rear back and smack that shoe right across his big dumb face. His lip is bleeding. "I hope you burn your tongue off on the cheese."

Sal doubles over laughing, and strangely, for the first time since that awful Christmas party ten days ago, I feel something other than fear or pain or absolute rage.

I laugh too. "Sorry, Arti." I hand him a tissue from the desk. "It's been a tough one."

"No sweat, Mrs. Romero." He wipes his face and then takes the shoe from me, quickly slipping it back on. He turns to Sal. "You want me to put him in the trunk now, boss?"

"That'd be great," Sal says, the big smile resting on his face.

My mom-o-meter is ringing at five-alarm fire. "What the hell is he talking about? Put who in the trunk?"

Sal straightens his cuffs. "You've got twenty-four hours to *find* my money."

"I told you, I called the bank and—"

"It's not in the bank. It's not in your house. We checked. And it wasn't on that plane. Romeo was dumb, rest in peace, but not dumb enough to take my money out of state. Someone has it. My guess is someone in this room."

"The hell I do," yells Rom and starts to leave. "Ma, let's get out of here."

Sal shoots Arti a hard look, and he makes it to the door before Rom, despite being twice his size. "You're coming with me, kid. Easy or hard, don't make no difference to Arti."

"Take him where? You're not putting my baby in a trunk!"

"He deserves a lot worse than that." Sal tips his head at Arti, who grabs Rom and hauls him out the door.

"Wait, stop!" I scream, running after Arti. "Damn it, come back here!"

The music hits me in a wave. I run right into a table, spilling several drinks. The stage lights are bright and throwing off my vision.

"Arti! Rom!" I scream and continue to rush and crash and then rush again.

"Krystle, wait," I hear Sal call from behind me, but I'm already halfway across the big room.

As the opening notes of "Roxanne" by the Police begin, I nearly motorboat Meredith's perfect boobs as she leaps in my way. "Watch out," I yell, trying to get around her.

"What the hell is going on?" she shouts.

"Arti took Rom out the back."

"What did he do now?"

"They think *we* hid the money." I grab her arm. "Come on. Arti!" I yell again, but he's way ahead of us now. We have to dodge a couple other half-naked girls, and I spill a drink being held by a very concerned bartender.

"What's going on?" she asks.

"I'll be right back!" Meredith yells as I pull her harder.

"Take my coat!" The bartender's heels click behind us.

Sal yells for her to get back behind the bar, but no one slows down as we rush toward a big metal door just slamming shut with an EXIT sign glowing red.

"This way," I scream, dragging us there.

We burst through the door and gasp as we're blasted with cold air.

"Arti!" I watch as he slams the trunk of a Cadillac, and I barely see a flash of Rom's black hair. "You no-good son of a bitch!"

I start to run, but someone grabs me around my waist, pulling me back. I hit at the big muscular arm, but it only squeezes tighter, dragging me toward the door.

I wrestle away. "Let go, Sal!"

He obeys, and I try to catch my breath. Meredith is doing the same and is wrapped in a coat with the bartender's arm around her. They both have some sympathy in their eyes, even though I know they probably think Rom deserves it. Hell, Rom's no angel, not even in his mother's eyes, but he shouldn't be punished like this for his father's mess.

Sal throws my coat around my shoulders. "Inside."

Meredith pauses a moment as if she wants to stay and help. I nod for her to get inside, and she and the bartender quickly leave.

"You too," Sal says once we're alone.

I pull back from his grip, not caring about the cold or anything except my Rom. "What the hell are you doing to do him?" I slam my fist into his big chest. "He just lost his father! Have some compassion!"

Sal closes the top buttons of my fur and doesn't let go, keeping us almost nose to nose. "You need to listen, Mrs. Romero. You had extra time on something that's considerably overdue. That is unheard of from me. Compassion doesn't even begin to scratch it."

I look up at him, his hot breath streaming into the night air like a bull. "If I find that money, I'll get Rom back? Unharmed?"

"He'll be alive," Sal says.

I nod, but everything inside me is screaming. I know Rom's a dumbass, but he's my dumbass, and I'd do anything for him. I couldn't begin to guess why he'd lie about the money being on the plane, and just what, keep it?

Well...I could guess a few reasons.

Still, he'd never do it. Maybe Romeo or one of the other partners hid it. "I don't know where I'm going to look..." I stop when my voice cracks, and I suck in a deep breath of cold air and remind myself who I am. What I've done to get here. This won't stop me. I start to run through places I need to check out. "You mind if I take Meredith? I've got a lot of ground to cover."

"Whatever it takes."

"Thanks," I say, meaning it. Sal is doing me a favor. Four million is serious money. You don't need to be from the Hill to know that much. And I know a lot more. "Where do I bring the cash when we find it?"

"Come by my place," he says. "Big New Year's Eve party. But you gotta dress the part, Mrs. Romero, or we can't let you in."

I get even closer. "You will if I have four million dollars."

He makes a pleased little sound in his throat. "I'd almost pay all that to see what you wear to get past the door."

"I can handle it."

"I hope so," he says, something near sadness on his face. "Be a real tragedy for your boys to lose both parents."

My mouth falls open. I try to take a step back, but he's still holding me by my coat. "You couldn't," I whisper. "You wouldn't."

"I could and I would. I hate making orphans, but not as much as I hate having four million dollars stolen from me. And if Rom didn't do it alone, everyone will pay. No matter how cute the thief."

JUSTINE

New Year's Eve is never a night to work late, but the bosses being dead has granted everyone permission to leave early. I don't hear a single voice as I guide JJ past the empty reception area and through row after row of vacant cubicles. Three dozen lawyers usually work here. Yet no associates man their desks. The lights are all off. Although I can't see much, I don't turn them on. One of Ponterelli's men could be hunting here. The space doesn't feel empty so much as still. It reminds me of a held breath. I fear the explosion of its release.

"Is Daddy here?" JJ whispers.

His big eyes beg me to contradict myself, to confess that Jack never died and has been tucked away at work, waiting for me to finish crying and cursing while digging through every drawer, closet, and cabinet for a scrap of something—anything—that might be owed to the mob.

I crouch beside him. "Honey, Daddy isn't on this earth any-more." I refuse to say *in heaven*—not exactly because I don't believe in some sort of afterlife but because I resent the idea of Jack rising up to leave us in this hell of his creation. "We're here to look for something important, remember?"

JJ grips my hand as I resume our march through the fifteenth floor. The firm commands the entire space, and my husband had one of the four corner offices, albeit on the side sans Providence River. I lead JJ there by memory, navigating via the light creeping through closed blinds.

Jack's door is ajar. Pushing it back reveals a ludicrously clean desk that couldn't possibly belong to any lawyer, let alone my husband. Juris Doctors are not known for their organization. The typical attorney's desk is topped with manila folders, lined note-books, Post-it-Note tagged loose-leaf, and highlighted papers. Jack was the type to wallpaper flat surfaces with research, to construct skyscraper cities of file folders. Yet all that is left on his tabletop is an IBM PC and two photo frames, each lying facedown.

The computer is useless to me. Not only do I not under-stand how it works, but I have to assume that whatever Ponterelli wants is not on it; otherwise, it would be gone along with the rest of Jack's files. That mobster made clear that what I'm looking for is tangible and portable, something my husband could have brought home.

I pick up the nearest picture frame. Inside is a wedding shot.

When we married, I was four months pregnant, though my pose covers any baby bulge. I lean into Jack, a mermaid atop a wave of lace and silk. He kisses my cheek. We were happy once, weren't we?

The other frame is empty. It contained a photo of Jack, JJ, and me in front of the new house. Whoever cleaned off my husband's desk took a souvenir. Something to remember me by.

I expect that the same person scavenged Jack's drawers, but I attack them anyway. Not a single folder hangs from the metal tracks in the file cabinet. However, the pencil drawer seems promising. It's stuck.

Jostling it back and forth loosens the jam. After the fourth shake, the drawer cracks open. I slip my hand inside and claw for whatever is gumming up the works. My pinky snags fabric.

A hard pull releases it. My prize falls into my palm, silken and unsubstantial. Or maybe not. I drop it on the table.

It's a *thong*. A strip of satin meant to sit in the crack of someone's ass. No doubt who this belongs to. It's even her color—bright red.

"What's that?" JJ whispers.

"Garbage."

JJ points to a wastepaper basket beneath Jack's desk. "There's the—"

The office lights flicker on. I point beneath the table and mouth one word to JJ: *hide*.

He doesn't need to be told twice. As he dives under the desk,

I scan for a weapon: a letter opener or a box cutter, something sharp that I can stab into one of mustache man's steel-blue irises. Jack's bookcase has been emptied, but something on the floor beside it catches my eye. It's large. Reflective. Round. Shades of amber and brown swirl inside, recalling scotch in a glass.

I scoop up the object. It's about as heavy as a crystal tumbler. In my hands, it won't do much damage. But it's all I've got.

I curl my fingers around the paperweight like it's a hand grenade and hunker down behind the door. Adrenaline heightens my senses. At this moment, I am not Justine: waifish ex-model and mother. I am a beast capable of striking, scratching, and smashing whoever dares enter.

Low voices become audible. The tones are high and agitated. Female. Familiar?

"Check every crevice! Closets. Cabinets. Under the freaking carpet."

"That kind of cash takes up space. We're talking about a big bag."

"Or a key for a safety deposit box."

I peer around the doorjamb. Krystle half runs, half stumbles through the alleys between cubicles, headed to Romeo's office on the opposite side of the hall. She wears heels and a black dress with big white polka dots like evenly spaced bullet holes. A broad belt cinches her waist. Her outfit is the antithesis of what's beneath my coat. Krystle looks like she's come from somewhere important.

She flings back the door to Romeo's office and screams. "*Porca troia!*"

I don't understand Italian, but I can tell by her tone that whatever was said is not the kind of thing to translate around kids. JJ, fortunately, is still under the desk, which is where he should stay until I figure out what's happening. I take a tentative step into the main room and close the door behind me.

"They stole it all. There's nothing left. Nothing of my Romeo. *Dio, ti prego. Per favore* help me. I'm going to kill Salvatore Ponterelli."

Drawers open and close, punctuating her statements. When Krystle reemerges in the main room, she turns to me. "What are you doing here?"

JJ doesn't need to hear the full answer. I cross the room, explaining as I go. "Some mobster threatened me. He said Jack had something belonging to an associate of his."

"No shit. His share of the four million. Sal insists it didn't blow up on the plane."

"It can't only be the money. He said I *personally* needed to find what he wants, or else he'll come after me." I lower my voice. "He'll come after JJ."

Krystle doesn't seem to be listening. She's striding toward the exit. I follow her, easily keeping pace thanks to my sneakers.

"I've torn apart the whole house, but there's nothing," I explain. "Jack's office has been cleared out. You know these guys. I thought you would be talking to them, getting them to understand our situation. Can't you tell them we don't have what they want? Tell them—"

"Connections are useless when you're talking about four million dollars."

She picks up pace like she has no intention of helping me. For all I know, she's going to march out of this office and disappear. I grab her arm. "Krystle, please. They'll come for my son!"

"They already have mine!"

"What?"

"Sal took Rom. Threw him in the trunk of a car. If anything happens to him…"

For the first time, I truly see Krystle's emotion. It's visible in the red laced through her eyes, the stiffness of her body. When that mobster stepped on her hand, she wasn't scared; she was indignant, insulted, furious. That anger is gone now.

Krystle yanks at her dress lapels. "Look. They want their money. We have to find it and give it to them. They'll back off once we do."

"Well, there's nothing in here."

We both turn toward the new voice. Meredith stands outside the room closest to the firm's entrance. It's the least significant of the corner offices, the kind given to a new partner without her own client base. The one with the most to prove.

"It's been completely stripped. Robin used to keep a photo of me in one of her drawers. They even got that."

A door slams. We all duck as if the sound were a gunshot.

The exit is so close. Still, I can't escape. My son is beneath his father's desk.

"There's nothin' in Peter's office either. Anything in Jack's?" Camille's unmistakable voice comes from the opposite corner. Since her husband died, she's dropped the *g* and the Boston Brahmin accent. Her pronunciation is all deep-fried now.

I want to tell her it's none of her business. Instead, I answer honestly. "Just trash."

Krystle's nose flares. "Okay. Okay. Let's think." She puts her fingers to her temples, a psychic channeling a vision. "It's not at our homes, and it's not in their offices. They'd be crazy to leave four million out on the floor with all the associates, so we can forget that. If Vince had it, he would have given it to us."

"We can't be sure." Camille says it, but I'm thinking the same thing.

"He's family," Krystle snaps. "I'm his niece, and he's Rom's goddamn godfather. That means something to people like us."

"Does it?" Meredith places her hands on her hips and gazes up at the tile ceiling. "Because Sal's still coming, even though Rom swears that money blew up on the plane."

"Rom." Krystle whispers the name, half curse, half prayer. "Jesus Christ."

Her gaze zeros in on the room closest to her husband's former domain. Rom's office is almost as big as his father's. A glance at Robin's space confirms that her "corner" was significantly smaller and on the side without river views. The firm might have had a female partner, but it certainly hadn't been treating her like an equal.

Krystle's legs follow where her eyes have already gone. We all hustle behind her, soldiers on the same mission: Find the money. Give it to the gangsters. Get home—alive.

The absurdity of what I'm doing strikes me as we walk. "I still don't understand how Jack ended up owing the mob anything. I know Ellis Corp. was Jack's client, but he always handled legitimate corporate business: real estate contracts and lease agreements."

Camille shoots me some side-eye like I've missed the obvious. "I was surprised at first too, but now that we've been digging into it, it's pretty clear that the mob controls construction in Providence. The money was probably an initial investment to get things started with this mall project. All the big unions here—garbage, construction, deliveries—answer to Sal. Ellis Corp. probably needed him to get folks going on the build."

"But Ellis Corp. would pay all those guys on the books," Meredith pipes up. "Building is its business. I'm sure they have their own construction guys on the payroll, and they would want to document all payments to subcontractors for tax reasons. With a huge development like a mall, the government is going to be looking over your shoulder. All the paperwork would need to be in order."

Krystle snorts. I expect the sound to be sarcastic, but she actually looks impressed. "I guess you passed your business class in stripper school."

"They needed it for the land then," Camille says, annoyed to have her theory discredited by the likes of Meredith, especially when she was trying to make me feel stupid.

"It can't be the land," I counter. "Ponterelli owned it. He gave it away for a dollar so that the mall could be built and bring jobs to town."

Krystle makes the same nasal exhale. This time, the sound is definitely sarcastic. "Oh, please. Where'd you hear that? Salvatore Ponterelli is no philanthropist."

"I have a friend who lives by the construction site, and she told me all about it. She says there was a big press conference."

"I remember something about that on the news," Meredith says.

"He must have gotten a ton of great publicity," I add. "Everyone on the South Side thinks he's a man of the people."

Krystle scoffs. "Sal is always working some angle."

Meredith pauses. Her eyes glitter, more green than gray now. The proverbial light bulb has turned on behind them. "That's what this is! It's an off-the-books payment for the land. Sal wanted to *appear* to give away the property for good PR and probably a big tax write-off. But of course, he wants the money for the actual value. The law firm handing over the cash from the partners' personal assets eliminates any evidence of a transaction between Ellis Corp. and the mob."

"But then how was the firm supposed to explain the missing four million dollars?" Camille folds her arms over her chest.

"Small businesses can certainly launder money." Meredith speaks with the confidence of an independent contractor who probably doesn't report all her cash payments. "Believe me. The firm could've said they were returning an unused retainer or something. The government doesn't look that hard as long as you're not writing it off as a loss and you're still paying your taxes. I'm sure Ellis Corp. would have turned around and given them the four million right away and a lot more for undetermined legal fees."

Camille blinks as though Meredith has slapped her. "That jerk had me thinking that *he* was doing *me* a favor."

"Who?" Krystle asks.

"Martin Ellis," she hisses. "I met with him to ask for a loan, as promised, just until the insurance settles. The whole time, that bastard knew he *owed* us this money."

Krystle looks over her shoulder, her hand on the doorknob to Rom's office. "Is he going to help us?"

"I'm working on it." Camille taps a red nail against her painted lips. "He wanted me to look around for a report. I think Martin's concerned the mob is trying to get one over on him by not doing due diligence or something."

For a moment, I wonder whether Ponterelli's thug who's after me is seeking the same thing that Ellis wants from Camille— albeit for a different purpose. The mob must have taken all our spouses' files to ensure that their attorney-client privilege extended through death. Something in them probably had the potential to derail Ponterelli's under-the-table property sale to Ellis Corp.

Before I can voice my suspicion, Krystle opens the door to Rom's office and ushers us inside. Her urgency reminds me that the four million dollars due tomorrow has to be our top priority. Whatever documents the firm had on the mob won't matter as long as we pay Ponterelli and don't damage his interest in this mall. Ellis Corp. getting a raw deal doesn't compare to my son's life.

As with the other offices, barely anything is inside Rom's— though his space doesn't appear as thoroughly cleaned out. A long-handled umbrella leans in a corner stand. On Rom's desk is an upright eight-by-ten of him smirking in a Brown University cap and gown. A plastic-wrapped stack of manila folders lies beside the frame as well as several magazines. There's an open *Playboy* of bare-breasted Madonna and a worn copy of the *GQ* with Richard Gere smoking on the cover. The lead article: "Six High-Powered Ways to Generate a More Forceful Image."

"It doesn't look like they've been through here," Krystle says, opening the top drawer of her son's desk. "There's a pack of Barclays and a little bag of confidence booster. Somebody would have nabbed that."

Over Krystle's shoulder, I can make out a micro-sized Ziploc with the remnants of white powder. Behind me, Meredith mumbles, "Of course there is."

If she hears her, Krystle doesn't engage. She drops to her

knees and yanks the bottom drawer. It doesn't budge. Krystle tries a second time before standing and then slamming a pointy-toed pump into the furniture.

"Let me have a crack at it." Camille crouches down to the lower cabinet. Before pulling the handle, she reaches for one of the bobby pins tucking her blond waves behind her ear. She bends it ninety degrees and then scrapes a crimson nail against the end, picking off the rubber. She slips it in the drawer lock, jiggles it, and then withdraws the bent pin.

Krystle throws up her hands. "That never works."

"I'm preparing my tools. Give me a second."

Camille repeats the process with another bobby pin. Once she has two bent at right angles, she slides them both into the lock. She holds one straight while working the other up and down.

After a moment, there's a sharp click. Camille frees the drawer, beaming like she just wowed the judges in the talent portion of some beauty competition.

"Did you learn that behind the jewelry counter?" Krystle asks.

Camille stares at me as she answers. "I'm a woman of many skills."

The paperweight is still in my fist. For an instant, I consider throwing it at her face. I'd probably bust the straight bridge of her nose, maybe knock out one of her gleaming white teeth.

But I can't do any of that because there, in the drawer, is a bulging black gym bag.

Camille pulls it out and then drops it on the table with a

deafening thud, the final act of her magic trick. Krystle rips back the zipper.

Christie Brinkley grins from the cover of another *Playboy*. Krystle dumps the bag on the floor. Porn magazines spill onto the ground.

"We're dead." Krystle drives her hands into her frizzy red curls. "They're going to kill Rom. They're going to kill us."

She might be right. Even if the police want to help, going to them now would mean living my whole life looking over my shoulder for a murdering kidnapper. It would mean putting JJ's life at risk. I can't do that. I'd rather hand over my son to my in-laws and surrender to Ponterelli's men myself. If the Mafia has me, they won't hurt my kid. They'll have to be satisfied with my blood in exchange for my million-dollar share of the debt.

Meredith strolls to the corner of the room and picks up the umbrella. She pokes the *Playboys* with the silver end as if they're a dead animal. "Where else would Rom hide something?"

"He wouldn't." Krystle is full-on crying. "I should never have doubted my baby. You can't imagine what a sweet boy he is. Just yesterday, he gave me a grand to help out."

Meredith spins the umbrella, a dancer's move out of place in this setting. "So he *does* have some money. How'd the mob miss that?"

"It was only a grand. Rom hid it in the ceiling tiles in our base—" Krystle gasps. She tips her head back and stares up toward heaven. When her head lowers, her tears are gone. "Give me that umbrella!"

She snatches it from Meredith and stretches toward the ceiling, tipping on her toes. The umbrella doesn't quite hit the tile. "Damn it!"

"Move over, honey. I got this." Camille takes the umbrella from Krystle and stabs at an overhead square. It easily makes contact. In her heels, she towers over me the way my husband once did, and he was a tall man.

The tile flips up and falls at her feet. She moves to the next one and curses under her breath when it's empty too.

"Hit that one," Krystle yells.

"Back off, Strawberry Shortcake. I know what I'm doing." Camille tosses her hair and continues down the line. On the fifth one, there's a dull thump. "We got something!" She smacks it again like she means to hurt it.

The tile falls, along with stacks and stacks of cash. They rain down on Krystle, green manna from heaven. Our salvation. "Holy shit." Meredith steps toward where the cash has landed. I spot Ben Franklin peeking from behind a thick rubber band.

Krystle drops to the floor and grasps two fistfuls. She mutters in Italian as she gathers the money. Every few seconds, she stops to swipe at the corner of her eyes. I wonder whether love or betrayal propels her tears.

Meredith sits down next to her. She runs her hands along the stacks of hundreds. "I don't think it's four."

Krystle points at Camille. "Keep poking."

The umbrella strikes tile, and more money pours from the

ceiling. This cash is the cause of my husband's death. If Meredith is right, then the firm promised to pay the mob under the table for the land. But Rom absconded with the millions, leaving us in debt and without alternatives.

"Rom hid the money," I whisper this fact to myself, its implications still materializing.

Krystle continues piling bills. "I can't believe he wouldn't tell me when so much is on the line. Rom must've thought he was helping out."

"He got them killed."

Krystle is suddenly on her feet, her index finger aimed at me like a gun muzzle. "Don't you dare blame him. Rom worshipped his father."

"It's the only explanation for why the plane blew up," I continue. "Sal knew the money wasn't on the plane because our guys must have told him that someone stole it. When Sal demanded the cash anyway, the partners all probably went to New York for an emergency loan or something. But they didn't get it, and Sal punished them by—"

"Sal didn't kill my husband," Krystle roars. "And Rom would *never* have done anything to hurt his father. Never!"

"The proof is in the pudding, honey," Camille says while flipping tiles. More stacks tumble to the floor. "The money is here."

Krystle whirls to confront Camille. "But we don't know *why* it's here. Once the plane went down, Rom could have realized our lives were in danger. He could have been trying to protect me and his brothers in case we needed to split." She gestures to the cash littering the floor. "We don't even know that they were killed over this money."

"Why else would the mob murder them?" Camille's voice raises as she jabs the umbrella in Krystle's direction. "Your son stole—"

"It doesn't matter. None of it matters!" Meredith still kneels beside the cash. "They're gone, okay? Robin, Romeo, Peter, Jack—they're all dead. And we will be too if we don't give Sal Ponterelli every bill on this floor by midnight tonight. So everyone shut the fuck up and start stacking."

She's right. The reason Jack is dead doesn't matter as much as making sure JJ and I don't suffer the same fate. I drop the paperweight to pick up the deflated duffel. "We can use this."

Meredith resumes counting while Krystle and I load. After twenty minutes, every ceiling tile has been flipped, and the bag on the desk can't zip shut. It reminds me of a geode, green crystals protruding from the center.

"I think it's four million exactly," Meredith says, her face a little flush.

Krystle lifts the bag by the handles, grunting as she raises it an inch. "Feels like it's all there."

I don't know how she knows this, nor do I want to know. But I accept that this is the kind of information in Krystle's arsenal, just as I now see that Meredith is some sort of financial expert and Camille is a thief. Part of me is jealous. I'm the only one without a secret superpower.

"I have to get this to Sal right away." Krystle stands straighter. "I need to buy back my kid."

"No way," Meredith snaps.

"Don't worry—I know Sal. He won't hurt me."

Meredith looks at Krystle like she's insane. "I'm not *worried*. He has to be clear that this money is the debt from all of us, paid in full. Not to mention he doesn't seem to have much love for you. He tossed your son into the trunk like a cheap suitcase."

"We all have to deliver it," Camille agrees. "All four of us."

"And we'll need to do it someplace crowded in case he decides we're not worth keeping around once we've paid." Meredith directs her attention to Camille and me as if to fill us in on something that Krystle must already know. "Sal's New Year's Eve party tonight will be packed with witnesses. We'll all give it to him there, at his house."

Before I can agree, I hear a small voice in the next room. "Mom? Mommy?"

The sound makes me wince. JJ's been hiding all this time, no doubt wondering what the hell happened to me, probably worrying what would happen to him if I died like his daddy. I'm a terrible, horrible mother.

"Baby, I'm right here. I'm coming." I shoot the women an apologetic look. I'm sure they're all asking themselves why I brought my kid to search for mob money, why I bring him everywhere. Don't I have a single friend or family member who can help me?

Camille gives me a curt nod. "Go."

I rush into the main room, and JJ stands in the center. Tears shine in his eyes but not on his cheeks. He hasn't been crying—at least not a lot.

I carry him back to Rom's office. As much as I want to leave with my son, my work here is not done. Camille is right. We all have to deliver that money together.

"Do you have someone to watch him?" Camille asks as I reenter.

Again, I want to tell her to mind her own business, but JJ's presence makes me hold my tongue. He wouldn't understand why I was being nasty. I don't want him thinking that's a normal way to answer a simple question.

I set him down on the carpet. He looks at each of the women in turn. Krystle in her polka dots and smeared eyeliner, Meredith in a copious amount of blue eyeshadow, and Camille looking regrettably like Brooke Shields in her boot-cut Calvins and a red button-down. His gaze predictably rests on Camille.

"If you don't, I can have Kimberlee do it," she volunteers. "My stepdaughter. Fifteen and more responsible than she looks, thankfully."

Krystle and Meredith stare at me, waiting for an answer. I hate the one that I have to give, but I've no choice. I can't exactly ring Jack's grieving parents and ask them to watch my three-year-old so that I can go to a New Year's Eve party. They'd file for custody. Now that I have this money, I don't have to give it to them.

"Thanks. That would be helpful."

Camille crouches to JJ's level. "Does that sound good? You'll have a sleepover with Kimberlee at my house."

JJ looks from Camille to me and back to Camille. "Is she nice?"

Camille mashes her mouth like she's spreading lipstick. "She's a teenager, and she's a bit sad. She recently lost her dad too." She sniffs. "But I think she'll be very nice to a handsome young man like you."

One of her long, red nails tap my son's nose. He smiles at her, wrapped around that painted finger just like his father undoubtedly was. I pull him close.

"All right then." Krystle breaks in, perhaps sensing that I am reaching my boiling point. "We all head to Camille's to drop off the kid."

"I have to go home and change." Meredith glances at my footwear. "And so do all of you. They won't let us into the party dressed…down."

The tracksuit and sneakers I'm wearing are beyond dressed down. But I'd wanted clothes that I could run in, just in case.

Camille looks at me as though she can see it through my bulky coat. "You can borrow something of mine."

Meredith puts a hand into the black bag, grabbing a stack of bills. "This is my collateral so you don't go without me. I'll be at Camille's in a half hour."

Her cut is just enough for Camille to zip the bag all the way.

She hoists it over her shoulder. "I'm parked around the corner. The red Alfa Romeo."

She strides from the room, knowing that we have no choice but to act like lemmings—especially me. Whether I like it or not, Camille and I are aligned. We both wanted Jack. We both don't want to end up dead.

CAMILLE

I hear the music as soon as we pull into the driveway. Floorboard-shaking, window-rattling music blaring from inside the house, that Foreigner ballad they constantly play on the radio. It thunders behind multiple layers of brick and glass.

I glance across the console at Justine and smile. "Looks like Kimberlee beat us here."

As usual, Justine doesn't say a word. Even with the threat of some mobster chasing her, even though riding with me was *her* idea and not mine, she's back to silently seething—about the fight, about sharing the air in this car, about leaving JJ with a stranger related to her husband's mistress, even if only by marriage. She pops out of the car, then pats around for the lever to flip up the seat.

Lights flash on the back window—Krystle pulling into the driveway behind me, a decision she made after taking one look at the tiny back seat of my Alfa Romeo Spider. But JJ climbed right in. He fits snug as a bug, like the seat was made just for him.

I twist around, smiling in the dim overhead light. "Kimberlee's going to take really good care of you, I promise. Maybe you two can watch a movie or something. And I think she's got a puzzle up in her room somewhere. Make sure to ask her, okay?"

He stares back, silent like his momma. He's old enough to have picked up on his mother's animosity toward me, but it's clear he doesn't share it. He watches me with his father's eyes, blue and open and curious. Jack was that way too. He liked forming his own opinions.

Justine stretches a hand in his direction. "Come on, sweetie. Let's get you inside and ready for bed."

"But I don't got my pajamas."

"You don't *have* your pajamas, and that's okay. You won't be here long. I'll be back to get you in a couple of hours. Until then"—she smiles and wriggles her fingers—"you get to sleep in your underwear."

JJ's face brightens like she just offered him a handful of lollipops, and he drops his little hand in hers. He really does look like Jack. The hair, the square chin, that adorable little pucker in his left cheek. How does Justine do it? How does she look at this little boy all day long and not think of him?

Krystle bonks on my window, her voice carrying through the glass. "Hurry it up, Camille. I'm freezing my tits off out here."

I grab my keys and the duffel bag from the trunk, and the four of us hurry up the walk.

Inside the house, the song is reaching a crescendo, Lou Gramm's wails backed up by the New Jersey Mass Choir. I slide the key into the lock and push the door wide, and it's like standing in front of the speakers at a concert.

"Jesus Christ, Kimberlee! Turn it down!"

Wherever she is, no way in hell she heard me. I don't even hear me.

I usher everybody inside, park them in the foyer, then drop the duffel onto the marble. I hold up a finger and scream, "Wait here!"

I flip on the overhead light and step to the cabinet on the living room wall, punching the off button on the stereo. The house plunges into silence so complete, it's a whole new noise ringing in my ears.

Kimberlee shoots upright on the couch, blinking at me over the back. "What the hell? I was listening to that."

"No, you weren't. The neighbors ten houses down were listening. You were busting out your eardrums. And JJ's here. Come say hi."

She rolls her eyes, which are red and puffy. "Who?"

"JJ. The little boy I called you over here to babysit. He's here." I pause, taking in her pinched expression, her shiny cheeks. They're wet, I suddenly realize. "Everything okay?"

"Oh my God, Camille. You are such a loser." She swipes the

corner of the afghan over her face, dragging a black smear down both cheeks. "You owe me for this, big time."

They're the exact same words she used when I called her from the office, though this time, I don't push back. This is a girl who lost her father in the worst possible way. Whose only remaining parent is on the other side of town, drinking herself into a stupor while her daughter lies on a couch in her dead daddy's house, bawling about heartache and pain and her lonely, lonely life. I'm not the person she wants to show her what love is, but the least I can do is let her be.

With a sigh, she drags herself off the couch and seems to snap out of it.

She greets "Auntie Krystle" with a kiss to both cheeks, then leans down, planting her palms on her knees. She gives JJ a toothy smile. "I'm Kimberlee. Looks like I'm your date for tonight."

JJ wraps an arm around his mother's thigh, looking up with undisguised panic. "I don't know her. My throat hurts. I wanna go home."

Justine chews the inside of her lower lip, but Kimberlee doesn't seem the least bit insulted. "Hey, you know what my daddy used to do whenever I didn't feel so great? He'd take me into that kitchen over there, sit me at the table, and make us both a banana split. Banana splits are magic, you know. They cure me, every single time."

JJ frowns, his cute little forehead crumpling. "A banana what?"

"Something with way too much sugar in it," Justine says. "I don't think—"

"The sugar is the best part. That's what makes it so delicious!" Krystle says, her voice high with exaggerated excitement.

Kimberlee nods. "What's better than ice cream and chocolate sauce and…" She pauses, taking in JJ's dubious expression. "Hang on. Are you telling me you've never had a banana split?"

He nods. Shakes his head. Bounces a shoulder. "I dunno."

Kimberlee straightens and holds out a hand. "Come with me, little guy. I'm about to change your life."

The promise of ice cream does the trick. He takes Kimberlee's hand and lets her lead him into the kitchen.

Krystle hikes a thumb at their retreating backs. "I'm just gonna give Kimberlee a hand, seeing as I'm already wearing my best dress. You two better hurry though. Meredith will be here in fifteen."

"She better be," I mutter, though I still have my doubts.

Justine is chewing on her lip again. "Maybe this isn't such a great idea."

I laugh at the absurdity. "Which part? Going to a party hosted by the person who probably put out the hit on our husbands? Walking into a room filled with mobsters and four million dollars stuffed in a bag? None of this is a good idea, with the sole exception of leaving JJ safe at home. Kimberlee will take good care of him, I promise. They have a few things in common."

One in particular. The reminder of their shared tragedy

wipes some of the fear from Justine's face, smears it with sadness. It seems surreal to be standing in my foyer with this woman, my dead lover's wife. We stare at the kitchen doorway, where low chatter is punctuated by the clanking of plates and utensils.

Justine turns for the stairs. "Let's get this over with."

I grab the duffel and lug it to the second floor. At the top of the landing, she steps aside for me to pass, and I lead her down the hallway to the master bedroom, where I dump the money just inside the door.

"Sorry for the mess. I was in a hurry this morning."

I wasn't in a hurry, because where would I go? I don't have a job or a grumpy teenager to chase out the door, no girlfriends swinging by for boozy lunches. I slept until noon.

Justine stops in the doorway, wrinkling her nose at the unmade bed, the Laura Ashley sheets and comforter that spill off the mattress onto wall-to-wall carpeting strewn with clothes and kicked-off shoes. Her bedroom is probably pristine, decorated within an inch of its life like the ones you see in magazines. Her gaze lands on this morning's breakfast, black coffee and a can of Carnation Diet Plan, lined up on the nightstand next to a messy stack of Polaroids.

Jack's Polaroids.

Shit.

After I got home from Hemenway's last night, I lugged Jack's briefcase from the crawl space in a fit of desperation and dumped it on the bed. I was searching for the report, but then I let myself get caught up in the pieces of Jack pressed between the work files. A crumpled tie in a blue that matched his eyes. A strand of golden-brown hair, glittering against the red felt. A to-do list in his neat scrawl, reminders about settlements and due diligence and to book a trip with Justine and JJ to somewhere sunny.

That last one almost killed me.

I spent the rest of the evening blubbering over those pictures, imagining him shuffling them in his broad hands, wondering which one he loved the best.

Now I step into Justine's line of sight, backing myself up to the dresser. "The closet is through there," I say, pointing to a set of double doors. With my other hand, I swipe the pictures into a drawer. My heel bumps up against something solid, and I don't have to look down to know it's the hard edge of Jack's briefcase sticking out from the bed. I give it a good kick, shoving hard until it's concealed behind the dust ruffle. "Never mind. I'll just show you."

In the closet, Justine runs a finger down the line of colorful dresses. She stops at one, picking up a black and gold sleeve, rubbing the fabric between her fingers.

"I don't know what you're making that face for," I say. "That happens to be couture."

"Just because some saleslady tells you it's designer doesn't mean you should actually wear it. If you want a little black dress, you go to Hubert de Givenchy."

"Like this one?" I pull a gown from the rack, a Givenchy dripping in rhinestones and capped with sleeves of white mink.

Peter paid an obscene amount for it, but only after I dropped to my knees and gave him a blow job, right there on the dressing room floor.

Justine takes it in with begrudging admiration, and I feel a punch of pleasure. The fashion model approves of my dress. Victory.

I hold it out to her. "You want to wear it to the party? The model who wore it on the runway was taller than you, but it might fit."

Her eyes turn hard, and she thinks about it for a beat or two. "That depends. Did you wear it on a date with Jack?"

Without a word, I hang it back on the rack.

Justine turns back to the dresses with a huff, reaching for a translucent Thierry Mugler from his Zénith collection. It's a fabulous piece, one that would be stunning on her.

"Not that one either," I mutter.

She steps down the line, stretching a hand to a pink sleeve.

"Or that one."

She whirls around, throwing up her hands. "Oh my God, Camille, which one? Which one did you *not* wear while screwing my husband?"

As much as I want to tell her *not many*, I manage to bite my tongue. I step farther into the closet, pulling out a burgundy Dior with a puffy skirt. The tag still dangles from a sleeve, its price marked down three times before I snapped it up late last year at the Lord & Taylor semiannual sale.

"Fine. Give it here."

I hand her a fresh pair of black pantyhose, then take my time slipping into a hot-pink Valentino with a plunging back and jeweled neckline. I shimmy the silk up my body, reaching for the side zipper, when Justine snatches a pair of black heels from the rack and bolts for the door.

"Guess this means we're not gonna do each other's makeup," I call after her.

No response, just the swish of her stockinged feet stomping across the bedroom carpet.

I slip on a pair of silver pumps and follow in her fumes down the stairs.

In the kitchen, Krystle is seated at the table next to JJ. She's helped herself to a Diet Coke from the fridge and a spoon from the drawer, which she's using to shovel the last of JJ's leftovers into her mouth. A white napkin is tucked into the neckline of the polka-dot monstrosity she calls a dress, hanging over her boobs like a paper bib.

"Do you want my cherry? This one tastes funny." JJ picks up a bright red blob from the table with sticky fingers. His chin is sticky too, chocolate and caramel and ice cream that's dribbled brown puddles onto his shirt.

"Thanks, buddy. Maraschinos are my favorite kind." Krystle pops it into her mouth, then smiles across the dirty cups and bowls at Kimberlee. "You make a mean banana split, young lady. Excellent job."

Kimberlee grins. "Thanks. It's my dad's recipe."

"Her daddy died too, in the same airplane as *my* daddy. They blewed up." JJ's words are sad but not his tone, hopped up on sugar and cream.

Krystle pats his hand. "And it's a goddamn tragedy." Justine gives her a sharp look, and Krystle smiles. "Pardon my Italian, sweetheart."

Justine moves closer, armed with a wet paper towel, and uses it to mop up JJ's face. "It's already been a half hour. Do you think Meredith ditched us?"

"She'll be here," Krystle says. "Don't you worry."

I make a throaty sound, and Justine's gaze meets mine across the table. She did the math too—Meredith's collateral was a half dozen stacks of cash, which amounts to sixty, maybe seventy thousand dollars, more than she likely earns in a year and enough to mess up our plan. I see the thought cross Justine's expression and think, *Finally, something we can agree on.* She doesn't trust the stripper either.

The doorbell rings, and Krystle sits back with a triumphant huff. "There she is. Told you so."

Kimberlee pops out of her chair without prompting, which makes me wonder what Krystle said about Meredith and what the four of us are doing here. At least tonight she won't *look* like a stripper. Kimberlee has enough bad influences in her life.

I hear Meredith's familiar voice, the taps of high heels moving closer across the tiles, and here she is. Tiny strips of black and red lace that barely cover her privates, Robin's white-fox fur hanging from her shoulders, heels halfway to heaven. Next to her, Kimberlee is beaming, and suddenly, this hot-pink dress Jack loved so much makes me feel frumpy.

Meredith's gaze bounces from Justine to Krystle to me. "Maybe I should have been more specific when I said *party*."

MEREDITH

Y ou said to dress up!" Camille protests.

She's dressed up all right. Except Camille looks like she's on her way to Barbie's Dream Oscar Party, not a New Year's bash at a mobster's mansion.

Which, I have to hand it to her, is still a step up from Justine and Krystle's attire. Justine looks ready for high tea in that puffy taffeta frock, and Krystle, despite my clear instructions, didn't bother to change out of the polka-dotted dress she's had on all day. She's not even wearing makeup, just a smudge of hot chocolate sauce on the corner of her mouth.

I sigh, pinching the bridge of my nose. "Yeah, dress up like—"

"Like a dime-store hooker?" Krystle gives my outfit a disdainful once-over.

Justine's son coughs. Fuck, I forgot he was here. I'm the worst with kids; luckily, Robin was even less interested in starting a family than I was. Not that it matters anymore.

Justine crouches to check on him. "You okay, sweetheart?"

He nods, staring up at us with wide eyes. Justine whispers something to Camille's sullen stepdaughter, who takes little Jack Junior by the sugar-sticky hand and leads him into the next room. Soon the sound of ABC's Times Square celebration broadcast rings out loud enough to drown out the rest of our conversation.

"Look," Krystle says. "This is a business meeting. That's it. We go, we give Sal his money, we get my son back, and we get the hell out. We're not going there to party."

I shake my head. "We need to blend in. You want to draw attention to yourself while you've got millions of dollars in cash on your person? They'll rip you apart. That is if they even let you in the front door dressed like that."

"We should listen to her, Krystle," Justine says. "She's the only one who's been to one of these parties before. We have to get inside the house. We want as many witnesses as possible."

"What kind of party is this anyway?" Camille asks. "I've never been invited."

Keeping my voice low so I don't traumatize the minors on the other side of the wall, I fill in my fellow widows on Sal Ponterelli's monthly free-for-alls of beautiful girls, boys, booze, powder, and pills. Krystle looks queasy, probably wondering if her beloved firstborn has ever attended one of these sordid events. (The answer is yes, but only once: Rom took too much X, tried to tongue-kiss a city councilwoman, and got tossed out in the snow before the clock struck 11:00 p.m.) Camille seems intrigued, while Justine barely reacts at all. If she used to frequent fashion parties in New York, the Ponterelli mansion's brand of debauchery might seem relatively tame. Or maybe she's just too nervous about her son's safety and the money drop tonight to care.

"Fine." Krystle looks at Camille. "What else you got in that overstuffed wardrobe of yours?"

Camille leads the way to her walk-in closet, which is about the same size as the apartment I lived in before shacking up with Robin. A colorful explosion of couture covers every surface—all stunning and all totally wrong for where we're headed tonight.

"Help yourselves," Camille says, peeling out of her hot-pink gown. Underneath, she's wearing high-cut lace panties and a matching push-up bra in the same searing color.

"There, that's perfect." I gesture at her. "Wear that."

She looks at me like I've lost my damn mind. "It's below freezing outside."

"Put a coat over it." I grab a herringbone duster from the other side of the closet. "Something with pockets big enough to fit some of that cash."

Now for the other two. An anxious buzz builds under my skin. Even if we dress the part perfectly, even if we get into the party and return Sal's money without incident, there's no guarantee we'll be safe. If he's telling the truth and the mob wasn't behind the plane crash, if all they want is the money—well, that just means our dearly departed partners must have left even *more* enemies behind for us to deal with. Enemies who might demand a price much higher than four million bucks.

But I can't think about that now. One crisis at a time. Get them dressed, then get Sal his money before midnight. That's the plan, and we have to stick together and stick to it.

I open the top drawer of Camille's dresser, and sure enough, it's stuffed full of a lingerie boutique's worth of lace and satin. "Here," I say, holding up a strappy negligee that looks like it might suit Justine. "How about—"

"Absolutely not." Justine folds her arms, shooting Camille another scorching glare.

"Unless you're planning to staple six of those skimpy things together," Krystle says, "you're not getting me into any of that shit either."

I hate to admit that Krystle's right, but it's true: there's no way in hell any of Camille's designer sexpot wardrobe will fit her. It's not like we can go shopping though; even if we had the time to spare, it's New Year's Eve, so everything is closed. We're going to have to improvise.

Camille and I start grabbing any remotely stretchy pieces and tossing them Krystle's way. Justine flicks through the racks, her mouth fixed in a sour twist, and finally selects a garment that looks like chain-mail armor laid over a black slip.

"Only if you lose the liner," I tell her.

Justine stares at me. "Are you serious?"

What part of *drug-fueled Mafia orgy* do these people not understand? I snatch the dress off the hanger and rip out the black fabric so only the skimpy bronze overlay remains. Camille lets out a little whimper at my crime against fashion, but she doesn't try to stop me.

Krystle holds up a leather skirt with gold embroidery that looks a couple of sizes bigger than the rest of Camille's wardrobe.

"Oh, I forgot about that! I was gonna have it altered." Camille shoves another item at her, a strapless corset made of pleated gold lamé. "Try it with this."

Krystle holds it up to her chest and stares down at the curved neckline, which looks like golden wings swooping out to support her tits. "What kind of bra do you wear with *this*?"

"You don't," I say. The skirt is floor-length, which is not ideal, but paired with that plunging top, it just might pass muster. And we could hide some cash under all that leather if we need to.

It takes a fair bit of teamwork to get the corset strapped on her—me, Camille, and Justine all yanking on the laces, Krystle bracing herself in the doorway like Scarlett O'Hara—but it works. As long as Krystle doesn't lean over or breathe too hard, she'll be good.

Camille gets her makeup kit next—all designer too, but even the most expensive products can look cheap if you pile enough on, and that's exactly what we're going for. I've already sweated half of my makeup off during our impromptu makeover session, so I reapply, savoring how smoothly her Chanel spreads over my face compared to my usual Maybelline. Justine does her own face with expert flicks of liner, while Krystle lets Camille paint her eyelids gold to match the corset.

Now we only need one more accessory to complete our party looks: all that damn cash.

We dump Rom's duffel out on the bed, and I add my collateral back to the pile.

"How are we supposed to hide anything when we're dressed like this?" Justine asks. She's ended up in the most outrageous outfit of all: that metallic netting is almost the same shade as her skin, so she looks practically naked.

"I've got some really big purses," Camille offers.

"They'll search our handbags. I don't trust anyone seeing that cash before Sal," Krystle says. Then she looks at me. "Right?"

"They'll frisk us too." I shake my head. "Some security guy sees that kind of money, says right this way, and then we're dead."

"What about our coats?" Camille picks up the herringbone duster, which ended up on the floor in all the commotion. "We could sew the cash into the lining."

"You know how to sew?" Justine asks.

"I couldn't always afford all this couture. Once upon a time, I made my own."

It pains me to think of ripping up Robin's fox fur. She loved that coat. Sometimes when I'd get home late from the club, she'd be waiting for me in bed wearing it, a bottle of champagne chilling on the nightstand.

But I'm in this situation because of Robin. Sacrificing her coat is a small price to pay, considering the mess she left behind.

"Do it," I tell Camille.

She slices into the coats like a surgeon, and we slip the stacks of cash inside each of them, lining them up neatly so they lay as flat as possible. Then Camille sews the seams back up in a flash, her stitches so precise you'd never know the difference. The final few stacks that wouldn't fit in our coats, Krystle tapes around her thighs under that floor-skimming skirt; I suggested her hips instead, but she said that's the last place she needed extra padding.

By the time we're done, it looks like a bomb went off in Camille's closet. We put the bulked-out coats on over our skimpy party clothes and crowd in front of the three-way mirror for a final check.

The four of us look good but cheap as hell. You'd never guess we're packing a million dollars each.

"Ready, ladies?" Krystle says.

Camille, Justine, and I all nod. Time to ring in the New Year—or die trying.

KRYSTLE

O nce the Providence mayor and a leggy local news reporter are escorted inside, it's our turn at Sal's Castle Dracula tucked away in the woods of East Greenwich.

We stand in our call-girl finest in front of huge wolf sculptures looming on either side of the massive wooden front doors.

A no-neck bouncer without a clipboard steps in front of the snarling statues. "You like them? Wait until you see the real ones inside."

"Please." I roll my eyes.

"Just wait, Red." He winks at me and turns in Meredith's direction. "Now, who the hell are your friends?"

"Sal invited them. Fresh meat."

"Boss didn't say nothing to me about it." He looks us up and down. "What's under them coats?"

I open my money-lined fur to expose more cleavage than I

ever thought possible. I'd never pick this top, and it sure as hell wouldn't pick me, but we've made this devil's bargain and both want to make it out of here with every stitch intact.

While it may be slowly squeezing me to death, this is by far the sexiest and most scared I've ever felt.

Whatever it takes to get my son back.

The bouncer gives me a small eyebrow raise, and his gaze goes back to Justine. I poke her hard in the back. "Show 'em the goods."

She slowly unwraps the trench. The guy whistles, and I can't blame him. She's in a chain-mail dress, which I only ever saw in magazines. What do you know, Justine *is* New York model hot. Even if she doesn't act it.

He pokes a finger through one of the holes near her cleavage. "This is giving me some ideas, wild thing." He tugs on her coat. "I want the whole show."

Justine freezes. I shoot a worried glance at Camille, who sees it too.

"Hey, big man." Camille sidles up next to him and opens her coat. "I wore this for you," she purrs at the doorman in her pink lingerie. "Heard you're a tough judge of *character*."

I loop an arm into Justine's and pull her back.

"Character?" I say to Justine with a smirk, trying to get her back into the game. "The kind you get from a plastic surgeon."

The door guy is mesmerized by Camille the centerfold, so that's something.

I stick out my chest and try for a pout. "You letting us in or what?"

He reluctantly turns from the Camille show to find Meredith. "They screw up, it's your ass, Tina."

The front door opens, and I hear the party before I see it. The opening guitar riff of "Money for Nothing" is blasting as we follow Meredith inside.

But we're not quite at the party—yet. It's more like a cave, dark rock walls and stone floor. Our heels echo, and then we all stop at the same time. There is a huge oil painting of Sal and four wolves.

"Is that how he got the nickname?" Justine asks. "He just really loves wolves."

"His mother's surname was Lupo. It means 'wolf' in Italian," I explain. "Though that's not the only reason he's called *the wolf*."

Two guys are blocking our path to large stained-glass doors that are closed but rattling from the music. "Open them purses and coats. Drugs only, no weapons, no cameras, no recording devices. We break them. Then we break you."

Luckily, Meredith knew this was coming, so the purses are clean. The glass doors swing open, and Sal appears. His tuxedo fits like a second skin across his muscular shoulders, centered with a silver bow tie.

"I'll frisk this one. Privately." He winks at me and holds out his hand. "*Mrs. Romero*, right this way."

I glance back at the girls with an encouraging nod but keep

going where I'm told. I say a silent prayer he's taking me to Rom.
Sal's fingers are loosely threaded through mine as he pulls me
into a huge living room.

"Welcome to my bacchanal, baby," he whispers in my ear.

I'm nearly blinded by the white: the giant living room is an
octagon of white walls, white shag carpet, white leather furniture, and even a silvery-white stereo system in front of a white
grand piano. As my eyes adjust, I notice the sunken living room
has white and black marble tiles. There are red touches too. A
large sculpture on the wall and giant red leather lounger where a
Rhode Island senator is getting a lap dance by a gal in not much
more than tinsel.

She's not the only one. Blond twins are wearing thongs and
mini–New Year's hats, but not on their heads. Several other
nearly naked girls are dancing with men and women in the
sunken living room. There's a long coffee table with two blonds
doing lines with a woman in a business suit. They start to undress
her, and I turn away.

I'm not sure I could ever get used to these kinds of jiggles and
giggles. But the room is packed with familiar faces, some people
from the Hill, but others from downtown. Lawyers and doctors
and East Siders who don't seem to mind mingling with people
from the Hill when it's at this fancy house with plenty of booze
and boobs and drugs, oh my.

Rom is nowhere to seen, not that I expected him to be mingling. There's a scream in my chest that's been building since the

second he was taken. I have to know my son is okay. Even if he did something really, really stupid.

"May I take your coat?" Sal is watching me as his hands come to my collar. "See, I'm learning."

"We're going to want to take that with us." Sal drapes it over his arm, and I strike a pose, hands on my hips. "Well? Best I could do on short notice."

"I like it." His gaze assesses Camille's too-tight corset and the long leather skirt I hope is hiding the cash well enough. "Course, you look a little curvier around the thighs since the last time I saw you. Not that I'm complaining."

I gasp, my hands reflexively going to my ass, and then realize he can tell the money is holstered to my legs. "You son of—"

He cuts me off by spinning me once as the sax blasts to "Careless Whisper."

"Any chance of a dance?" he asks.

I shake my head firmly, tired of his nonsense. "Where's my Rom?"

"Straight to business? Okay then. Let's go to my office."

I glance back to see Justine refuse to give her coat to the busty girl.

Sal lifts my coat on his arm. "This has gained some weight too since yesterday."

Before I can answer, he puts his other hand on the small of my back, and we head toward a side door. Down a long hallway, there are a few Hill guys milling about. One is playing solitaire at a small table in front of a door. Another two stand at the end of the hallway like they're waiting for us.

"Hello, Mrs. Romero," says Arti as he opens the door. "Hey, boss, that broad wants to see you about the problem she's having."

"Later," Sal says as we enter a room that's definitely not an office.

"What the hell are we doing in your bedroom?!" I screech.

I hear Arti laugh as the door closes. Sal throws my coat onto the mattress. "This is where I do my best business."

"Not with me. You think I'd sleep with you after what you've done?"

"The money is mine," he says. "What are you so heated about?"

"My son, for starters. My dead husband for the chaser. And threatening to do the same to me, yesterday, if you don't get that money."

"Krissie," he says as if well and truly wounded.

"Don't you call me that." I shove him, and there's a growl, deeper than any dog I ever heard. I snap my gaze around, and there's a goddamn wolf baring his fangs. "Jesus, Mary, and Joseph! What the hell is that?"

"Daisy, heel," he says firmly, and that beast obeys, plopping onto her haunches. "She gets jealous if I bring another woman in here. Especially one as feisty as you."

"You *actually* have a wolf?" I whisper in complete shock.

"I have four, actually. Rose, Marigold, and Petunia. The ladies of the house. My girls are babysitting your son. No charge."

I have to squeeze my eyes shut for a moment. "Can I please see Rom?"

"Your kid is fine." Sal points at the wolf. "Daisy, bed."

My mouth falls open as the wolf heads over to one of four red satin cushions in the corner. "You're Cocoa Puffs crazy," I murmur and take a deep breath. "What next?"

He takes a step back from me and crosses his arms. "Take off your skirt, Krissie."

"I'm not sleeping with you, Sal."

"A shame, but that's not what I'm after. At the moment." He steps behind me, and I feel his warm hands where the corset meets the leather. "I'm unzipping, sweetheart."

"I can do it," I stammer.

"I'd rather though. You look like a present in that gold getup." He tugs at the zipper and slowly starts to slide it down.

I'm glad I have on Camille's slutty underwear, even if it's slightly stretched. Then I feel guilty and grab his hand tight. "I refuse to let the man who killed my husband see my ass."

"Krissie, you aren't serious?" He starts to unzip again, but I squeeze his hand tighter. "Okay, listen good, sweetheart. I'm not saying your late husband and I didn't have some things to discuss. I'm not saying I wasn't going to break his arm. The ice was definitely thin. But I was *never* going to kill Romeo."

I twist around to look at him. "You sent your goons after us. Why not blow up the plane too?"

He laughs as if I'm a child. "Kill four lawyers? On a plane

taking off in New York territory, not even my own turf. Do you know what kind of favors I'd need for that?"

"But you said you knew the money wasn't on the plane. You knew you could blow it up."

"Sweetheart, do you think I want the FBI and FAA and who the hell knows sniffing around here? Yeah, that juice is not worth the squeeze. It wasn't me, Krissie. For your sake, I hope the explosion was an accident."

I want to believe him. I'd been praying for the same myself. Unlucky after more luck than we deserved. "The insurance company says the plane was new. It's likely the engine was sabotaged—"

"Insurance company? I wouldn't trust a word. They don't want to pay you. That's their angle. They'll drag their feet and point fingers. You'll be lucky to ever see a penny from them."

"On your father's grave, Sal. You didn't kill Romeo?"

He doesn't blink, doesn't hesitate for a moment. "I swear to you, Krissie."

"Okay." I let out a long breath because I didn't ever really believe it, but I feared it.

"We good?" he asks, stepping behind me.

"For now," I say, turning to see what he's up to.

"Stay there. I'm unzipping again, though I don't mind the view at the moment."

I spin around and face him. "For that, you tell me exactly what they were buying from you for four million dollars."

"I'm not talking unless I'm unzipping."

I let out a huff and turn back around, making sure Daisy is still in her satin bed. "Was it your land? For the mall? But you pretend it's a donation?"

"You've always had brains, sweetheart. Yeah, they wanted my land. I was happy to part with it for the right price. They scraped it together, supposedly, and it was going to be under the table. That way, it looked like I donated it for some community goodwill."

"Why did they need *that* land?"

"Good thing falls in my lap, I don't ask questions. Besides, I was done with that place anyways."

"Done how?"

"In my business, as you know, I have occasion to bury things. As did my father. When something is free like the land seems to be, people don't sniff around as much. Win-win."

I let out a little gasp as he slides the zipper enough that my skirt drops around my feet.

"This is how I wanted to start 1986. Give me a little turn, Krissie."

I step out of the skirt and put my hands on my waist. I spin slowly, liking the spike of something I tend to resent in other women. Owning my body. Owning that the male gaze isn't always one of rejection. Finally, I stop, and there's less of a grin than something lupine. Maybe it's the money strapped to my thighs, and maybe it's not. "And I didn't even need a pole."

"No, you didn't, sweetheart." He heads over to a white marble-top desk across the room and opens a drawer. He returns with a gold letter opener.

"What the hell is that for?"

"Shouldn't hurt. Much." He drops to his knees and glances up. "Anything else I can do for you while I'm down here?"

I toss my head. "Hurry?"

He does, actually, and it's only a couple of minutes before all the cash is off my body and in a neat pile beside him. "Ready to go to bed?"

"Cute," I say and follow him over there. The letter opener slices my coat. We stack the money on his mattress, and I try to keep cool. Finally, it's all there, and he quickly runs fingers along the green.

"Plus, what was on your thighs, that's one million."

"We each brought our share. Now give me my son back." I march over to my clothes and he follows, offering his hand. I take it to step back into my skirt.

"I'll do the honors." He zips it up before I can tell him to back off. "Are the other ladies wearing theirs as well?"

"Don't look so excited. It's in their coats. I doubt they'd be as willing to make an idiot of themselves as me."

"Is that what you were doing?"

I snicker. "Obviously."

"I wasn't laughing." He watches me as if waiting to see my next move.

"Rom."

"You make me wish I'd had a mother, the way you fight for that numbskull." He heads back toward the bedroom door, opening it to reveal Arti standing there smoking, looking anxious, with an annoyed Donna Moldova in all her queen-of-the-kooky-crystals glory. Her eyes grow wide as I sashay past her from Sal's bedroom.

I pause with a smirk. "How's my aura now?"

She gives me a withering look.

"Take Donna to my office," he says to Arti.

"You do have an office," I say and point a finger at his chest, but he only winks as Donna stomps past us farther down the hall.

"Go find your girls." Sal leans against the door. "Have a drink. Mix and mingle. Make some friends, but don't get too friendly. We'll do the exchange in a bit. I got a pain-in-the-ass pressing matter to deal with."

I glance at the wolf in her bed, her master with a million on his, and then rush down the hallway. I've got pressing matters of my own.

Rom is here somewhere, and wolves or no, I'll be damned if I wait one more second to find him.

JUSTINE

They all want to take my coat. One of the bouncers tried first, jamming his fat fingers into my barely covered breasts and demanding to see the rest of the chain-mail sheath. The city's mobsters, lawmakers, and wannabe players didn't travel to the suburbs on New Year's Eve for the trees. They came for the views. And the gangsters manning the door are making sure wool drapes don't ruin them.

Camille saved me from exposing any more of myself. She dove in front of the tit poker, flashing her pink bra and panties like she was auditioning for *Playboy*. At first, I figured she was competing with me as always, making the case that she's more attention-worthy than Jack's wife, that any man—not just my husband—should choose her over me. But the way her smile twitched as the bouncer's eyes devoured her made me realize that she was taking one for the team. Without her, my coat and the million dollars pooled in its hem would never have been allowed in.

Since I've been inside, no fewer than ten men have asked me to shrug off my trench and stay awhile. Were it not stuffed with hundreds, I might be tempted. The mansion is warm enough for all the naked strippers not to freeze. I'm sweating and itchy, though that might be from nerves.

As I mill around the crammed space, I'm hyperaware of what I'm schlepping. The twenty pounds of bills stuffed into my coat's silken lining pull the fabric toward my ankles and smack my calves, giving me a jolt with every clacking step I take on the great room's checkered marble floor. I'm a chess piece that can't decide where to move.

Everywhere I look, there's cocaine. The drug is sprinkled atop Lucite tables and combed into snow trails on cocktail trays. Powder is dusted on the décolletage of the dancers and topless waitresses. I guess my jittery behavior blends right in.

"Hiding in plain sight?"

A sharp tug on my sleeve punctuates the question. I whirl around on Camille's one-size-too-large heels and nearly face-plant into a bloodred necktie. It's been pulled loose so that the Windsor knot hangs between a pair of pecs pressing against a white button-down.

I stumble back, but it's too late. The man's hands are already beneath my coat, gripping the indents of my waist, driving metal into my bare skin. I look up at his face as he stares down at mine. Heavy lines crease the sides of his closed-lipped smirk. He's shaved for this party, but the same thick brows shadow the same steel-blue eyes.

My stalker has found me.

"I have it, okay?" I say as Bon Jovi wails from wall-sized speakers on the other side of the room, but I don't raise my voice. The mobster is close enough to hear me breathe. "I found Jack's share of the cash."

His brow lowers.

"Krystle is talking to Sal right now. We made the deadline. He'll have it by midnight."

I attempt to pull away, but his fingers press deeper into my sides. I look over my shoulder for help—an interested guy wanting to play the hero or maybe Camille armed with her aggressive sex appeal. The bejeweled lady from the Christmas party reflects too much light from an overhead chandelier. She gestures wildly, apparently arguing with one of Sal's enforcers. Behind her, I spot Camille's blond waves.

"Hey." One of the hands releases my waist. Before I can move, it's against my chin, directing my head toward him. He's staking a claim for the crowd, and he wants me to acknowledge it. "I'm right here."

"I know."

"You're cold."

The hand still on my side travels up to my breast and back down again as if to warm me. But fear has electrified every nerve in my body. I'm burning up.

"You're clean-shaven."

It's a dumb retort, but I don't have anything else to say. It's all I can do not to scream.

His smirk breaks open into a smile, as if my observation was intended to be funny. "Changing looks can be necessary in my line of work."

The fingers on my chin fall to my clavicle. He presses a thumb into the notch at the base of my throat. I brace myself for a blow that will leave me coughing and choking. Instead, he traces the bone to the shoulder while his eyes follow suit, a butcher seeking the best place to cut. "You changed too."

He reaches my shoulder and pushes off the wool. The coat tumbles to the crooks of my elbows. His gaze drifts to my bronze-caged cleavage and then meanders to the sand-colored underwear the same tone as my skin. He steps back, letting me go to get a better gander.

"Not exactly what you wore to the construction site. But I suppose you were in mom mode then. Can't bring a kid here. Is your boy with his grandparents again?"

I shudder. "He doesn't have anything to do with this."

"I should hope not."

Behind his shoulder, I spot Krystle. Her red hair appears aflame against the white-wall backdrop. The leather skirt pasted onto her bottom sits askew, as if she'd shimmied into it in a hurry. She looks right and then left, probably searching for the rest of Sal's millions.

Despite present company, I exhale. Though Krystle insisted that Sal wouldn't kill us, I doubted her until this moment. If the man had ordered the murder of our husbands, what was to stop him from getting rid of us as soon as he got what he wanted? Krystle's living, breathing presence means that maybe she was right. And Sal just might be true to his word.

"There's Krystle Romero. She just gave Mr. Ponterelli her share and is looking for us to do the same." I step around Sal's man. "You'll find out that everything's fine in a few minutes. Excuse me."

I skate toward Krystle in Camille's giant, slippery stilettos, shouting for her attention. She catches me with a stare that conveys *shut up* better than a finger to the lips. Immediately, I stop yelling, though I continue rushing to her corner of the room.

"I'm so relieved that you're okay." I keep my voice low. "Should the rest of us go in now? I can leave the coat with him and—"

"He said he'd get the rest in a little bit. There's something he has to do."

"What? I can't keep fending off folks who want this coat off me. We have to give him this money. He made us fear for our lives over it. He killed our—"

Krystle shakes her head. She's not looking at me so much as through me. "He didn't. The plane probably malfunctioned. Accidents happen."

I don't believe it. Small aircraft crash sometimes, sure. But it can't be a coincidence that our spouses' plane went down while they were in the midst of brokering a multimillion-dollar deal with the Mafia. There's no use in fighting about it now though. All that matters is getting my kid out of the mob's crosshairs.

"What can be more important than four million dollars?" I whisper. "I want to get out of here. My son—"

"*My son*'s still here," Krystle hisses. "Sal thinks we can just mix and mingle while they turn Rom's fingers into Kibbles 'n Bits. I'm going to find him. And Sal's not seeing another dime until Rom's safe. *Capisce?*"

Though her fist now waves in my direction, I know the person she's really threatening isn't standing in front of her. Tears well in her eyes, not of fear but of fury. Seeing them melts something inside me. I'm no longer frozen in terror. I'm enraged. These people have threatened our boys—our flesh and blood. Krystle and I are no longer wives, but we are still mothers. We have the same job.

My son is safe until midnight. Right now, I need to help find hers.

"I'll look too."

Krystle's defiant chin retreats to her neck. "No offense, but you're not exactly incognito in this crowd."

She might mean I'm the only Black person here, but I take her statement as a compliment. I don't want to blend in with mobsters, corrupt politicians, and cokeheads.

She glances around the room, seeking someone who could actually be of some use.

"Let me do something, Krystle. It's your kid."

Her blue eyes zero in on me like she finally sees something worth exploring. There's recognition in her gaze. Respect.

"You want to help? You're a fashion model, Justine. Take off that coat and sell that damn dress! The more people staring at you, the fewer folks wondering where the hell I've gone off to."

Krystle is sprinting away before I can agree. With her gone, I feel less protected but just as angry. The mobster from minutes earlier eyeballs me from across the room. Krystle's right. If he's focused on me, he won't be thinking of her or Rom. And if the whole crowd is watching me, he won't be able to make any unwanted advances.

I peel off the coat, fling it over one shoulder, and strut toward the center of the room.

Determination maintains my balance. As I walk, I hear murmurs and male grunts of approval. I feel the X-ray heat from dozens of eyes, straining to see through metal mesh. The attention isn't enough though. My nearly nude dress is only a mild distraction in a room where 25 percent of the female guests wear pasties and thongs.

A gleaming baby grand is positioned in front of a wall-size entertainment center. The unit spinning the compact discs has a thumb-size button with a shining green light in its corner. I march over and slam the heel of my hand into the power switch.

It's a CD player, so there's no record scratch. Still, the whole room seems to stop along with the Hooters' earwig of a dance tune. A man in the corner starts toward me, not so much angry as annoyed. He must think I'm drunk and bumped into the stereo by mistake.

I slide onto the piano bench, drop my coat next to me, and play a florid run up the G-scale. I like G major. It's in the sweet spot of my range, and it's easy to remember the key signature. There's only one sharp: F. Tonight it stands for the four-letter word that I want to shove into the mob's face along with the letter *U.*

The crowd is really paying attention now. Even the mobster has halted his mission to restart the tunes. Through the empty triangle beneath the piano's raised lid, I see interested or at least curious expressions. Folks weren't expecting live music. Maybe they're thinking that Sal went all out this year with the help. A piano-playing pole dancer!

Camille is among the group, though she appears more flabbergasted than fascinated. She thinks of me as Jack's dull wife— the pretty face that he got pregnant who'd promptly turned into a stroller-pushing pumpkin. Her impression brings a jazz standard to mind, one of those that I learned behind my childhood piano teacher's back. "Let's make some whoopee," I shout.

I sing Ella Fitzgerald's version in Eddie Cantor's more accessible key of G. It allows me to showcase my rumbling chest voice while climbing to the octave on every ending "ee," letting it ring loud and high for laughs. It also allows me to look directly at Camille as I sing/speak the verse that I most want her to understand—the part about the husband stepping out on his wife after they have a kid while the discarded woman sits alone, caring for the house and child, waiting for her love to call while wondering why he's so "*busy*."

As I croon the words, anger and pain round out my tone. I hope Camille can hear the emotion. I want her to really understand the unfairness of her actions. No new mom overwhelmed with washing dishes and baby clothes—not to mention feeding, caring for, and loving a kid who can't even go to the bathroom alone—should have to compete with a young, sexy woman able to direct all her attention to *making whoopee*.

I finish off the song on a lighter note, bringing the tempo back to its jaunty speed as I sing about the judge who will send the cheating husband to jail if he doesn't hand over his entire salary and then some to the mother of his kid. "*It's far, far cheaper to stay and keep her*," I sing, adding my own spin on the lyrics. "*Forget about the whoopee!*"

The crowd erupts in laughter and applause. I hop up onto the piano bench, less carefully than I should, and execute a girlish courtesy that undoubtedly flashes half of my behind to everyone in back of me. There are cheers and whistles. Calls for an encore. For a moment, I forget that I'm in a mobster's mansion with a coat worth a million dollars and my life. I am my old self: sexy and sassy, perhaps a little cheesy, though in a way most men find cute and endearing. I remember the good parts of all those rock-n-roll parties, the impressed faces at my improvised melodies over guitar riffs before things devolved into some drugged-out front man suggesting that he would introduce me to his manager—in the morning.

A hand appears to help me down from the piano bench. I accept it without checking who it's attached to, simply happy to have a spotter to bring me down to earth. When my feet touch the floor, I realize my mistake. He's there, staring at me with that smile that lacks any warmth. He looks at me like he's window-shopping and I might be something he wants, depending on how easy I am to steal.

I grab for my coat without taking my gaze off him. He reaches for my neck but then changes direction, selecting one of the long, dark curls falling to my shoulders. Slowly, he extends it toward his chest, pulling the shaft straight. He lowers his head to the lock and inhales.

His face cracks into a smile. This one is different from the others. It's not performed. I see both top and bottom teeth. He's almost laughing.

He releases my hair. "Smells sweet, like almonds."

"Sal is busy, but he said he'll get around to taking the money. We have it all."

"I like that song. 'Makin' Whoopee.'" A smirk twists the edge of his mouth. "You sing it good, and the ending is funny."

My stalker is not like Sal's other cronies, I realize. Those guys have been focused on doing their boss's bidding. This man is more interested in what he wants.

I opt to take a page out of Camille's book. Flattery will get you everywhere. "Thank you for the compliment. I'm happy that you enjoyed it."

He licks his bottom lip. "Though you know that judge was wrong."

I strain to keep my plastic grin. "What do you mean?"

"The guy didn't have to stop with the whoopee. He could have just killed her."

CAMILLE

I lean against a marble column, clutching a glass of champagne and watching a couple of topless girls hoover up an impressively long line. A year ago, I would have plucked that rolled-up hundred out of their painted fingers and shoved myself between them. Hell, a *week* ago I probably would have. This party is my kind of debauchery, and honestly, I'm disappointed that I didn't know it was a monthly thing before tonight.

But after that performance Justine just gave, I can't seem to get in the mood.

Making whoopee, my ass.

What on earth could I possibly say to make her understand? That, okay, maybe my relationship with Jack began with a whole lot of whoopee but that it quickly turned into something more? That we often fantasized about how our lives would look if our spouses didn't exist and we could be together? That I loved him, and I'm pretty sure he loved me back?

Or maybe I could tell her that our first kiss happened on a night like this one—a raucous concert after-party at the Living Room downtown. Both of us were drunk and flying solo, me because Peter hated the Ramones and Jack because of JJ.

"There's not a sitter on the planet who's good enough," he said with a roll of his eyes, which made it clear this policy was his wife's. That was how he talked about her that night and every time since—in the most roundabout way possible, so that both of us might actually forget he had one.

And I tried, good Lord, how I tried.

In the beginning, it was easy, when the lust was overwhelming enough to smother the thoughts of poor, beautiful Justine at home alone, flipping channels and trying not to think about why her husband's meetings stretched longer and longer into the evenings. There was no room in my head for her, only thoughts about how much I wanted Jack, and I didn't know what to do with that. Wanting *things*, sure, that's been a constant for as long as I can remember. But never have I ever wanted anything like I wanted him.

"I never knew my father," I told him once, our bodies still slick with sweat, our feet still tangled in the thousand-count sheets at the Copley Plaza in Boston. He'd just finished telling me about JJ's latest milestone, and it was obvious how much he adored his son. And it wasn't just the contrast to my own absent father that was making me emotional. I was beginning to wonder if Jack's love for JJ meant he'd never walk away from Justine. "He left when I was little," I said. "I don't even have a picture."

It wasn't the entire truth. My dad didn't leave. My dumbass mother just didn't know which loser to inform he was about to become a father. But I certainly spent my entire life feeling abandoned by *her*, constantly checked out on cheap booze and whatever pills she could scavenge, too comatose to play with me or often even to feed me. It doesn't take a genius to figure out that with all these men I've spent my entire life chasing, it's really just my father I've been aiming to catch, the nameless, faceless prince I've been praying would swoop in and save me.

That night with Jack, the words poured out of me with surprising ease—the most truthful ones I've ever shared with a man about my past. The real me came out of hiding that day, even if only for a tiny peek, and it didn't send him bolting out of bed. He squeezed my hand and passed me a cigarette, and he *stayed*, and it was intoxicating. That moment really did a number on me.

On *us*.

"Camille Tavani, who let the likes of you in?"

At the nasally twang, the champagne turns sour in my stomach, and I put the glass down on a side table. Donna Moldova, heiress to the Donnabelle Jewelry Company and a royal pain in my ass. Why is she everywhere I turn lately—at the Christmas party, the memorial mass, and now here? I'd really hoped once I stopped working for her all those years ago, I'd never have to see her ugly mug again.

Like most guests, she's gone all out for this party, in a flowing kimono that has a lot more fabric than it should, though it dips low in the front to show off plenty of cleavage. A red silk flower is tucked behind an ear, and her makeup is slapped on thick and loud. I'd say she's trying too hard for the occasion, but this is how she always looks, overdressed and overdone.

A shirtless waiter passes, and I grab the first two drinks from his tray, taking a giant gulp of the clear one. Hooray, it's vodka. "Keep moving, Donna. I am nowhere near drunk enough for this conversation."

She smirks, pretending to look around. "Does Sal know you're here? Maybe I better warn him so he can hide his valuables."

I ignore the dig, gesturing instead to the shiny stones hanging from her every body part—wrists and earlobes and every finger on both hands, that stupid moonstone piece she's known for dangling from her neck, the biggest gem trapped in her bosom like a hot dog in an overstuffed bun. "Haven't you heard? Christmas is over. You can finally put away those tacky decorations."

"Still jealous, I see. You've always wanted what I have, the jewels and the cars and the name, though you never wanted to work for it. Not when seducing my clients and having sticky fingers is so much easier. And by the way, you're looking particularly…slutty." Her gaze rolls down my body, seven pounds lighter since the plane crash.

"Now who's jealous? And you seem to have conveniently forgotten. I have a little secret of my own." I smile, and she scowls. She knows exactly what secret I'm talking about.

"Not one you can prove."

"I wouldn't be too sure of that if I were you. There's a stack of Polaroids hidden somewhere real good that says otherwise."

It's a lie, of course. I only have one stack of Polaroids, and as much as I'd enjoy watching her face twist with envy at all that glorious skin, I can tell from the way her forehead crumples that my words are enough. Donna doesn't need photographic evidence, and I know what I saw. A truckload of waste leaving her warehouse in the middle of the night is *not* headed to a legal dump. She swipes the second drink out of my hand and takes a big chug.

"And besides," I say, "I don't know how many times I have to tell you, I didn't take that stupid tennis bracelet. Gwendolyn had the keys to the diamond case too."

"Gwenny is my cousin. Unlike you, she isn't a thief."

My eyes bug at the last word. "Keep your voice down, would you? Otherwise, I might start shouting something about the trucks I saw leaving the warehouse at all hours of the day and night. Don't forget, I got 'em on the Kodachrome."

I only saw one truck, and at sometime just past 2:00 a.m., when my date dropped me back at my car. But Donna doesn't correct me, so I know I'm not wrong. There was more than one truck.

She squints, and her mascara is a mess, thick and clumped in the corners. "I thought you said Polaroids."

"Whatever. The point is I have evidence."

"Yeah, well, so do I."

"Then I guess that means this here's a standoff, doesn't it?" I drain my drink and press the glass in her empty hand. Her fingers curl around it before she can stop them. I wriggle mine in a wave. "Enjoy your evening, Donna. Oh, and you might want to wipe that lipstick off your teeth."

She leaves in a huff, and I turn back to the party raging behind me, scanning the room for the other widows. I'm still carrying a million bucks in my coat, and it wouldn't be awful to find someone to talk to, someone I can drag to a couch in the corner and unload all my feelings about Jack and the trucks and Donna on and maybe even receive a tiny bit of sympathy in return.

But if the other widows are here, I don't see them. I search in the shadowy corners. Meredith said this was the kind of night where anything goes, but what she meant is everything. *Everything* goes, including the full-on foreplay happening right here, in this very room.

"Are those people turning you on?"

I jump a little at the voice, the nearness of it, the heat coming off the body just behind mine. The wrongness that it doesn't belong to Jack.

Martin Ellis, leaning against the same marble pillar I rested on earlier, one ankle crossed in front of the other. He's traded his suit for a pair of dark pants and a light-blue shirt, unbuttoned halfway to his belly button. A glass of brown liquid dangles from a hand.

His eyes rake me from head to toe, then back up again, his gaze slow and thorough. He zones in on the two tiny pink scraps of lace that La Perla calls a bra, and his lips quirk in a lopsided grin. "They are, aren't they? They're turning you on."

I swat his arm. "It's cold, you pervert. *You* try standing here in your underwear and tell me how warm it makes me feel. And by the way, I'm mad at you." I cross my arms, then, when his gaze dips to my lifted breasts, drop them back by my sides.

"At me? Why? What did I do?"

"You made me believe the missing four million dollars was *my* problem when really, it was yours."

"Is that so?"

"Yes. It's so. I happen to know that the money was an off-the-books payment for the land so Sal could get paid, look like the hometown hero, and get his tax write-off at the same time. And let me ask you this: What was the firm charging you for brokering this deal? Because considering the seller, I'm betting it was more than four million. A *lot* more."

He pushes off the column and takes a couple of steps in my direction. The room is big and wide, but the music and the people and the flashing lights and Martin moving closer shrink it down to the size of a broom closet. This man is devastatingly handsome, but it's his confidence that makes him so seductive.

Even here, in the head mobster's house filled with CEOs and politicians, he shines.

And like it or not, I *am* newly single.

He cocks his head, his hazel eyes narrowing just a bit as he studies me—my face this time. He looks pleased, or at the very least impressed. "You're smarter than you look. Has anyone ever told you that?"

All the damn time. My mother, when I forged her signature on the financial aid application and finagled a free ride to the University of Georgia. Her endless string of skeevy boyfriends, reeking of fried food and stale sweat, their hands grabbing me even when they were sober. All the male teachers and college professors who took one look at me and thought I was good for only one thing. When you are born onto a sinking ship, you either drown or you figure out real fast how to build a lifeboat.

I smile, tossing a long curl over my shoulder. "What I'm trying to tell you is we fixed your problem. The four million is here, in this very room even. It's being delivered as we speak." I pause, waiting for his reaction, for his gratitude, but he doesn't look happy at the news. He doesn't look all that surprised either. "This is the part where you're supposed to thank me for finding the missing money. Didn't your mama teach you any manners?"

"What about the report? You were supposed to find it for me, remember?"

"Sure, but that was back when I thought I needed you to

front the money to the mob. But like I said, that problem's been solved. You're welcome." I touch a fingertip to the center of his chest, pressing against skin and bone. "Looks like you're the one with the little bitty problem now, big guy."

"Think again, Camille, because it's not just my money on the line here. I can't move forward on property that hasn't gone through the proper due diligence—especially given the seller. If that report doesn't materialize in the next day or two, I'm going to have to pump the brakes. And just so we're clear, no mall means no fee to the firm for brokering a deal, which means you four are out a million apiece—no return on investment. I know Sal, and he doesn't do refunds."

Well, hell's bells. I hadn't thought of it like that. The widows and I need that mall deal, or else we need to hang on to that cash—or what's left of it, at least until the insurance comes through, and who knows when that'll be? I glance around for Meredith and Justine, thinking maybe I can stop them before they fork over their coats. Maybe we can convince Sal that it's Martin who owes him this money, not us.

"But I looked everywhere, even in"—I lean close, lowering my voice to a whisper—"you know, Jack's things. It's not there. It must have burned up on the plane."

"I have it on good authority that it didn't."

"I'm telling you, Martin. I don't know where he put it."

He smiles again, but it's different this time. Colder. Almost dismissive. Disappointment sits like a rock, hard and heavy, in my belly. This isn't a flirtation. It's a business transaction, and somehow, I'm on the losing end.

I sidle closer, threading my hand around his elbow, hooking it over his bicep. "Come on, sugar. Don't look at me like that. I'm trying to help you out here."

"Then help me find the report. Because until then, I'm not dropping another penny into this deal." He shifts his big body, the movement untangling us and putting us nose to nose. "Not even for such a beautiful package."

MEREDITH

The baby grand is silent now, but there's an even bigger crowd gathered around. Two women are making out on the white lacquered top, wearing gold body paint and nothing else. Not even Justine's perfect body and honeyed voice could manage to pull focus from *that*. One of the painted girls slaps the other on the ass, and a flutter of fifties rains down around them—a reminder of just how much I'm missing out on coming here as a guest rather than the entertainment.

I turn away from the show, slipping down one of the shadowed hallways that splits off from the living room. This house is a labyrinth. I've been here dozens of times, and I'm sure I still haven't come close to seeing it all. Sal keeps some areas off-limits to his guests, of course. Wherever he's stashed Rom, it's going to be well away from the party crowd and possibly behind multiple locks even Camille can't pick. That's Krystle's problem, not mine.

There's a couple ahead of me in the corridor, a potbellied guy with a thatch of silver chest hair and a girl with a *Flashdance* physique who looks young enough to be his daughter. I slow down until they disappear behind a door.

Farther down the hall, I see a woman alone—an unusual sight at Sal's parties. She tosses a glance over her shoulder, and I stop in my tracks.

"Frankie?"

My bartender friend is more dressed up than I've ever seen her, stiletto boots replacing her usual shitkickers, a handbag with a chain strap slung over a leather minidress that hugs curves I didn't even know she had.

"What are you doing here?" I stride toward her. "How did you get in?"

"I have my ways. I thought you said you were busy tonight. Who were those two women you and Krystle came in with?"

"The other wives." Behind Frankie, one of the bedroom doors swings open, and a muscular guy in bondage gear spills out, white powder dusting his Tom Selleck mustache. "Widows, I mean. The other widows. From the firm."

"So the four of you came here together?" Frankie asks. Bondage guy stumbles past us, probably in search of more blow. "I'm surprised you're all in the mood to celebrate, so soon after... well, you know."

Celebrating? This is the last place I want to be. I should be ringing in the New Year blackout drunk and sobbing in Robin's bed, not sober as a judge and sneaking around a Mafia boss's mansion with a million dollars hanging around my shoulders. I can't even untangle the grief from the anger anymore. I miss Robin so much, it feels like my heart's on the floor with a heel through it. But if I saw her right now, I might just kill her myself for putting me through this.

I can't explain all that to Frankie—not without ruining my makeup and blowing my cover.

Frankie's dark eyes sweep over my body. "Aren't you a little warm in that?"

I cinch Robin's fur tighter around me. With the money in the lining, the coat won't close over my chest. "I'm fine. You really shouldn't be walking around all by yourself. It's not—"

"I was looking for a bathroom. This place is confusing as hell."

"There's one around the corner. Third door on the right."

"Thanks. Maybe I'll see you at midnight." Frankie winks and starts walking away.

I've got enough to deal with tonight without taking on babysitting duties, but I'd never forgive myself if something happened to her. I'll just make sure she finds the bathroom okay.

When I turn the corner, hustling to catch up with Frankie, she's already passed it right by. She stops in front of a totally different door—the only one without mood lighting glowing around the edges or moans and music reverberating from inside—then withdraws a long metal object from her boot and sticks it in the keyhole.

She's picking the lock, but not with a bobby pin. That's some kind of specialized tool. She came prepared.

One expert twist of her wrist, and the door pops open. I was already sweating under this damn fur, but now it feels like Niagara Falls running down my spine.

"Frankie!" I call after her. But it's too late; she's already ducking into the darkened room.

I have no idea what's back there, but it's clearly something Sal doesn't want his guests to see. Cursing myself for letting yet another beautiful woman lead me astray, I follow Frankie inside.

"What the hell are you doing?" I ease the door shut behind us as silently as I can. "You can't be in here. If Sal sees you—"

"You should go find your friends, Meredith."

Frankie has a small flashlight in her hand now, and the weak beam illuminates the space enough for me to tell it's an office— Sal's office, if all the wolf paraphernalia in here is any indication. On the desk sits a bronze bust of a wolf head, and the wall behind it boasts a blown-up photo of a pack running through the woods, the ornate picture frame flanked by heavy velvet drapes.

Say what you will about the man, but you have to appreciate his commitment to a theme. Rumor has it Sal Ponterelli's entire back is covered with wolves too, a trio of them howling at a full moon tattooed between his shoulder blades. I wouldn't know: unlike the majority of my coworkers, I've never slept with the man. And even though Sal's parties feature sexual encounters on just about every mountable surface in his mansion, Sal himself always takes his conquests back to his personal suite. Either he's a secret gentleman under all that swagger, or he's into some *really* freaky shit that he doesn't want prying eyes to see.

Whatever the case, we shouldn't be in his office. And Frankie should *definitely* not be rooting through his desk drawers with that flashlight clenched between her teeth.

"What are you doing?" I ask again.

She sets the flashlight on the desk along with some file folders and a spiral-bound book. "Don't you want to know what kind of man we work for?"

"Not really." I'm Providence born and raised, so I knew what I was getting into when I applied to dance at a Ponterelli-owned establishment. The club was still a step up from the gig I had at the time; I got my ass grabbed and my tits ogled there too, for far less money per hour and a much worse boss.

When people find out I'm a stripper, they always want to pathologize it, hear my tragic backstory. The truth is the worst thing that's ever happened to me was Robin's plane going down. Stripping has always been a business proposition to me, the most efficient way to make a lot of money in a short amount of time. And if my parents were going to disown me for anything, it would have been me coming out as bisexual at sixteen. Compared to that, my choice of profession was a relatively easy pill to swallow. I'm pretty sure my mom's still holding out hope that I'll meet a nice man while spinning around the pole.

Frankie opens the book—looks like a financial ledger,

columns of handwritten names and numbers—and takes a few papers out of the folders, arranging them on the desk. Then she opens her purse and produces a Polaroid camera.

"Whoa!" I rush toward her. "What the fuck, Frankie? How did you even get that past the bouncers?"

"I told you. I have my ways." She snaps a photo and withdraws the print, shaking it as the image develops. "Look at this."

She holds up one of the documents. It's a financial statement, rows of steadily increasing dollar amounts showing revenue from the strip club—except it's way too much, thousands more on each date than the Wolf Den ever pulls in. I've been there long enough to know.

"So? Obviously, he launders money through the club. He launders money through all his businesses; that's what they're for. If it bothers you so much, go tend bar at Bennigan's."

Frankie looks at me with wide eyes. Not like she's shocked. Like she's calculating.

"You know, Meredith." She brushes her fingers across the fur coat, tracing down my arm. "You're a good person. No matter how much you'd like to pretend otherwise."

We're both in shadow, the flashlight beam pointing away, so even this close, I can barely see her. Just the halo of her hair, the curve of her lips. This is a terrible idea, maybe the worst one I've had yet tonight. But if I might die anyway...

I lean in, my eyes falling shut.

And then snap them right back open, because there are footsteps in the hall. Voices too—outside the door.

"Hide!" I whisper. Frankie flicks off the flashlight and shoves it back in her purse, along with the photo and the camera. I stick the folders back in what I hope was the drawer where she found them, then grab her hand and drag her behind the drapes. The thick fabric is still settling around us when the office door opens and the lights switch on.

"You want me to finish him off, boss?" a rough male voice asks. Arti.

"No." That one was Sal—and he sounds irritated. "Not yet. They've got the money, and I'll have it by midnight."

"You sure? For all we know, that bitch might—"

There's a harsh *thwack* like Sal might have smacked Arti across the face. "That's enough. Krystle Romero may have raised a thief, but she's a goddamn lady, and we respect ladies in my house."

"Yes, boss," Arti says, much softer this time.

"Find the other three and bring them to me," Sal says. "I wanna get this taken care of so I can enjoy the rest of 1985."

The door opens and shuts again. Sal's still here though. I can't see him through the gap in the curtains, but I hear the desk chair creak as he sits down and leans back. Frankie's pressed up against my side, the hem of her leather skirt brushing the strip of bare skin above my stockings.

I shift my weight carefully, trying not to bump the curtain

or the windowpane. Except there is no windowpane. No wall either. As my eyes adjust, I realize there's nothing besides empty space back here. The drapes were concealing another corridor, continuing deeper into the house.

I nudge Frankie with my elbow, jerking my head in the direction I want us to go. She nods, breath rustling my hair, and we start creeping down the hidden hallway. I listen for any hint of movement from the office behind us—Sal's chair pushing back or footsteps approaching—but there's no sound other than the thudding of my heart.

Eventually we find ourselves at the top of a dimly lit staircase, nowhere to go but down. It feels less like an escape route and more like we're hapless prey walking deeper into the open maw of something with teeth.

Frankie starts down the steps, but I stay on the landing, grabbing for her arm. "Maybe we should go back," I whisper.

I'm panting from terror and exertion and the weight of this damn cash-filled coat. Frankie's exhales are even—awfully relaxed, considering the situation she's gotten us into.

"Oh, come on, Mere. Where's your sense of adventure?" She tosses a wink over her shoulder and keeps heading down the stairs.

This bitch is crazy.

And so am I, because I keep on following her, down into the belly of the beast.

At the bottom of the stairs, we push through another set of

heavy drapes and into a room so big our footsteps echo. There's a huge fireplace across from us filled with smoldering logs and a dimly glowing swimming pool in the center of the floor—the only sources of light. Despite the fire, it's cold in here, and for the first time all night, I'm glad to be wearing Robin's fur.

Frankie gets out her flashlight again and sweeps it around to get more detail. The space looks even more like a cave than the entryway: faux rock-textured walls, little fountains running down them into the pool. Lining one wall is a long table, covered with—

"Holy shit," Frankie says, focusing her light. The surface is stacked with all sorts of loot: millions in cash, guns, bricks of cocaine. Between the larger items, diamonds and rubies and a few smaller milky stones glimmer in the flashlight beam.

I step closer, resisting the urge to stuff a few of those jewels in my bra. It's not like Sal, leaving all this unguarded, even if you do have to take a secret passageway from his office to get here.

"This is…" Frankie takes out her Polaroid again. "Wow. *Wow.*"

"We need to get out of here." This doesn't feel right. It feels like a trap. "Frankie, let's go."

"Just a second." She lifts the camera to her eye, walking back to fit as much contraband in the frame as possible.

"Frankie."

"I said one second." She presses the shutter button, and the flash goes off.

Illuminating the teeth of a very large wolf.

"*Frankie!*"

The wolf lunges, snapping its jaws just short of her arm. Frankie stumbles back, colliding with me, barely keeping hold of the camera.

Growls rumble in the dark. More wolves, prowling toward us.

I back up, one step at a time, pulling Frankie with me. "Give me the flashlight. No sudden moves."

She hands it over, and I point it toward the snarling sounds, the light wavering in my shaking hands.

There are three wolves, giant silvery beasts with broad shoulders and sharp eyes, all wearing collars and chains that attach to the wall by the fireplace. They can't reach us if we stay right where we are. But if we get close to that table or anything else in the room, we're dinner.

"Okay," Frankie says. "You were right. Let's get the fuck out of here."

"Wait!" a voice calls after us.

Frankie and I both look around, trying to find the source. It sounded male, scratchy, and weak, coming from somewhere above us. I swing the flashlight up.

There's a balcony on the wall about fifteen feet in the air, between us and where the wolves are chained. And slumped on it, gripping the railing with bruised fingers, is Rom Romero.

Rom's eye is swollen shut, dried blood smeared from his nose to his chin. He looks so miserable, even I can't help feeling sorry for the guy. He reaches through the bars to wave at us, and the wolves jump and snap like he's offering them a tasty treat.

"Help me," Rom cries. "Please, Meredith. They're gonna kill me."

KRYSTLE

First it was being nose to nose with a wolf. Then it was stripping down to my skivvies in front of a mob boss. But now, seeing Justine bibbidi-bobbidi-boo into Cher at the piano has really shocked the shit out of me.

Hugging the wall, I slip behind one very distracted goon and hurry down a white shag-carpeted hallway. There are more oil paintings, and I recognize the gray coat of Daisy along with three other wolves that don't look any friendlier.

I open the first door to find what I believe is called a devil's three-way. Two guys on either side of one gal, who is the meat between these two slices. I'm never eating a sandwich again.

"Join us!" shouts a man, and I slam the door.

Listening before I open the next room, there's a loud snort and giggle. I move on toward another few rooms—passed-out girl, guy getting whipped, more cokeheads—and finally, there are some stairs.

I decide to go downstairs, because who has wolves in the attic? Seems a basement situation. I picture Rom surrounded by Daisy's snarling sisters and hurry.

On the basement level, there is more muscle at the end of the hallway. He's guarding a steel door. I throw myself behind a huge vase at the foot of the stairs.

He's flipping through a magazine and seems distracted enough. I hustle over to the first door, which is thankfully wide open. Inside is an empty billiards room full of dark wood and smelling of leather.

There's a giant pool table right in the middle, and I grab the eight ball off the table. I make sure the guy isn't looking, then I launch it toward the end of the hallway. The ball smacks a wall and bounces over to hit a door I didn't see. Jumping under the table, I listen as the guy hurries past.

A walkie-talkie crackles. "Heard something, boss. I'm going to check outside."

Might as well be an engraved invitation. Once the door slams, I hustle down the hallway. My mom instincts have me nearly screaming for my son.

I heave open the metal door and am surprised to see the warm glow of a swimming pool in the center of a dark and cavernous room. I choose to go right, making it around a table with money and drugs. Oooh, and jewels. In fact, lots of moonstones, and I wonder if some of this comes from Donna herself. What's she need to pay Sal this kind of money for? Still considering the connection as I hug the wall, I run smack into a familiar set of boobs.

"Meredith," I screech, shocked she's here with that bartender from the strip club—Frankie, I think. "What are you guys doing here?"

"Shhhhh," they both say.

I blink and crane my neck to see around them. My eyes are adjusting, and I see this is a huge two, maybe three-story room made to look like a cave. A small fountain drips down the rocky wall into the pool as steam floats on the shimmering surface.

"This is what happens when you never marry," I murmur.

"SHHHHH!" they say, louder.

What? I mouth, and that's when I see it.

Three sets of eyes glowing in front of the barely burning fireplace. The wolves. This must be where they have Rom.

I grab Meredith's arm, and she reads my mind, pointing up. I keep looking, past the plants and rocks and water until I'm almost at the ceiling, and there's a little rounded balcony.

There's my son.

Clamping a hand over my mouth, I keep from screaming his name, or I might as well call out *Buon appetito* to those damn wolves.

"He's fine," Meredith whispers. "I mean, not mint condition, but definitely alive."

That is not the kind of proof of life a mother wants. I pull away and scan the cave walls for a door or ladder or stairs or, hell, gym rope. Whatever it takes to be sure Rom is okay. "Rom, it's Mom!" I whisper as loud as I can. "Do you need an inhaler, sweetie? I brought an extra. Don't ask me where."

He groans, but it's the whiny one, not the I'm-in-deep-shit one.

I take a step, and it echoes. The three wolves instantly move, and I reach out for the gals and scoot us back.

"They're on chains," the bartender says.

"Who the hell is she?" I ask, giving Meredith a look.

"I'm Frankie, nice to meet you," she says as if we're greeting each other at Sunday school.

I wrinkle my nose at the Polaroid camera she's holding. "Taking a picture so it'll last longer?"

Frankie shoves the camera in her purse. "We're about to bounce. There's a set of stairs behind that curtain that leads to Sal's office."

"Too risky," says Meredith. "How about the door Krystle came through?"

They're missing the point. "We can't leave without Rom. I know he can be a doofus, but he's my son. I love him more than anything. Please, you have to help me."

Meredith glances at Frankie and then me, not hiding the conflict in her eyes. "We'll come back for him."

"No!" I yell, and that's all the wolves need.

The largest one charges us, and we scream and fall back as she leaps in the air. Thankfully, the chain snaps her back from making my face an *aperitivo*.

We're all gasping and scurrying in reverse on the stone floor. The chains are long, making half the room their territory. One of them runs to the closest edge of the pool and howls up at Rom, whose perch is just over her. If he tried to jump into the pool, he'd break his leg on the stone before being eaten alive.

"How can we get out of here now?" Meredith hisses. "Their chains cover the door you came through."

"We can make it on this side of the pool," Frankie says, glancing around at the blocked stairs, narrowing her eyes toward the shadows under the balcony holding Rom. "Maybe there's another exit over there."

"Do you really want to take that risk?" Meredith points up toward him. "Why don't we find a way up there? You can pick the lock to get out."

I blink at Frankie. "You pick locks?"

"Sure."

I glance around the room and search for something one of us—okay, one of them—could climb up.

The wolf continues to growl and doesn't move back.

"Rom!" I whisper-yell. "You need to help us! Can you drop one of those curtains down?"

He moves, pulling himself to the edge of the balcony. His eye is bruised, but otherwise, he looks fine. "What, Ma?"

"The curtain! Drop it down, sweetie! On the side opposite the wolves."

"No doy, Ma." Rom gets up quickly, and there's more easing

in my chest that he's really okay. He flings the curtain over the side and ties it around the metal rail with a firm knot. Guess ten years of sailing camp finally paid off.

The curtain falls, hitting about four feet above the center of the pool. One wolf jumps for it, but she's short a few feet.

"Are you kidding?" Frankie puts her hands on her hips. "I'm not climbing up there. If I fall, I'll be a wolf snack."

"I thought you were all about adventure?" Meredith says, something suspicious in her gaze. "I'll help you, Krystle."

I take off my heels and leather skirt, and Meredith stays in her hooker getup, so now we're both in panties and tiny tops.

"At least give her your fancy lockpick," Meredith calls as we walk around the edge of the pool. My heart has not slowed down since I stepped foot in this house, but now I'm pretty sure it's about to explode.

Frankie looks truly conflicted but hands over the large metal pick. I stick it in my gold corset and put one foot into the pool.

"Shit!" I squeal as the water hits above my knees. "It's colder than a penguin's pecker!"

Meredith sighs but still steps in. "Let's hurry."

The three wolves mirror us wading into the pool. Their chains stop just short of where the curtain hangs above the water. They're snapping and snarling, but we reach it safely.

I lift up onto my tippy-toes, but I'm at least a foot short. One wolf starts to howl, like an alarm. "Shhhh." I splash water at her, but that just makes her howl louder. "Damn it, we gotta move."

Meredith sloshes and kneels on one leg, cursing under her breath. "Heave ho."

I step onto her knee and take her hand as I try to balance. My wet foot falls and splashes us both. "Let's try that again."

This time, I use her hand and her head to balance. I mean, it's right there.

"Ow! That's my hair!"

I get both feet on her knee and reach. "It's still short."

"Jump or something!"

I keep wobbling and then jump, completely missing the curtain and landing with a splash. The wolves are close, but not close enough to reach us. Not that you could tell by the way we're gasping in panic. "Oh my God...oh my God..." I nearly jump into Meredith's arms.

"What now?" She shivers against me.

My teeth are rattling. "You have to boost me."

"What? How?" She swipes where her hair is dripping down her face.

"Boost her, Meredith!" Rom yells from above. "She needs a boost."

"Yeah, I got it, man." She focuses on me. "How the hell do I do that?"

I grip her shoulders. "Get an ass in your face, that's how. You're used to it, right?"

Meredith sticks out her jaw. "You know, I can bounce outta here with Frankie and leave you to the wolves."

"I know," I say quickly, my teeth chattering. "Thank you. You could, but you didn't. Really, thank you."

The wolves are howling as Meredith dips down into the water. She gets her arms under my thighs. She heaves up once, I bounce, and I still can't reach.

"Bend with your knees or you'll break your back!" Frankie yells.

"Not helpful!" I yell.

"Yeah, get over here, Frankie," Meredith says in a tone that could lead to a spanking and probably has.

Frankie obeys, throwing off her hooker boots and hiding her purse before wading into the water with a few colorful phrases. They each have a thigh and heave at the same time. I shoot up like some kind of circus clown out of a cannon. I grab the curtain just as they lose their grip and fall into the water with a muffled yelp.

My arms are already shaking as I wrap my legs tightly around the swinging curtain. With an active-labor grunt, I pull myself up. The wolves are really losing their minds now. Their howls are replaced with vicious snarls and barks.

"Hurry, Mom!" Rom yells. If I had an ounce of energy to spare, I'd tell him to piss off.

I pull up again, making it maybe another few inches. Then a few more. This is going to take until 1987.

Focusing, I figure out how to keep my balance better with my feet pressed into each other. God only knows what kind of boiled frog legs I look like. "Rom, try to pull it up!"

He tugs and makes a really unflattering noise. What do they think I weigh? A metric ton?

Suddenly, the wolves are quiet. I only hear Meredith and Frankie sloshing below me. I pull myself a little farther up with a grunt.

"I knew you'd come right for him, sweetheart," calls a deep voice. "Romeo, Romeo, wherefore art thou Romeo? Cause his mommy is coming to save him."

Sal's laughter fills the cave room. I glance over to see him standing at the water's edge. Arti is behind him, holding Camille and Justine by their bare arms. Their coats aren't with them.

I guess he chose this opportunity to get us all together and get his money.

Sal snaps his fingers at another guy in the corner. "Grab that coat. Get it to Tino."

Meredith takes a couple of sloshy steps in the pool, moving toward her coat on the side. But almost as soon as she starts, it's hauled off.

"Yoo-hoo!" I yell.

"You want me to catch her, boss?" Arti asks.

"Not unless you want another smack in the face." Sal's shoes hit the floor with a light thud. Then a belt buckle and the swish of falling pants. "Hold tight, Krissie."

He's in his white shirt and bare legs. I narrow my eyes to get a better look and almost lose my grip. "Shit!" I squeak.

"Easy," he calls as he hurries through the water with a sloosh. "You'll break your neck at that height."

I look down to see him behind me as I try to stop wiggling on the curtain. I can't bear to imagine the view.

"Quit looking at my ma's ass," Rom yells.

Maybe I should just break my neck.

"When you fall, try to keep your arms and legs out," Sal calls up. "Like Christ on the cross, so you don't break my nose."

"Sure!" I yell, suddenly terrified of a potentially deadly fall. This would be a lot to explain to a coroner.

"Okay, ready?" Sal shouts.

"If you're not too busy," I snap, seconds away from my arms ripping off my body. The wolves would love that.

"On three, Krissie. One, two, three."

I close my eyes and let go. It's only a second of falling, but I gasp as I try to keep from smacking Sal.

His arms are right there, holding me steady and tight against his chest. My hands reach around his neck, and for a moment, I breathe in the safety of someone else being there for me. It's been a while.

Of course, he did kidnap my son and get me into this mess in the first place. I glance up at Rom scowling down at us, open-mouthed. Maybe for good reason.

Sal carries me over to the side of the pool. When the wolves growl, I stick my tongue out at them. Pardon me for enjoying a little chivalry and maybe some strong hands on my ass.

He places me on the floor and snaps at Arti, "Get them towels."

Arti ambles over to a small corner and brings back a stack of towels the three of us grab as we drip everywhere. I hand one to Sal, and he winks.

We get back into our clothes, though Frankie never took off her tight dress. I'd imagine pliers would be required. And poor Meredith just has to stand there shivering.

"You all right?" I ask Camille and Justine.

"Did you almost kiss him?" Camille whispers with an impressed gleam in her eyes.

"Shut up." I launch a towel at her face.

"Arti, where's Tino?" Sal barks.

With that question, one of the other guys who'd ransacked my home swings open the door. Behind him, someone rolls a rack over to us. I recognize the remains of Camille's, Meredith's, and Justine's coats, freed from their linings. There are also several furs that look like they fell off a truck beneath the Tri-Store Bridge.

"Got these extras for you," Sal says. "Go ahead. You're turning blue."

You don't have to tell me twice. I go for a long white mink and nearly moan as I slip into the smoothly lined arms and pull up the collar. Camille opts for a brand-new chinchilla, as does Meredith. But Justine takes her old coat, the lining in tatters where one million dollars was stashed.

"The money was all there, boss," Tino says.

Sal looks relieved. "You want your son back? I think our business is done."

I turn toward the ladies, aware we all risked a lot to come here, including our dignity. Yes, it was part self-interest. But when I needed help, they caught me too.

"Ma, come on. Make Sal get me down," Rom whines.

"Not until you answer my questions to my satisfaction." Meredith steps toward me, wrapped in fox fur, with her high boots back on. I wouldn't mess with her. "Why did you steal four million dollars and leave us holding the bag?"

"Hey!" Rom yells. "I did not steal that money!"

Camille walks up beside Meredith and me. "Usually, sugar, when people are given four million dollars, they don't keep it in their ceiling, where it's less secure than their spank bank."

"I mean, yes, I hid it… Okay, I did do that." Rom sounds nervous, and I'm glad. "It's just… I don't want to say any more."

"You entitled prick," Meredith says. "What you want has no place in our conversation. We've been chased and threatened and harassed for this money. You'll tell us everything, or we'll leave without you."

"You will not," Rom says. "And I'm not a prick."

Rom looks at me to save him, but finally, I realize that's not what he needs. "A couple more nights here are fine by me," I say, meaning it. "If he won't answer your questions."

"Fine!" he says, like the most petulant twenty-four-year-old who ever drew a breath. "Dad gave it to me, okay? Before he left for New York."

There's a fiery, burning lump in my throat. How dare Romeo

involve Rom in his shady dealings? Business is business, I get it, but there has to be a code. He knew I drew the line at our children.

"Did your dad tell you it was mine?" Sal asks without much judgment.

Rom looks away. "Dad told me to keep it safe. It was the last thing he ever said to me. So I thought I'd finally listen. After he was killed, I realized we might need the money to run."

Every mother's heart knows disappointment. The problem is the older they get, the more you wonder if the finger should really be pointed in your direction. "Let him out, please."

As Arti heads off to get Rom, someone slips through the door. A tall man with intense eyes. He's completely calm walking into this scene, like it's just another day that ends in Y.

The wolves begin to growl, low and angry, something even more terrifying than before. I hear Sal curse under his breath. "No offense, but this is a private party."

"Looks to me like this is the real entertainment," the man says in a deep, unnerving voice.

From the terror on Justine's face, I realize this was probably the guy who'd spooked her. "You can call him off, Sal," I say.

Sal doesn't respond but instead moves quickly toward his snarling wolves.

I yell toward the creep, "We've paid. No need to lurk! We're square."

The man smiles at me, and my stomach drops. "Are we

square?" He sounds like he knows something we don't, and it might just kill us.

"Yes," Justine says with a shaky voice. "I told you. The money has been paid in full."

"I never said I wanted money, Justine." He raises his eyebrows and faces each of us. "Perhaps I should also discuss it with Krystle? Or Camille? Certainly Tina. Or do you prefer Meredith? I didn't see your name on Robin's mailbox, so I wasn't sure." He's still grinning. "I want the report Jack was holding on to. The one from Vista Corp."

Recognition flashes on Camille's face. "We don't know where it is. I've searched."

The man directs his attention to Justine. "Then I guess I *will* have to help you look."

Chains rattle, and Sal has unhooked the wolves from the wall. He holds the three of them tight as they pull and snarl at the stranger.

"Seems you're upsetting the girls." He lets out a chain, and Daisy snaps her jaws as she jumps several feet closer to the man. "We'll see you upstairs."

For a moment, the man shows no reaction. Then a cruel smile. "See you soon."

Sal's hard gaze remains on the door, even after it's shut. The wolves calm down and circle him.

"That one of yours is really scary," I say to him, moving closer. "I should never have complained about Arti."

"Mr. Ponterelli," Justine says. "You have the money. We don't know about any documents. Can you please tell that man to leave us alone?"

Sal frowns deeply. "I'm afraid I can't do that." He scratches behind the wolves' ears, then moves his hands along their sides. "Good girls."

"But that was the deal! Isn't four million enough paper for you?" I stomp my foot. "What do you need that document for anyway?"

"You misunderstand, Krissie."

My gut tightens at an emotion I've never seen on Sal's face, not once in the decades I've known him: fear.

"He's not one of mine. I don't hire men I can't control."

Justine puts her trembling fingers over her mouth. "Who does he work for then?"

"Whoever is paying him," Sal says. "He's a contract killer they call the Tiger. But a man like him doesn't do it for the money, though he's paid more than most. All he's looking for is an excuse to kill."

We glance at one another. Even more danger was stalking us, and we'd had no idea.

"Krissie, if you've got something he wants, you better not stop until you've handed it over."

Justine is staring at the spot where he was standing. "Why the Tiger?"

Sal answers her question but looks at me, the fear thick, as if he might be saying goodbye. "He always goes for the throat."

JUSTINE

Camille drives with the top down despite the cold. Wind rips through the remains of my coat, stinging my bare skin beneath. I don't complain. The icy air is a balm for the images burned into my brain: Rom's bloodied nose, wolves snapping for human flesh, my stalker's predatory stare as he demands documents that none of us can find.

I turn my face into the current. It whips my hair and batters my ears, silencing even my own thoughts. Now that we've dropped off Krystle, Rom, and Meredith at Robin's place, it's just Camille and me. I have nothing to tell her anyway. Everything that needed saying, I sang.

We pull into the driveway of her Georgian mansion. The sprawling brick structure with its shuttered windows and scarlet door fits the woman beside me. It's a beautiful fortress. Most anyone driving by the home would admire it, though its exterior says little about what's inside.

Camille steers the Alfa Romeo into an open bay of her three-car garage. She lowers the gate before turning the key in the ignition, in case we need to suddenly reverse. We both watch the retractable wall descend. The mob is no longer after us, but the man on our tail is worse. Neither of us can be too careful.

The house is dark. Quiet. I pull Camille's heels from my feet and place them on her mudroom's stone floor, hoping to muffle my steps. It's nearly one in the morning. JJ is surely asleep. I don't want to wake him until I've shed this metallic skin and transformed back into his mother.

Camille removes her shoes as well while leaving on her new chinchilla fur, a thousand-dollar-plus apology from the man who had threatened to kill us. It's a beautiful coat, but I could never feel comfortable wrapped in a gift from Salvatore Ponterelli. The only present I want from that man is to never see him again.

"I'll change quickly, get JJ, and go."

I whisper the words, though I don't know how I'll follow through with them. My car isn't parked out front. I deliberately left the Mercedes around the corner from the Turk's Head Building in hopes of making it more difficult for the mob to track my movements. The ruse worked, somewhat. My stalker asked if Jack's parents were watching JJ, suggesting that he didn't know where I'd actually dropped him. Of course, he might know now. The Alfa Romeo isn't subtle, and neither is Camille.

"JJ's asleep." She offers a weak smile. "You should leave him."

My knee-jerk reaction is to shout, "Hell no," storm upstairs, and scoop up my son. Under no circumstances would I *leave* my child at the home of Jack's former lover, but especially not now. Camille might have had my husband, but she couldn't possibly take care of my baby. If JJ woke up scared in the middle of the night, she wouldn't know how to comfort him. She probably wouldn't even hear him crying. And there's no way that I would trust her to protect him if the Tiger were outside her door.

Camille must see something in my expression because she shakes her head. "Obviously, you can stay too. You can sleep on the queen with JJ or in another bed by yourself." She sighs. "This house has plenty of guest rooms."

She isn't kidding. Camille's place is significantly larger than mine, with a living room attached to an even bigger family room and a kitchen containing a breakfast nook big enough for a nursery school class. When I went upstairs to the master bedroom earlier, I passed at least four closed doors.

For the first time, I wonder why Camille doesn't have children. She's enamored enough with JJ to suggest she likes kids. Did she have conception problems? Or did she simply not want to bring a child into a loveless marriage?

It's not the kind of question that I could easily ask a friend, let alone a woman whose hair I tried to yank out a few days ago.

"Thanks for the offer." My answer is intentionally non-committal, though it shouldn't be. The truth is that JJ and I are likely safer in Camille's manor with its plethora of hiding places and neighbors on all sides than at our home, which backs up to a public park. Here, there's a chance someone would hear us scream. Whether I'm willing to say it aloud or not, I know I'm not leaving tonight.

I follow Camille into a butler's pantry bigger than most kitchens. An entire wall has been converted to store wine. Most of the bottles lay cork-side out, hiding the vintage. However, the center row has been angled to display labels.

"All that booze and blow at the party, and I didn't even get a good buzz," Camille says, perusing the section clearly reserved for the expensive stuff. She selects a bottle and raises it like champagne. But the look on her face is anything but celebratory.

"It's Bordeaux. Château Mouton Rothschild, 1962." She traces a red nail over the label. "Peter loved wine. He was saving this one for a special occasion."

She sets the bottle on the marble counter and produces a fancy corkscrew from a drawer. "All things considered, I should probably enjoy it. Never know what life will bring, right?" She plunges the metal tip into the cork and begins twisting. "You partaking?"

I want to refuse, but I don't even have the energy to support my ego anymore. I'm scared, sad, and, after a sleepless night searching for whatever Jack might have hidden, barely standing. I can't continue to shoulder my spite or spar with my dead husband's lover. Really, we have nothing left to fight over. Jack is gone. Neither of us can have him.

"Yeah, please," I mutter. "Thanks."

Camille points to a windowed cabinet. "Glasses are in there."

I select two of the largest goblets, partially because an aged wine should have space to be swirled, but mostly because I expect a generous pour for both of us. Camille doesn't disappoint, doling out a double portion of deep-garnet liquid into each glass. She sets the bottle down and raises her drink.

We clink without toasting. The standard *Happy New Year* would sound too sarcastic.

I close my eyes and take a long gulp. A lifetime ago, before breastfeeding turned me into a teetotaler and its aftermath made me a lightweight, I enjoyed wine. This bottle reminds me of why. It's sweet and tart and smooth all at once. The liquid slides down my throat, massaging my strained vocal cords before pooling in my stomach and dousing the anxious fire inside my belly.

"It's supposed to taste like small dark fruits. Blackberries and deep-red cherries," Camille says.

I open my eyes to see her reading the back label.

"When we were dating, Peter used to make a game of guessing the flavors. He'd have us both drink and then describe it. He was pretty good at identifying the right notes. His palate was more sophisticated than mine."

"It tastes like calm," I say.

Camille cracks a smile. "That would have been a witty retort for Peter when he was teasing me about not being able to tell terroir from treacle. He tried for years to make me refined enough to have dinner with his law school buddies and their wives. But those women never took to me." She snorts. "I guess you can take the girl out the country, but…"

Camille cuts herself off with another drink rather than finishing the phrase. I follow her lead and tilt my glass back. My recent break from alcohol, coupled with not eating in more than twelve hours, is turning every sip into a shot.

"Well, I'm not sure what terroir or treacle is. Though I know the sound of a man trying to make himself seem smart by slipping in French and British terms. At least we're savvy enough *not* to go into business with folks who feed their enemies to literal wolves."

Camille smacks her lips. "You know, Jack was wrong."

"About doing a deal with Salvatore Ponterelli. Yeah. He—"

"Well, that, but other things too." She looks up from the wine, tears clinging to the insides of her glass. "You didn't lose *all* your shine."

The compliment serves double duty as a dig, reminding me that my husband complained to her, no doubt following a night of wild sex in some swanky hotel. I actually don't think Camille intends the insult though. Her eyes are watery. Soft. I sense that this is her way of apologizing. She's just not particularly good at it.

"I got duller though," I admit as Camille refreshes my drink. "I concentrated on JJ to the detriment of my marriage. When I got pregnant, I became hyperfocused on how Jack and I were going to be these great parents—*so* much better than my folks.

My parents divorced before I hit elementary school. I guess my dad never really looked back, and things got complicated after my mom remarried. I felt discarded."

In spite of myself, I make eye contact with Camille. She nods along, as if she can empathize.

"I was so determined that JJ never feel like that," I continue. "So I made everything secondary to being a mom and making sure that Jack stayed. I learned to cook instead of constantly ordering in. I traded concert tickets for toddler sing-alongs. I moved *here*, a city where I don't have any friends or job prospects, so that my husband could be a big shot. I gave it all up—all the things that Jack really loved about me, a lot of the things that I loved and admired about myself."

I stare into my glass. "It's crazy. But when I was performing in that horrible house, surrounded by strippers and mobsters, I felt more like me than I have since moving here—maybe more than I have since giving birth. I was suddenly, I don't know, worth a damn."

Camille reaches for another bottle on the middle shelf. I recognize the merging blue heads on the label. Opus One.

"California cabernet by the same winemaker," Camille says, popping the cork.

I extend my glass and watch the ruby waters rise to its equator. Unsteadiness from the already-absorbed alcohol forces me to concentrate on not spilling as I bring it to my lips. This wine is also delicious, though I still can't tell whether I'm detecting raspberries, figs, or jam. Not that it matters. I'll be too drunk to discern much of anything soon.

"You know that song you sang?" Camille looks directly at me. Her eyes remind me of antique porcelain plates, cobalt blue bleeding into white. "I never intended for you to be home alone with a kid while I…you know. I didn't think of you. I guess I didn't allow myself to think about you. I only cared about me and my crappy marriage and how I wanted to feel good and valued for a change. Jack made me happy."

I drink, anticipating the usual swell of anger at hearing her speak my husband's name. But it's not there. I'm too tipsy. Too tired.

"I regret…I can't regret Jack. I loved him, so I can't. But hurting you, hurting Peter…"

As she drinks, I finish her sentence in my head: *it wasn't the plan.* And, of course, it wasn't. Only psychopaths set out to cause others harm. Most people do their damage simply by focusing on what's most important to them, to the detriment of everybody else. We're all "most people"—save, perhaps, for the Tiger.

"Peter dropped out of the sky knowing about the affair." Camille gazes into her wineglass like it contains Peter's reflection. "I regret that."

Her admission snaps me from my alcohol stupor. Peter's awareness that his wife was sleeping with his business partner adds another dimension to our husbands' plane crash. I picture the man whom I'd met several times: the rooster comb of styled curls. Hazel eyes with a devilish glint. Perma-smirk. How would such a proud alpha male stomach the shame of being cuckolded by his own junior partner? It could be the kind of thing to make someone cut a fuel line in a fit of despair and rage, determined to kill himself and his enemies in the same fireball—taking everything away as the ultimate revenge.

"Peter didn't seem like the kind of guy to know something like that and not act on it."

"Oh, I'm pretty sure he intended to humiliate me at the Christmas party." She pauses to wipe a streak of wine from her lower lip. "I heard him on the phone before they left for New York. He was shouting about it being over and asking Jack if he wanted to be involved with *garbage*, telling him that he thought he was better than *this*—meaning me. He mentioned proof."

"What proof?"

Camille doesn't look me in the eye. "I accidentally on purpose left a pair of underwear in Jack's office one day when we…" She drinks to keep from underscoring her actions. "I guess he found it and was going to wave it around in front of the other partners and spouses."

The memory makes me take another swig from my glass.

"I found a red thong when I was searching through Jack's office. If Peter intended to confront you, I doubt he would have left it in Jack's drawer. And I have to believe that Jack would have come clean to me if Peter had called accusing him."

"Are you sure?" Camille says.

What I'm about to say makes me shake. "Jack loved me. I know he did. And I understand that he might not have been *in love* with me. I get that he felt neglected and wanted someone who was more fun and exciting to paint the town with."

Camille's mouth opens with an objection. I raise a hand, a stop sign forcing her to yield to my oncoming traffic.

"I even recognize that he might have had real feelings for you," I continue. "But I know from the way he was when he came home, the laughter we still shared, the talks about our future kids. He loved me as his wife and the mother of his son. There's no way that Jack would have let me walk into that party to be blindsided. If he and Peter had that conversation you heard, Jack would have told me not to go."

Camille's mouth shuts. She taps a red-tipped finger against her wine-stained lips. "But if he wasn't talking to Jack…"

"Who knows?" I throw up a hand. "Maybe a client. Maybe another partner. It was probably about business."

Relief spreads across Camille's face. In spite of all the wine, the sight irritates me. The possibility that her husband didn't know of the affair makes her feel better about sleeping with mine.

"None of it matters," I grumble. "Jack was hiding something much more important than a mistress, some document that our lives are riding on." The words work like a strong cup of coffee. I'm suddenly sober and back to feeling the full mess of my emotions. "He didn't do any *real* work here, did he?"

My question is rhetorical, a snide way of implying that

all Jack's serious business happened at home or the office. But Camille doesn't notice. "There weren't any documents…in his briefcase."

The last word feels like a slap. "Swaine Adeney Brigg? Black leather, hand stitching? That briefcase?"

My voice crackles with each question, wet firewood starting to take. I'm angry again. He left the gift from his wife with the other woman.

Camille fingers her fur's lapel. The temperature in the room is changing. "Yes. But I checked it thoroughly when Martin Ellis first asked me to look for a document. There's nothing in there."

I picture the buttery leather and firm handle, the brass catches that the stuffy Bergdorf Goodman salesman painstakingly demonstrated how to operate. "That's because you didn't buy it. You don't know where to look."

CAMILLE

Upstairs in the bedroom, I fall to my knees in front of the four-poster bed, shove my hand underneath, and feel around for the briefcase. My fingers connect with the hard corner, and I drag it into the open.

"You'll need to take everything out first," Justine says from behind me. She's keeping her voice low, barely more than a whisper so as not to wake JJ and Kimberlee, both sleeping across the hall. "I'm going to change real quick. These chains are starting to chafe."

"Bring me some clothes too, will you? Something comfy."

She nods and disappears into the closet.

I turn back to the briefcase, flipping the twin latches on either side of the handle with a gentle nudge. I lift the top and stare at the details I've memorized by now, the bridle leather and hand stitching, the solid-brass hardware and velvety red felt. Justine really does have good taste.

But if there's a secret compartment in this thing, I still don't see it.

The overhead light hits the lone strand of Jack's hair, still lodged in the felt of the lid. Justine probably has hundreds of these things floating around at home, tangled in a brush or littering the bottom of a bathroom drawer. All I want is this little one.

I pinch it with two fingers and tug, and it springs loose.

With a lightning glance over my shoulder at the empty hallway, I open my nightstand drawer and carefully drape it across the pile of Polaroids. The closet light flips off, and I shut the drawer just in time. Justine emerges in the clothes she was wearing earlier, that blue tracksuit that should be hideous but on her looks like the cover-shoot outfit for a fitness magazine. Bright-white Tretorn sneakers hang from two fingers, their laces untied and dangling.

"This okay?" she says, holding up my favorite pink sweatshirt and a pair of gray sweats.

"It's perfect, thanks." I shed my fabulous new coat and, with a loving pet, drape the chinchilla carefully across the bed, then tug the sweatshirt over my head. It's almost as soft, warm and fleecy from a million washes, and big enough that it hangs over my butt. The sweats I toss to the carpet beside me.

"Are you sure the report's not in one of those?" Justine says, pointing to the stack of manila folders.

I pick them up and dump them on the carpet, tossing her a look over my shoulder.

"What am I saying? Of course you're sure. You've already looked, probably a million times."

I pat her on the knee, a silent gesture for *it's fine*. "Now show me what you're talking about, because I've studied this bad boy from top to bottom, and I have no idea what I'm missing."

"That's because Swaine Adeney Brigg made this briefcase to hide twenty rounds of ammunition, some gold coins, two knives, and a tin of what looks like talcum powder but is really tear gas."

My hand, which was scooping up the pens and loose change, stills.

"Didn't you ever see *From Russia with Love*? This is the same briefcase James Bond used to kill the bad guys on the Orient Express. Well, minus the weapons." She runs a finger along the top inside edge, over a leather label engraved with the company's name. "We had a real good laugh about that one, that Jack wouldn't need the ammunition in his current job. He liked to joke that his clients could be jerks sometimes, but they weren't the murderous kind."

I make a sound deep in my throat. "He should have talked to Peter then. He would have set him straight, though he never thought the mob would turn their wrath on him. He figured sticking to legitimate business meant he was safe. Well, that, and he knew where the bodies were buried."

"Not all of them though."

"Not all of them. Clearly." I pick up the rumpled blue tie and, with a pang, pass it to Justine. "Here. You should have this. I'm sorry I kept it from you, but...well, *you* know."

She drapes it over her lap, letting out a long, sad sigh. "Jack loved this tie. He said it brought him luck. Anytime he had an important meeting or a big case, he'd strap this thing on and pray the rosary before he left the house. He wasn't even all that religious, but the gods of law are temperamental, he said. He made all sorts of little offerings."

"Like refusing to get his hair cut when he was working a big case? Because that's what Peter did, and one time it got so bad he looked like a bum in a three-piece suit. And he only used pens with blue ink. For some reason, black was bad luck."

"Because it's the color of death and mourning. Jack did the same thing."

We fall silent as the wine turns sour in my gut. All those little offerings, and in the end, none of them worked. Jack and Peter are both dead, possibly because of whatever's in this briefcase.

I upend the damn thing, dumping the rest of Jack's stuff on the floor. "Now what?"

Justine slides the case in front of her knees, snapping shut the lid and clicking the brass latches back into place. She points to the rectangular buttons on either side. "See how these are vertical? For the secret compartment to release, they have to be horizontal."

She gives them both a ninety-degree twist, then nudges the

buttons with her thumbs. The locks flip open once again, but when she opens the top, the false bottom comes with it.

"Well, hot damn," I whisper, staring into a second compartment. A neat stack of papers bound with a black spiral coil sits in the center underneath a thin box, light blue and tied with a white bow. The box every woman on the planet wants to receive.

"At least it's not from that vile Donna," I quip, and you'd never know from my tone that there's an invisible vise around my chest, making it hard to breathe.

Justine looks at me, unsure, and I know what she's thinking—maybe this gift isn't for her but for me. After all, Jack left the briefcase in my car, and looking back on it now, I see why. It was the night before the New York trip, after we'd stolen a couple of hours in a hotel along the highway. Before he kissed me goodbye, he'd wedged the briefcase behind my seat and told me he'd get it back later, and a flutter ran down my spine because that meant there would be a next time.

But he must have known the danger. Why else would he tuck the report in the hidden compartment? Why would he not tell either of us where it was or that it even existed? Knowing what I know now, I can't help but wonder if he gave the briefcase to me in order to get it away from Justine and JJ. He wanted to protect them, but he was willing to put *my* life in danger.

A tiny envelope is nestled under the white silk bow, and I pick it up and pull out the card, both of us bracing at the sight of Jack's neat scrawl.

Flawless like my diamond in the rough.

XO
—J.

Justine makes a noise low in her throat, one that sounds like a sob. "He used to call me that, his diamond in the rough. Back before JJ and the move and *you*."

I press a hand to my stomach and try not to throw up. *Smoking hot. So fine. His sexy little bedroom kitten.* These are the things Jack called me. Never flawless. Never a comparison to anything as timeless as a diamond.

She doesn't reach for the box, so I pick it up and put it in her hand, and reluctantly, she tugs on the bow. Inside the box is another one, darker this time and made of velvet. She peels it opens to reveal a necklace, the perfect diamond solitaire on a golden chain.

"This is just like him, you know," she says, mostly to herself. "He buys me the absolute most perfect gift I could ever imagine, and then he goes and gets himself blown up before he can give it to me."

She's crying now, big salty tears sliding down her perfect cheeks, and I think of my words down in the kitchen, *you didn't lose* all *your shine*. Maybe Jack didn't always see it, but that's because he wasn't looking. Justine is still gorgeous. She still glows from within. All he had to do was open his eyes—which, clearly, he did.

"What am I supposed to do now?" Her voice is strangled. "I love him and I hate him and I wish he was here so I could slap him across the cheek and tell him I know. I *know*, and now I don't know what to do." She clutches the box to her chest and pitches her upper body forward, pressing her face into the carpet. "I am just so *angry*. I want to kiss him, and then I want to *kill* him."

And maybe it's the wine or the adrenaline crash after a crazy night or some kind of delayed response at the relief of escaping Sal's with all our fingers and toes intact, but a giggle bursts up my chest before I can stop it.

Justine twists her head, frowning at me through her tears and hair.

"Not gallows humor. Got it." I press my lips together and force my face to straighten. "Look. I'm about to tell you something that I'll probably regret later, something I would never have admitted to anyone before tonight, not even to myself. Scratch that. *Especially* not to myself. But one of the last times Jack and I were…*you* know, he said he owed it to JJ to 'do what has to be done.'"

She straightens, frowning. "What? That doesn't make any sense."

"I think he just meant supporting his family with a salary. Working hard. I don't know. But the point is he was over the moon for your son, and you just told me downstairs you two talked about future kids. And judging from the way he felt about JJ, I know that he wanted them. With you."

She stares at the diamond, glittering against the navy felt, her brow crumpled with pain and yearning, and that's when I make a silent vow. Justine will never know about the Polaroids in the nightstand. She will never know the size of his grin when I gave them to him or how he carried photos of me naked around in his briefcase. I've caused this woman enough pain. No matter what happens next, I will take those pictures to my grave.

"What I'm trying to say is Jack was never going to leave you, Justine. Take it from the other woman, who at the time wanted nothing more. He was never going to choose me over you."

Her eyes fill with tears all over again, but she smiles. "Thank you. I know that wasn't easy for you to say or even admit, and it doesn't let Jack off the hook, but it...I don't know, softens things, I guess."

"Good. Now can we please see what all the fuss is about?"

I gesture to the briefcase, and now that the Tiffany's box is gone, I can see what we missed before. The report, on Vista Corporation letterhead, the orange and green logo set over a landscape of trees. Next to it, an embossed seal signed by a notary, and slashed in big black letters across the middle of the page:

Groundwater Sampling Results at the Terminal Road Site

Terminal Road. The future location of Providence's most notorious mall.

I flip through the first few pages—a long-winded explanation of method and objectives, a map of the land pressed between 1A and the Providence River, lots of scientific jargon I don't understand. Impatient, I turn the report over and start at the back, flipping until I get to a passage marked RESULTS.

From somewhere behind us, from deep in the dark hallway, there's a bonk, followed by quiet swishes on the runner. Footsteps.

My heart gives a hard kick and I freeze, but Justine is better prepared. She springs to her feet, her body poised to attack. I think of the phone, on Peter's side of the bed. Of Kimberlee and JJ sound asleep across the hall. Of the knives and the frying pans down in the kitchen, along with a hundred other possible weapons. And here I sit with empty hands.

Then a tiny body appears in the doorway, and my bones go slushy with relief. JJ is adorably confused, standing there with Kimberlee's Rolling Stones T-shirt hanging down to his knees, the decal tongue peeling and faded. His hair is mussed from the pillow, sticking up on one side like a lopsided mohawk.

He rubs his eye with a fist. "Mommy?"

"Yes, baby. I'm here. Did we wake you?" She stretches out an arm to him, moving closer.

He frowns, dropping his arm to his side. "I have an owie. In my—"

His words get sucked up in a strange rumbling sound, half burp, half moan, right before he projectile-vomits red and brown goo, all over my white Berber carpet.

MEREDITH

I toss a throw across the living room sofa so Rom doesn't bleed all over the dove-gray upholstery Robin special-ordered from New York.

I thought it might feel strange having him and Krystle in my home. The truth is, though, Robin's town house has never felt like mine, no matter how much space she made for me here.

Krystle helps her son limp the last couple steps and stretch out on the sofa, then leans over to examine his injuries. The structural integrity of her corset seems to have been compromised by our dip in the pool, and Krystle's ample chest is on the verge of spilling out.

"Jesus, Ma." Rom turns away, grimacing. "Can't you cover those things up?"

Krystle narrows her eyes. "*Those things* kept you alive for the first year of your life, you ungrateful little *cretino*. Get over it."

"You can borrow something," I offer. Krystle snaps to look at me. "If you want."

"Sure," she says. "Thank you. You got a first-aid kit anywhere?"

"Or painkillers?" Rom adds.

"I'll see what I can do."

I head back to the master suite and exchange my party wear for leggings and Robin's old Harvard Law sweatshirt. She let me steal it from her—and cut open the neckline so it slouches over my shoulders—ages ago. Since she died, I've worn it to bed every single night.

I grab a pair of extra-stretchy leggings plus an oversize cashmere sweater from Robin's side of the closet for Krystle, then go into the bathroom to scope out the medical-supply situation. There are bandages and disinfectant under the sink—and yes, a bottle of prescription painkillers left over from Robin's dental surgery last spring. Hopefully they're still potent enough to keep Rom quiet for a while.

Even with the vanity lights left off, my reflection in the mirror makes me cringe. My eye makeup is smeared with sweat and swimming pool water, and my curls have gone frizzy and flat. I would kill for a hot shower, but after what happened tonight, I'm way too paranoid. I can't help picturing that creepy contract killer's shadow on the curtain like Norman Bates in *Psycho*, my blood swirling down the drain as I scream and scream.

On the way back to the living room, I pause to peek out the window, searching the darkness for any sign of him. Nothing.

The only people outside are a few New Year's Eve revelers staggering up Constitution Hill. The State House is a ghost on the horizon, white-marble facade glowing even with the lights switched off for the night.

I hope Justine and Camille made it back safe. Though none of us will be truly safe until we give the Tiger what he wants.

Back in the living room, I find Krystle dabbing at Rom's cuts with a dampened kitchen towel. I set the first-aid supplies and the folded clothes on the coffee table. "Either of you want something to drink?"

Krystle says "No," just as Rom sits up with an impassioned "*Yes.*"

"All I have is tea and soda," I admit. I haven't gotten around to replenishing Robin's bar after my solo pity party—God, was that really last week? It feels like a lifetime ago. Even sneaking around Sal's mansion with Frankie seems like a distant memory. I still don't know what the hell she was up to, with that lockpick and Polaroid camera. Clearly, bartending isn't her only area of expertise.

Rom makes a face and falls back on the sofa. "Then no. Never mind."

Krystle picks up the pill bottle to read the label. Rom takes it from her, taps a few out into his palm, and dry swallows them before curling in toward the cushions.

Just like Rom to cause all this trouble, then fall asleep and leave the rest of us to handle business. Robin said that was how he was at the office too—literally: she caught him asleep at his desk, drooling on a legal brief, on more than one occasion.

"I was thinking—" I say, but Krystle puts a finger to her lips.

"Let's let him rest. I'm going to go change."

By the time she returns from the bathroom, Rom is already snoring. Robin's sweater looks good on her. They have similar coloring, actually, except Krystle's hair is brighter red, while Robin's was closer to copper-penny.

"So the report," I begin again. "That creep was convinced Jack had it. What if Robin had a copy too? She liked to keep backups of everything important in her home office."

As insurance in case one of her sexist-pig colleagues tried to screw her over or take credit for her work, but I'm not going to get into all that with Krystle.

"You didn't check her office yet?" she asks.

"For the cash, I did. At the time, I had no idea about the report. I wasn't looking for it."

Krystle gives a weary shrug. "Worth a shot."

I lead her up the stairs to Robin's office, which is in the loft space that looks out over the town house's open-plan living room and kitchen. When I searched the room before, I tried to put everything back exactly the way I found it. I'm sure if Robin were here, though, she'd find plenty of picture frames to level and knickknacks to straighten.

That was Robin: perfectly organized, everything all lined up the way she wanted it. Not only in her work—in our relationship as well. We never fought, because she'd douse my feelings with ice-cold logic until I couldn't remember what I'd been so upset about in the first place. Robin knew what she was doing, always, and it was easier to go along with her plans than to make my own.

Now look where it's gotten me. For someone who refused to tolerate messiness when she was alive, Robin sure left me a hell of a mess to clean up after her death.

Krystle runs her fingertips past the line of framed photographs on the credenza. Most are of me and Robin—snuggled up on the white sofa downstairs or sunburned and smiling on a beach far away from here—but there's one of Robin at the law firm too. It was taken the day she made partner. Romeo Senior stands beside her, arm around her shoulder like a proud papa, his grin even bigger than hers.

"Romeo was so impressed with Robin, you know." Krystle picks up the photo. "Her first day at the firm, he came home and told me, 'This dame'll be running the place before we know what hit us.'"

"Robin admired him too." That's the truth, whether or not Robin would've wanted to admit it. When she complained about Romeo, it was different, tinged with genuine affection. He could be boorish sometimes, but he respected her. He took her seriously. And he tried to teach her everything he knew—including, apparently, how to make shady deals with the mob.

"He always said she was the best kind of lawyer: one who could fight in the dirt and then get up without a speck on her. I could never understand why she didn't get married. I kept trying to set her up with all the eligible bachelors I knew, until Romeo told me to knock it off. None of them were good enough for her, he said. For someone to catch Robin Calder's attention and keep it—" Krystle looks at me with genuine warmth, and I try to blink back the tears burning in my eyes. "Well, that someone would have to be really special."

"I don't know what to think anymore. I thought Robin loved me. I thought I knew her. But she kept so many secrets from me, I don't even—"

"She loved you, Meredith. The way you're feeling right now, it doesn't mean you love her any less. You can love someone and hate them all at once." She glances down the stairs in the general direction of her sleeping son. "No matter how much a person fucks up, how much stupid shit they do, if you can't help loving them anyway? That's how you know it's real."

The tears are flowing freely now. I dab at them with the tissue, and Krystle turns away, giving me a moment to pull myself together. There seems to be a silent agreement between the two of us that we're not at the hugging stage yet. Fine by me.

Krystle sits down at Robin's glass-topped desk and starts thumbing through the filing cabinet underneath. "Robin and her labels." She shakes her head. "I remember she took it upon herself to redo the firm's whole filing system a couple of years back, because they weren't giving her enough client work to keep her busy. Romeo couldn't find anything for weeks. He likes his piles."

She flinches at her own use of the present tense but doesn't correct herself. I toss the crumpled-up tissue in the trash can and crouch down next to the cabinet. The folders are all alphabetical—typical Robin—so I skip to the back, looking for *Vista*.

And there it is. *Vista Corporation*, printed in the embossed type from Robin's label maker. It can't really be that easy, can it? I open the folder, and sure enough, right on top is the report. *Groundwater Sampling Results at the Terminal Road Site*.

If Robin had a copy of the report all this time, neatly labeled and sitting in an unlocked file drawer, why did the Tiger need to harass Justine and her little boy? Why break into Sal Ponterelli's wolf-cave basement to threaten the four of us? No one's even tried to search Robin's home as far as I know; her basic anti-burglary system wouldn't be able to stop a pro like the Tiger.

"May I?" Krystle asks, admirably restraining herself from snatching the report out of my hands, which I can tell she's itching to do. I hand it over, and she flips through the pages.

"What is it?" I ask.

"An environmental study on the land where they want to build the mall. For any building project to go forward, they have to have one of these. It's standard procedure. This doesn't make any sense though."

She holds up the report, open to a page titled RESULTS. I don't know what the technical terms listed there mean, but they're all followed by the same green label. NORMAL.

"So it says the land is okay to build on?"

Krystle nods. "Right. It's all fine. That's what doesn't make any damn sense. Why hire some elite contract killer to track down *this*?"

The rotary phone on the desk rings, and Krystle jumps up so fast she knocks Robin's chair over. It must be two in the morning now or even later. Who the hell would be calling at this hour? I pick up the call, bracing myself—for heavy breathing, whispered threats. The Tiger waiting in the trees to confirm the location of his prey.

But it's only Camille on the other end of the line. Guess she isn't getting any sleep tonight either.

"Meredith." Camille sounds breathless, her voice pitched higher than usual with stress. "Is Krystle still with you?"

"Yeah, she's right here." I hold the phone out to Krystle. "It's Camille."

Instead of taking the receiver, she cozies up beside me so we can both listen in. "We found the report in Robin's office," Krystle says. "At least we think it's the right one."

"Justine and I found something too, in Jack's briefcase. But now we're at Rhode Island Hospital. Her son…"

Camille trails off, and I'm picturing the absolute worst: that poor little boy left bloodied, a vicious message from a vicious man. And I've had that damn report right under my nose from the beginning.

I tighten my grip on the receiver. "Is he okay?"

"I don't know yet. He threw up blood. Justine is talking with the doctor now."

"We'll be right there," Krystle says. "We'll bring the report."

"Good. Please hurry."

She looks at me, and I nod. We're truly in this together now.

KRYSTLE

Did we do this to Justine's baby?

This is all I can think as Meredith whips into the Rhode Island Hospital ER parking lot in Robin's BMW. I've silently argued with myself the whole fast drive. Maybe it's appendicitis. Maybe an ulcer. Do kids get those?

No matter how I scrape my brain for *General Hospital* plots, I can't ignore my gut: this is our fault.

"Here's good," I say, wiggling my finger.

"I see it, I see it." Meredith slides into a spot a few rows from the entrance.

I don't know why they chose this ER. The crowded conditions make the paper every few months. There's talk about building a new one, but that doesn't help the parents crammed into the small children's ward tonight. Prayers on their lips and tears in their eyes.

I've said those prayers and cried those tears. When Rom wasn't much older than JJ, we had a terrifying moment. He couldn't breathe. He turned blue. I knew if he didn't make it, I wouldn't either.

But his asthma condition is not the same as what Justine is dealing with tonight. Sure, I felt bad that I hadn't noticed Rom's wheezing or coughing. But if that creepy killer they call the Tiger has done this somehow, he'll see real quick how momma lionesses go for the throat too.

I'm relieved that we dropped Rom off at my oldest sister and brother-in-law's house. At the moment, that's the only protection I have.

"I hate hospitals," Meredith murmurs, maybe to me, maybe not. She inhales deeply and then pulls the keys out of the ignition.

It doesn't take us long to get inside. We're nearly running as we push through the doors and into a wave of heat and chaos from the people crowding around the admission desk and packed in every available waiting room chair.

New Year's Eve. Couldn't pick a worse night in the ER. The room is full of drunks and fighting couples and bleeding faces and broken bones.

We don't have time for this shit.

I grab Meredith's arm and pull her across the room. Two nurses are arguing with a drunk woman who seems oblivious to her real gusher of a nosebleed. I maneuver us around them and slip into a hallway. There's an arrow on the wall that says

CHILDREN'S WARD, and my heels are clicking fast as we zip past occupied gurneys and frantic nurses and yelling doctors. Meredith starts to move faster too, and we finally see the small sign outside two swinging doors.

We barrel through, and there's Camille, standing in front of a large glass window in her new fur coat.

She spots us and starts hustling our way. "Oh, thank you, Jesus!"

Instinctively, the three of us half hug, half cling to each other.

"Was it the Tiger?" I take Camille by the arms. "Did we do this to her baby boy?"

"I don't know. The doctor is going to look into what caused… the blood."

"Oh my God," Meredith whispers. "Was he…poisoned?"

"Maybe." Camille lets out an anxious breath. "Kimberlee is fine though, so I don't know."

"Where are they?"

I hurry toward the window where Camille was standing. A nurse rushes out, and then a doctor rushes in. The room is packed: narrow beds, crying children, beeping machines, and scared parents wedged among the panicked staff.

"They have to put a scope down his throat," Camille whispers from behind me. "To see…where he's bleeding."

Meredith leans against the window, tears in her eyes. "Poor Justine."

The three of us stand there in our furs, staring into the chaos of the room. There's a swell of emotion threatening me. A lot of it goes back to those terrifying moments in the hospital with Rom twenty years ago. My chest tightens, and I'm starting to feel hopeless.

But I know how to cut it off. To bring everything I'm feeling to a boil that will actually be worth a damn—I find my white-hot anger.

"Listen up, girls," I say like General Patton. "We will make this right for Justine and her boy." I toss my head back and point over at a bench. "This way. Get the paper, Mere, so we can figure this out."

I march over and sit my angry ass right in the middle, ready to Sherlock Holmes this clusterfuck. They follow, each on either side of me.

Meredith pulls the report out of her purse. "Here's the copy Robin kept in her desk." She shows the document to Camille and points at the "To:" line. "Vista Corporation studied the land the mob donated as part of the due diligence to build the mall."

I point at the title. "'Groundwater Sampling Results at the Terminal Road Site.' It's a standard environmental report. The firm has done them before for other projects."

"Wait." Camille snatches the paper. "It's the same report!"

I glance at Meredith, disappointed before I even say it. "But it shows the land is normal. The Tiger won't kill anyone over that. There has to be something else that he wants."

"Jack had the same report *hidden* in his briefcase." Camille reaches into her purse, pulls out her own identical document, and puts them side by side. "Robin's is a copy of the original Vista memo that Jack hid. See the notary seal?"

I tap the corner with the raised circle. "They always notarize the original."

"Martin made sure to mention that seal specifically." Camille flips to the last page. "Wait, how did you know the land is normal?"

I snatch the paper from Camille, and Meredith leans over me. There at the bottom of the page, where it says RESULTS, there is no "normal." Instead, I read aloud, "Highly toxic carcinogen levels. Land must be remediated before construction."

We all inhale sharply at the same time, and then Meredith whispers, "Robin was given a fake."

"It has to be the mob." Camille snaps her gaze back and forth between the papers. "If that land is worthless, they don't get the money. Martin Ellis made it clear that he isn't going through with the deal without seeing the results of this report. He definitely sensed that Sal was trying to hustle him somehow."

I shake my head. "But Sal had no idea what the Tiger was doing there. He didn't know anything about the report. He's not that good of an actor."

"Says you." Camille's lips press together. "Having abs doesn't make someone honest, Krystle."

Before I smack her six ways to Sunday, Meredith interrupts. "Okay, but the Tiger wants the report, right? So maybe whoever is paying him is a company polluting the area. They want to make sure nobody finds out the land is toxic."

I'm considering Meredith's stripper logic, which I'm learning is sharper than most, when a doctor with a cart zooms past us. He opens a blue curtain at the very back of the room. There's Justine, but no way she sees us. Her whole being is focused on her son. She soothes her small boy but also holds him tight.

"What can we do?" Meredith whispers.

"If her baby was poisoned, we'll make them pay."

JUSTINE

I lie on the hospital bed with my child atop my chest, his arms and legs pinned by my limbs, his head restrained by my hands and chin. I've contorted into a toddler-size straitjacket. And I hate it. I hate that instead of calming my kid, I am charged with restricting him. I hate that he's in this crowded pediatric ward surrounded by thin blue curtains that can't muffle all the cries, monitor beeps, and shouting nurses. Above all, I hate Jack.

I wish that he'd appear in this hospital room so that I could claw his flesh, beat my fists against his chest, and scream that his selfishness put us here. He's the reason I didn't realize our son was sick until JJ was vomiting blood. He's the reason there's a doctor approaching with a snakelike camera destined to slither up JJ's tiny nostril and then slide down into his throat. He's the reason our child is trembling with fear and I'm vibrating with rage.

I want my husband to feel my desperation and disgust. I

want my fury to have a target other than myself. Because no matter what Jack did, I failed my son. I'm his mother, and I didn't protect him.

I can't protect him now. The camera resembles a medieval torture device. But I have no choice other than to constrain and cajole as the doctor approaches. Scary as he may seem, the man before us is the only god listening. I've become an immediate disciple. I'll follow any instruction. Obey any command. Anything for him to save my son.

"Okay, sport, so like I said before, this might feel a little uncomfortable, but that stuff I sprayed in your nose should have everything all numb." The doctor punctuates this last word with a forced smile and flex of his endoscope's long, black cord. "It shouldn't hurt a bit."

JJ jerks violently, slamming his skull into my jawbone. I force myself not to recoil from the blow, to pretend everything is fine and I've been totally convinced by the doctor's conditional phrasing and fake chumminess. "It'll feel like a tickle," I promise.

My son is no sap. He tries to kick his legs, which are buckled to the bed by my own heavier calves. "No! Mommy! Mommy! No!"

The doctor pulls back. "Hold him, or we really will have to call the anesthesiologist."

I already have my kid in a modified full nelson. Still, I squeeze my forearms closer together, pressing JJ's limbs more firmly to his sides. The doctor has already explained that putting JJ under will cost precious time. The sooner he determines where the blood is coming from, the sooner he can stop it.

"Please, baby." Whereas JJ's voice sounds strangled, mine barely surfaces from underwater. "Please be calm, just for a minute."

Maybe my son senses my desperation—or terror simply overloads his system—but he stops struggling. The doctor takes advantage, shooting the camera up JJ's left nostril. I watch inch after inch of black cable disappear into his nose. Meanwhile, the doctor stares at the attached monitor, which sits atop a rolling medical cart, facing away from me.

"Oh." The doctor inhales sharply. It's the sound someone makes after a gut punch.

I crane my neck toward the screen, even though I've no hope of my seeing what's on it from this angle. "What is it?"

"The bleeding appears to be from JJ's pharynx"

I don't know how to respond. Obviously, any bleeding is bad. But there is awful, and then there is catastrophic. Is bleeding from there better than the other possible sources of injury? Should I be relieved or petrified? My prayers require direction.

"His throat is very inflamed," the doctor continues. "It looks scalded."

I mentally flip through everything my kid has consumed in the past twenty-four hours. There was the Kraft mac and cheese at lunch—a favorite meal that he'd never reacted badly to before—and the Hot Pocket pizza I defrosted before heading to Jack's office. I was so busy searching for whatever the Tiger wanted that I didn't cook any real meals.

But it wouldn't be like me to serve JJ something from the microwave without first checking the temperature. I even break open Hot Pockets to release the steam. Could I really have been so distracted that I gave my three-year-old piping hot food?

"Would melted cheese do that?" I ask.

"No."

"I went out for New Year's Eve. He was with a fifteen-year-old sitter. Maybe she gave him hot cocoa or something?"

The doctor reconsiders the image on the screen. "This wouldn't be caused by food. It would result from strong acids or bases. Chemicals. Something you might keep under the kitchen sink?"

He looks back at me, his downturned mouth full of damning judgment. I deserve it. I'm a terrible mother. I left my nursery schooler in a strange house with God knows what hiding in God knows how many unsecured cabinets, in the care of a young teenager still reeling from her father's death. What was I thinking?

That a mobster would kill me if I didn't hand-deliver my share of a four-million-dollar debt, of course. Even that excuse doesn't erase the pain my son is in. If JJ got into something that caused permanent damage, I will never forgive myself. I will already never forgive myself for those first few moments after he vomited when I was more embarrassed than alarmed, when I dismissed the chocolate-brown and maraschino-red stain on

Camille's snow-colored carpet as the result of a little kid chowing down on a banana split past his usual bedtime. For nearly a minute, I was more concerned about owing Camille a new rug than JJ's well-being. I will never be able to swallow my hesitation or the fact that I needed to hear my child's squeaky, pained cry to realize that he needed medical help.

The doctor begins removing the endoscope. As soon as the camera is out, I release JJ, sit up, and turn him to face me. His pupils are large and afraid.

I brush his curls back from his forehead, the way I do when putting him to bed. He looks even more like Jack without his hair falling into his face.

"Sweetheart, it's going to be okay." I force out the words even though the man with the medical degree has given me no indication that anything will be. Even though Jack is dead, a contract killer is after us, and I have no idea whether I will wake up to see the sun tomorrow. I need to believe what I'm saying is true. I need JJ to believe it.

"Mommy needs to know though. Did you open any bottles that you weren't supposed to?"

JJ shakes his head.

"Did you think, maybe, that something in a bathroom looked like soda or candy, and you had a little taste? It's okay, baby. You can tell me."

He croaks out a single word. "No."

The doctor doesn't believe him. He steps to the edge of the

bed, looming over both me and my child. "These kinds of burns often come from ingesting household cleaners or metal degreasers. Son, did you get into anything that was used to wipe down the counter or maybe take the tarnish off silver? Something that your mommy might rub on spoons to make them shiny?"

JJ clearly has no idea what the doctor is talking about. He shakes his head a second time and then stares up at me, wordlessly asking for me to speak on his behalf. I hug his head to my chest. "He said he didn't, and JJ is not the type of kid to take things without asking."

The doctor's lips shrink with disapproval. He thinks either one or both of us is lying. But I know my son. The truth is that he's far too shy to explore a strange house without permission.

"Well, since we don't know what he had..." The doctor trails off, giving me another chance to supply an answer.

"We don't."

"Then I suppose we'll have to give him activated charcoal and hope that neutralizes the acids."

The man crouches beside his medical cart and digs in one of the cabinets beneath the monitor. When he rises, he is holding a pill bottle that reminds me of JJ's Flintstones vitamins, all bright colors and large letters.

"These are chewable. They taste like coconut and honey."

He places the bottle on his knee and presses down on the lid. It opens with one wrist rotation, betraying his experience with childproof caps. Two pills are plucked from the jar and passed to me. "You'll take two with a big glass of water. After that, you'll get some sleep, and in the morning, you'll take two more with another giant glass of liquid. Okay, bud?"

Though the doctor still speaks directly to my child, JJ refuses to look at him. His face is buried between my breasts. I pet his head while nodding along to show the doctor that I am taking mental notes. "These will stop the bleeding?"

"They will make things better, but only time will heal his mucus membranes. His throat will be sore for the better part of a week, and he'll have some stomach upset too from the medicine." The doctor smiles, a forced "buck up" expression for my kid's benefit. "He'll need plenty of ice cream, ices, and bland foods."

Promising dessert does nothing to grab my son's attention. The doctor sighs, waving the white flag on his attempt to win over a little boy who will never see him as anything other than the enemy. I offer a weak smile in JJ's stead, a pitiful attempt at expressing my gratitude.

The doctor doesn't return it as he focuses on his new audience. In fact, his face falls into a deep frown. "Nothing acidic, spicy, or crunchy. Think yogurt. Smoothies. Boiled chicken. Rice is a good one. Basically, the BRAT diet, without the toast, though you can give other soft carbohydrates."

Bananas, rice, applesauce, and bread. The acronym isn't as easy to remember, but I get the gist. JJ can't have anything that might irritate or scrape his healing linings. For the next week, my three-year-old will be back on baby foods.

"Okay. But he'll eventually be fine, right? This charcoal and having soft foods for a bit will fix things?"

"What will fix things is putting a lock on your cabinets. But I can't write a prescription for that."

Though the sarcasm is unnecessary, I don't object. This doctor thinks his admonishing tone is deserved. In his eyes, I'm a negligent young woman who failed parenting 101: *childproof the home.*

There's nothing I can say to convince him otherwise—except, perhaps, for the truth. But I can't share that. I can't possibly tell this man that somehow, while I was at a New Year's Eve party, distracting gangsters with my lounge act and secretly enjoying it, a stranger used my child to deliver a painful message: the Tiger wants his report, and he always goes for the throat.

CAMILLE

I need you to tell me everything he put in his mouth," Justine says to Kimberlee, parked at my kitchen table between Krystle and me. Meredith sits at the end next to JJ, and despite the night we've just had, everyone is wide awake. All because of what's piled on the table between us. The real report. The fake one. A heap of momentous consequences we're all still trying to understand.

Kimberlee crosses her arms and frowns, looking a good two years younger with her face scrubbed clean of that heavy black liner. "He didn't eat or drink anything weird, I swear."

She's never been the merriest person to be around in the mornings, not that it's quite morning. The kitchen windows face due east, and they're a solid sheet of black, not even a whisper of dawn peeking over the trees.

"But the Tiger could have been here," Justine says to the table at large. "He could have planted poison in the food."

Kimberlee's gaze flits to mine with a not-so-subtle message. *Is this woman insane?* "I think I would have noticed a tiger."

"The Tiger is a man. I don't know his real name." Justine wraps an arm around JJ's shoulders and pulls him tight to her side. Ever since we left the hospital, she hasn't stopped touching him, smoothing down his hair or feeling his forehead for fever.

Krystle reaches down the table, giving Kimberlee an encouraging pat on the arm. "We're not accusing you of anything, sweetheart. Just tell us everything he put in his mouth."

"Well, you saw how he wolfed down most of that banana split, but all that sugar made him really thirsty. After everyone left, he washed it down with two, maybe three glasses of milk, but he didn't say anything about it tasting funny."

Krystle may be the oldest widow, but she's also the fastest. She pops off her chair and takes off in long, determined strides across the kitchen tiles. She locates the gallon of milk, empty save for the last few inches. She takes off the cap, sniffs. Chugs straight from the carton.

"Milk's fine." She dabs her mouth with a sleeve. "And Kimberlee and I ate the ice cream too. Did he eat or drink anything else?"

As one, the group turns back to Kimberlee, who tucks her hair behind both ears in a shy gesture, and I feel for the girl. Dragging her out of bed, interrogating her. Poor thing didn't ask for any of this.

"After that, we watched some TV, but he fell asleep five minutes in. He was still passed out when I carried him up to bed."

JJ confirms her words with a nod, staring across the table with big, grave eyes. He's still pale, but his cheeks are flushed pink, his lips twitching at the corners. I think somebody has a little crush.

"Are you sure he didn't get into anything he shouldn't have? Maybe some cleaner with packaging that makes it look like candy or something?" Justine says.

"Guys, come on," I say, sticking up for my stepdaughter. "Kimberlee babysits all the time. The mothers around here call her the baby whisperer. She wouldn't let JJ just drink from the bleach container. I mean, seriously."

"He probably got into something at home," Meredith says. "Kids do that, right? Drink the Mr. Clean under the kitchen counter."

Justine crosses her arms so abruptly, she rattles the table. "Not *my* kid. JJ has never done anything like that, and I didn't mean to accuse Kimberlee. It's just that none of this makes sense."

My stomach growls, loud and insistent, and I think back to the last time I ate. Yesterday's breakfast? Dinner two nights ago? These past two weeks have been a blur of missed meals and interrupted sleep. I wouldn't even know what day it was if not for New Year's.

I shove back my chair and stand. "I'm starving. Who wants something to eat?"

Hands shoot up all around the table, but no one's as fast as JJ's.

"I don't know," Justine says, hesitant. "Are we sure the Tiger didn't poison the food?"

"Because what's he going to do, lace every food item in this house? Take a look at my pantry. It's like a grocery store in there. He'd need staff and a sixteen-wheeler. Besides, Krystle and Kimberlee ate the ice cream too. Whatever JJ ate, it didn't come from here."

After a lengthy pause, Justine relents. "Fine, but the doctor says he has to stick to a bland diet, nothing crunchy. Yogurt. Applesauce. Hot dogs and boiled chicken. Things like that."

JJ makes a face.

I give him an *I-got-you* grin and step to the freezer. "Little known fact about Peter, that man loved his applesauce. He ate the stuff with everything. Pasta, salads, steak and potatoes—you name it, he dumped it next to any entree on his plate. But his absolute favorite way to eat it?"

"Applesauce popsicles," Kimberlee says.

I yank on the handle and pull a tray of Tupperware forms from the freezer. "That's right. He made them himself."

I carry the forms to the table and hand them to Justine, and she wriggles out a popsicle while I duck into the pantry, swiping packages from the shelves. Chips. Rice Chex. A jar of nuts and some cheddar crackers. I pile everything against my chest and grab a bottle of tequila from the bar. By the time I make it back to the table, JJ and Kimberlee are both sucking on Popsicles.

"The doctor kept talking about cleaning products," Justine is saying. "He said whatever burned his throat was chemical."

Krystle snatches the Rice Chex from my arms and rips open the bag, digging in like she hasn't eaten in days. "Let's just back up a minute. Camille's right. Whatever JJ ate didn't come from here, so it would really help us out if he could remember when his throat first started feeling funny." She pulls out a fistful of cereal and turns to JJ. "Sweetheart, do you think you can do that?"

JJ nods. He shoves the popsicle in his mouth, plunks an elbow on the table, cups his chin in a hand, and thinks.

Meredith is the first to lose patience. "No offense, but— who cares? The Tiger is still out there. He could be pulling into Camille's driveway right now. He could be creeping through her backyard this very second."

My gaze drags to the windows, still black with night, and I'm not the only one. Meredith is right. The Tiger could be on the other side, watching and planning his next move, and we would have no idea until he busted through the glass. A shiver shimmies its way down my spine, and I suddenly wish we'd chosen a room with curtains.

She reaches down the table, taking the tequila bottle by the neck. "I don't know about you guys, but I'd really prefer he not get his claws into my throat. We can better concentrate our energies on coming up with a plan."

"My *plan*," Justine says, stabbing a finger into the table, "my number one priority, is to protect my son. I can't do that if I don't know where the danger is coming from. You're not a mother, so you can't understand."

I rip open the bag of chips. "I'm not a mother, and I do understand. But you have to admit Meredith has a point. That report is a ticking bomb. It's only a matter of time until the Tiger figures out that we've got it."

At that, Meredith takes a long swig straight from the bottle. "Anybody who thinks this is over when we give it to him is seriously delusional. He's not going to just let us go on our merry way. He's going to—"

Krystle pitches a peanut at her face, and it bounces off Meredith's forehead. "Don't say it. Little ears, you get me?" And just in case, she flicks a glance at JJ before focusing her attention on Justine. "Retrace your steps for us, hon. Where have you two been besides home these past few days?"

"The grocery store," Justine begins. "The library, or I meant to go to the library. We ended up seeing a friend—"

JJ pulls the popsicle from his mouth with a soft *pop*. "When I was playing with Daddy's train!"

Silence. Even the chewing stops. We look to Justine for a translation, but she doesn't seem to understand either.

"My throat. That's when it hurted."

"My smart, smart boy." With a proud mom smile, Justine drops a kiss on top of his head. "The train set was Jack's. His parents gave it to JJ last Christmas, but it's complicated, and he doesn't play with it very often. But he took it out Sunday night—wait, no, it was Monday. I remember because it was right after our first run-in with…" Her words trail, and her eyes go wide with realization. "We were at Raquel's that day. JJ was playing with her daughter, Denise."

"Did he maybe drink something there?" The relief is unmistakable in Kimberlee's voice.

Justine swallows. "Water. *Lots* of it—the furnace was in overdrive, and her apartment was boiling. The water was a little weird. Cloudy and almost carbonated. Raquel said it was because the pipes are old, but—"

"It tasted like candy." JJ grins around a mouthful of popsicle.

Justine sucks in a breath. "So did the tea. I thought she'd sweetened it."

"So you drank the water too," I say.

"Yes, but not as much. He downed three glasses in a row. I only had a mug's worth. I don't even think I finished it. And mine was boiled first."

"I thought the doctor said JJ's issues would have come from cleaning products."

Justine ticks them off on her fingers. "Kitchen degreaser, nail polish remover, jewelry cleaner, laundry bleach…"

She's still talking, but whatever comes next, I don't hear it. I'm too focused on those two little words, smack in the middle of her sentence.

Jewelry cleaner.

I think back to my conversation with Donna at the party, to

the accusations we hurled around. My fib about the trucks I saw leaving her warehouse, her roundabout confirmation there was more than one. Donna would have plenty of jewelry cleaner lying around, and she *was* palling around with Sal at the party.

I gasp, punching the air with a salty finger. "Those trucks weren't Donna's. They were *Sal's*. He is the garbage king, right? They were *his*."

"What trucks?" Krystle asks, blinking at me like I've lost my damn mind.

"I saw a garbage truck leaving Donna's warehouse in the middle of the night. This was *years* ago. Think how much jewelry cleaner and chemicals she could have been dumping in the meantime. Decades, maybe more. Her family's been in business for generations."

Nods all around, because garbage collection in Providence is a money-making machine. Sal runs the union, and he controls the guys who set the routes and manage the many dump sites. He even owns some of the trucks, which means that could have been his I saw leaving the warehouse. People like to pretend it's a legitimate business, even though Sal has greased the palms of every city councilman. Everybody knows it's not just the garbage that's dirty.

Krystle sniffs. "I'm not saying Sal's shit don't stink, but he wouldn't poison innocent people. And there's no way Sal or his guys know everything they're picking up. They're paid to get rid of it, not perform scientific analysis."

"Whatever," I continue. "The point is those were *his* trucks I saw leaving the Donnabelle's warehouse at all hours of the day and night. And okay, so maybe it was one truck at 2:00 a.m., but Donna didn't deny it, so I know I'm not wrong. Kimberlee, run upstairs and see if I still have a bottle of Donnabelle jewelry cleaner under my sink, would you?"

As soon as she's gone, Krystle taps a French-tipped fingernail to the table. "You know, Sal *did* say something to me about things being buried under the mall land. He actually used that word, *buried*. I thought he was referring to bodies, but he could have meant garbage."

"But that still doesn't explain how the chemicals got into JJ's system," Meredith points out.

"The projects are across the street from the mall site, on land that the Ponterellis also owned." Justine sounds calm enough, but two pink spots have bloomed on her cheeks, and her hands, pressed together on the table, are shaking. "You can see the construction from Raquel's apartment. Her daughter, Denise, has been going through chemo for months now. She's not the only one. Lots of kids there are getting sick. If the ground is poisoned, chemicals could be seeping into the underground pipes."

"Well, fuck me, Watson." Krystle flashes JJ an apologetic glance. "Sorry, sweetie, your mom will explain it later. You know, gals, we may be in some trouble, but whoever was paying Sal to dump those chemicals is really in the fryer. The mall deal is toast once this report gets out. The poisoned land and water will be all over the papers. No one's touching that business with a ten-foot pole. Not to mention lawsuits, EPA, maybe jail time. Good riddance. I wouldn't slow my car down if they were crossing the street. Pumping kids full of cancer."

Meredith snorts in agreement, but then her brow scrunches. "If JJ got sick by the same polluted water that is causing cancer in kids, then why did he react to it so quickly? It might be something different."

Justine traces her fingers over her son's forehead. "JJ's always had a sensitive system. It's why I was so nervous about the banana split before. He drank a lot of that water in a short amount of time. Maybe the other kids built up a tolerance since it's all they've known. If they were first exposed as babies and spit up, their moms might not have realized anything was wrong. Kids under two throw up all the time."

The room falls silent. We stare at one another with wide eyes, the weight of our amateur sleuth work hanging heavy in the air. It's one thing to learn the land under the future mall is toxic, another thing entirely to believe it's the reason behind dead husbands and sick kids. My cheeks go hot, and my heart kicks into a hard, steady rhythm.

This is *huge*.

"Jack knew." Justine's words are fierce in the quiet kitchen. "Why else would he hide the report in his briefcase? He was carrying around a stick of dynamite."

One he stuck in my car, to get it away from his precious

wife and son. Justine's gaze finds mine across the tray of melting popsicles, and I don't like what I see there. She's done the math too. She pities me, dammit.

I sigh and look away. "Peter knew too. Obviously. I overheard an argument. It wasn't about me. It was about the report. He asked whoever it was if they wanted to be involved with that kind of garbage. He said he thought they were better than that. And now he's dead because of it."

"So did Romeo," Krystle sniffs. "That's why he told Rom to safeguard the money. They were in serious trouble, and they knew it."

"Robin wouldn't have gone along with that plan." Meredith's voice is loud and insistent, almost too much so, and conviction juts her chin. "I know her. She'd have wanted to stop the mall from happening."

No one disagrees, even though I have my doubts. Robin might have gone down with the others, but she'd stashed the fake report in her condo. I guess it's possible she didn't realize it was fake, but still. I haven't seen a lick of evidence she'd want to stop the firm's biggest deal from going through.

Footsteps sound from behind us, Kimberlee returning with the Donnabelle jewelry cleaner. Krystle waves her over, shoving the boxes and wrappers aside for the notarized report. "Bring it here, sweetie. Let's see what we got."

Between the two of them, it takes maybe thirty seconds. Half a crummy minute for Kimberlee to recite the list of ingredients and Krystle to match seven of them up to chemicals marked *hazardous* on the report.

I think of poor JJ, puking blood onto my carpet upstairs, of innocent kids battling cancer a few miles away. My hands curl into fists on the table. "That royal, royal bitch."

"Sal's not innocent either." Meredith looks at Krystle with a grimace. "I know you two go way back, but he's just as guilty as Donna. Maybe more."

"I'm telling you, Sal didn't kill our husbands or hire that maniac," Krystle argues. "Those are Donna's chemicals in the ground. The Tiger must be working for her."

"She's too cheap for that," I say. "A guy like the Tiger has to be expensive. I don't see it. And there are, what, a dozen more chemicals listed on the report? Hers isn't the only garbage being dumped."

Meredith chews on her lower lip, but she's nodding. "So now what? What do we do?"

I plant both palms on the table and let my fury at my former boss push me to a stand. "We confront Donna. She'll definitely know who else has dumping deals with Sal. And I know exactly where to find her."

"Let's go," Justine says as we stand together.

"Just so we're all clear," I say, already picturing the moment that's coming. "When we get to the part about how Donna's gonna spend the rest of her life rotting away in jail, I get to deliver the news."

MEREDITH

Camille tried to prepare us, but I still wasn't ready.

"Is she…" Krystle presses her nose to the front window of the Donnabelle jewelry store. "Naked?"

Donna Moldova is indeed greeting the New Year in her birthday suit. She's alone in the store, surrounded by enough candles to burn down the whole jewelry district, and engaged in some ceremonial gyrations I can't quite bring myself to call dancing.

According to Camille, Donna does this every January first—a ritual to bring good fortune in the year ahead. Maybe it worked for her in the past, but not today. This year, we're going to take her good fortune and shove it up her yoga-toned ass.

Because I think this woman is behind all of it: the secrets that got Robin and the others killed and the hit man on a mission to silence the rest of us. Even if she's not fronting his fee herself, I'd bet good money she knows exactly who is.

There's been no sign of the Tiger since our encounter in Sal's wolf cave, but that doesn't mean he's not here. We dropped Kimberlee and JJ off with Krystle's family for protection, and I just hope it's enough. Justine looked so pained leaving her son behind. But JJ didn't cry when she hugged him goodbye or when she handed him over to Krystle's sister with instructions to administer the rest of the charcoal pills the doctor prescribed. A kid that young shouldn't have to be that brave.

So we're all looking over our shoulders, fearing for our lives, and meanwhile, Donna Moldova is chanting and waving a smudge stick around her bare tits, not a care in the world. Her eyes are closed, but they pop right open when Camille bangs on the door.

"Open up, Donna!"

Donna screws her eyes shut like she thinks she can wish us away. Camille knocks again, and I join her, pounding my fist against the glass. No doubt this place has a killer alarm system; otherwise, I'd already be looking for rocks to hurl through the window. My last drop of patience dried up hours ago. We're getting answers now, today. This bitch is going to tell us exactly what happened to Robin and the other partners and why.

Finally, Donna sighs and comes over to the door—covering up first, thank God, in a silk robe that makes her look like a sorceress vacationing in Cabo. It's hard to believe this ridiculous woman would hire a contract killer. If I've learned anything these past few weeks though, it's that people aren't always what they seem.

Donna stares at us through the glass, folding her arms across her chest. "We're closed."

"We're not here to shop," Justine says.

"Really?" Donna smirks. "You don't want some earrings to go with that stolen bracelet, Camille? Or maybe a nice pendant?"

"Cut the shit, Donna," Krystle cuts in. "Let us in."

"Why should I?"

"Because we know what you did," I say.

Donna tugs the robe tighter around her. "I have no idea what you're talking about."

"The chemicals, Donna." Camille steps forward. "The garbage trucks. We have proof."

"You've got nothing. Once a lying slut, always a—"

Camille slaps the report against the window. "I may be a slut, but *you're* the liar. Now let us in, or we're going straight to the police."

Guess those are the magic words. Donna turns the lock.

Inside the store, the air is thick with fragrant smoke, sage and incense and all those damn candles stinking up the place. Since Donnabelle is closed for the holiday, most of the jewelry cases have nothing in them but black velvet trays. All the diamonds and platinum and other really good stuff must be locked up in the vault. There are still plenty of crystals on display though—jagged towers in a rainbow of colors set up like a skyline across the counter and baskets everywhere piled with polished stones of all shapes and sizes.

I pick up an opalescent sphere about the size of my fist, and Donna snaps at me, "Don't touch that!"

Just to see the look on her face, I juggle the crystal between my hands a few times before setting it down. Why someone would pay a hundred bucks for what looks like a shiny baseball, I'll never understand.

"Is there anyone else here?" Justine asks, peering deep into the strange, flickering shadows.

"No," Donna says. "I always do my rituals alone."

When we pulled in, the only cars in the lot were her sedan and the armored truck the store uses to transport valuables. But the Tiger could be lurking anywhere.

"Now let me see those papers." Donna tries to snatch the report out of Camille's hands, but Camille holds it out of her reach.

"Not so fast," Camille says. "First you're going to tell us everything you know about the Terminal Road project."

"The mall? I don't have anything to do with it, other than that they've approached me for a Donnabelle store. They offered me a prime spot. The spirits, however, are resistant. I don't make any moves without my angels' input."

"Come on, Donna," Krystle says. "We don't have time for this woo-woo bullshit. Your angels only have green paper wings."

Donna ignores her, still focused on Camille. "Talk to your friend Martin Ellis. You two looked awfully cozy at the party last night. I should have known a girl like you wouldn't take long to land on her feet. Or, should I say, on her—"

"Fine," Camille says. "Maybe I *will* talk to Martin. Maybe I'll tell him all about how you and Sal Ponterelli tried to sell him poisoned land and screw his company out of millions."

Donna has the audacity to look offended. "*What* are you talking about?"

"I saw the trucks, Donna. I know all about the dumping. The chemicals in your jewelry cleaner match up with the toxins in the report. We know it was you."

"I didn't do a damn thing."

"Then you paid Sal to do it," Krystle says. "Same difference."

"*I* didn't pay Sal to do anything. I paid your husband. Whatever happened to that land, it was all Romeo and your—" Donna looks at me, a nasty smile distorting that well-preserved face. "Well, I guess she wasn't really your wife, now was she?"

Yes, she was. Robin was my wife in every way that counted. She might have kept secrets from me, and she might have had some questionable clients, but in the end, she did the right thing. She must have. And she died for it.

"That was their specialty, right?" Donna says. "Romero, Tavani, Kelly, and Calder—they'll make your problems go away. No questions asked, no dirt on your hands."

She reaches under the counter, and we all tense, ready to spring into action, to take her down if we need to. But it's not a weapon Donna retrieves; it's a pack of Virginia Slims.

She lights one and takes a drag, revealing deep wrinkles around her lips. "It used to be no one cared what you did with your garbage. Then the government had to stick their grubby paws in. All those regulations and fines and fees—how was a struggling family business like mine supposed to survive?"

Something tells me this woman has never struggled a day in her life. She was handed her career on a crystal platter instead of having to fight for respect like Robin did every day of her too-brief life.

"So I talked to my attorney." Donna blows out a long stream of smoke—right into our faces. "I told Romeo about my little problem, and he said he'd take care of it."

"By hiring Sal," Krystle says.

Donna nods. "His guys take the garbage away, and then it's *their* problem. I didn't even know what they were doing with it. I didn't want to know."

"Those chemicals are making people sick," Justine says. "Did you know that? My son just left the emergency room with a scalded throat. Little kids just a couple of miles from here are dying of *cancer*."

Donna's eyes widen with what I guess is supposed to be shock. I'm not buying it. She had to know. And now she's trying to weasel her way out of taking any responsibility. Whether or not she's personally to blame for that plane falling out of the sky or that creep trying to kill us, she's got a hell of a lot to answer for.

"I wasn't aware of any of that. As if I'd cloud my karma with sick kids. This is all *her* fault. She just had to go and get greedy."

"'She'?" Camille asks. "Who are you talking about?"

Donna stares at her. "Robin Calder, of course. The mall deal was all her doing."

"No, that's not—" I shake my head, like I can erase her words. She's a liar. This woman is lying. "I mean, yes, Robin worked on the mall deal, but once she knew the truth, she tried to stop it. Romeo too—and Jack and Peter. They all tried to stop the deal from going through."

"Are you serious?" Donna bursts into laughter. "Oh God, you are."

"It's over, Donna." Camille's eyes shine with triumph. "We're gonna make sure you go to prison. For a *long* time."

"It was you, wasn't it?" I step closer. "You had that fake report made."

Donna's not laughing now. In fact, she looks more than a little frightened of me. "What are you talking about?"

"We found another copy that says the land is fine. It had to be you or Sal or both of you together."

"I told you—I don't deal with Sal. Well, except for the muscle. Robin's the one who suggested building the mall on that property. How do you know she didn't have the report made herself?"

"Why the hell would she do that?"

"To cover her own ass," Donna says. "To make sure the deal went through. So she could get paid. Money's all she ever gave a damn about. That whole project had bad energy from the beginning, and so did she. The darkest aura I've ever seen."

"Shut up." I feel a hand on my elbow, trying to hold me

back—Justine's or Krystle's, I'm not sure. Definitely not Camille's, 'cause she's right at my side, staring Donna down too. "You don't know anything about Robin or about me."

"I know Robin was a ruthless bitch who would do whatever was necessary to get ahead and then some." Donna glances through the window. "If anyone tried to pull the wool over her eyes, it was probably the last thing they ever did."

I can't deny that. It was one of the things I loved about Robin—her drive, her uncompromising ambition. Sure, she might have bent her morals sometimes, but she still had them.

Donna tries to push past Camille and me, heading for the door, but we block her way. I'm holding that stupid crystal baseball again, gripping it tight. I don't even remember picking it up.

"You and Robin must have made quite the couple," Donna says, a thin eyebrow arched. "You're even crazier than she was."

I pitch the crystal at her head. Donna ducks, and it crashes through the door instead, shattering on the icy asphalt.

"You *bitch*!" Donna's screech is even shriller than the alarm I just triggered. "That was a sacred orb, blessed by—"

Krystle rolls her eyes. "No one gives a shit about your sacred orb, Donna."

Two hulking security guards burst in through the back. "Took you idiots long enough!" Donna says, then points to us. "Get these women out of my store."

I recognize the men immediately: Arti and Tino, two of Sal's guys. I knew it. They *are* working together. There's more she's hiding.

Arti tries to take my arm, but I shove him off, rounding on Donna. "If you're so innocent, why do you have mobsters guarding you, huh?"

She turns away, silk robe billowing regally behind her. "Make sure they don't set foot on the property again. And clean up that glass and board up the window too."

"Yes, ma'am." Arti takes hold of Krystle, more gently than he did me. "Sorry about this, Mrs. Romero."

As the guys escort us out of the building, shoes crunching over the broken glass, Donna strides to her car without looking back. The store's alarm is still screaming, and I'd like to let out a good, long scream of my own. All this trouble, all this time wasted, and we still don't know for sure who's responsible.

Robin couldn't have covered this up. It doesn't make any sense. None of this makes any sense.

Donna gets in her car and slams the door. "You poisoned people," Justine shouts. "You—" She gasps, freezing like a frightened antelope.

"What's wrong?" Camille asks.

"He's here." Justine stares across the frozen expanse of the parking lot. In the far corner stands a tall, broad-shouldered man, staring at us from under the brim of a baseball cap. That intense gaze is unmistakable.

The Tiger. He's found us.

Arti and Tino see him too. They both draw their guns. "This is private property, asshole," Tino calls out. "You're gonna want to vacate the premises."

The Tiger smiles, like he's amused by their little show of bravado. He doesn't come any closer, but he doesn't back off either.

"It *was* Donna." Krystle curses under her breath in Italian. "That lying *puttana*. She hired him. She's been after us all along."

When Donna notices the man in her rearview mirror, she clearly recognizes him. But contrary to Krystle's theory, Donna doesn't seem happy to see the Tiger.

Her eyes bulge with terror, and she fumbles with her keys, frantically jamming them into the ignition. The car roars to life.

And then it explodes.

KRYSTLE

Well, I guess Donna didn't hire the Tiger to kill us after all. I'm not so ice-cold that it was my first thought as her car exploded.

Instead, as we all stare open-mouthed at the fiery remains of Donna and her car, I'm scared, sure. But more than that, I feel guilty. Romeo, and probably the other partners, got Donna's goose cooked.

"Mrs. Romero," Arti says, helping me off the ground. "You broads should get inside. Tino and I'll take care of that guy for you."

As Arti helps up a trembling Camille, I realize he doesn't look scared as much as angry. In my memory, I see a flash of Donna outside Sal's bedroom, waiting to have a word. She'd wanted protection. From the Tiger and whoever hired him. *That's* why Arti and Tino are here. And that protection failed.

Tino takes Justine's arm. She's become a statue, staring at the hit man. "We gotta get you inside, miss."

Meredith pulls on her other arm. "Hurry. We're not safe out here."

Justine takes a few steps backward, still not turning her petrified gaze from the murderer. "He's coming for us."

"Then come on!" Meredith grabs Justine by the waist and hauls her toward the broken door.

"It's not your fault," I say to Arti. "That man is a freak killing machine. There was nothing you could have done to—"

Arti's throat explodes, splashing blood all over the glass door and DONNABELLE logo. I scream as he drops to the ground, his hulking body like a giant doorstop.

"Get down! Get down!" I yell, and we land in a heap inside the store.

Tino steps between us and the parking lot, aiming at the Tiger, so we can safely get inside. I stifle a sob as we step over poor Arti.

Another shot rings out, and the window we're huddled under shatters. Then another, and Tino's throat rips open just as Arti's did. He drops to his knees and flops right beside his friend.

We scream in a panicked chorus. Crawling backward, we try to avoid glass as we get out of view. Except Justine. She's still standing in the window right by where Arti was shot.

"Get down, Justine!" I scream.

Camille grabs my shoulder with a firm squeeze, then rushes toward a back hall. "I'll be right back."

"What?" I yell and look at Meredith. "Help me get Justine."

We approach her from the side, like a cat stuck in a tree. "Come here," Meredith says in a sweet voice that's wholly unnatural. "Right over here."

"He's coming for us," Justine says like she's in a daze. "He won't stop."

I can't deal, so I rush Justine and yank her skinny arms. She's stronger than she looks, not moving much, and then, I see what she sees. The Tiger is closer to us now, standing proud in front of the car he just blew up. He looks relaxed and completely in control as the smoke and flames burn behind him. But the worst part is he's smiling. He's smiling right at Justine.

"Jesus, Mary, and Joseph, come on, Justine!" I yank her backward, and she gasps as if awoken from a bad dream.

"We have to run," Justine gasps at me. "Hurry!"

I take one last glance toward the Tiger just as he begins to move and stalk his prey again. "He's coming!" I yell over the alarm.

Camille rushes into the showroom. "I've got the keys. Hurry. There's a side door."

For a moment, I can't move, the smell of blood and bullets taking me all the way back to the Hill. I make the sign of the cross and whisper a quick prayer for Arti and Tino. They didn't deserve this either.

Now I'm the one being pulled as we rush through the main area with rows of cases on one side and windows on the other.

We stay crouched down, and the case we pass explodes. We scream and move faster. The next one is shot just before we get there, four bullets, and we all fall to the floor. He's playing with us.

After crawling the final feet through glass, we reach the side door. Camille heaves it open, and the bright morning sun blinds us for a second, but that's all we've got.

"The truck!" Camille motions, and we all start running toward the huge armored vehicle about twenty feet ahead. I glance to see the Tiger isn't outside but in the building, thank God. It gives us time to get the passenger door open and pile inside the long seat.

"Who can drive this thing?" Camille yells as she crawls over Justine and me to get out of the driver's seat. "Hurry! Who?"

"I can." I grab the keys and scoot over. I jam them into the ignition and the engine roars.

The store's side door flies open, and the Tiger steps outside. We all scream. I smack Meredith's legs so she's straddling the stick shift instead of blocking it, and I can actually put the damn thing in reverse. Then I change my mind.

"Hold on, girls!" I put it into drive and hit the gas, doing everything I can to run over this kitty. But he's too fast and leaps back inside as we zoom down the small alley that leads around the back of the building.

It's a dead end.

"Shit!" I screech and throw the truck into reverse.

"There he is!" cries Camille. "Gun it!"

I do, and he leaps out of the way again but lands on his face. "He's bleeding!"

The Tiger stands, and blood pours from his forehead. He's smiling like he's having fun. Then he pulls out his gun and fires right at us.

We're all crouched low as the front window glass is hit, but it doesn't shatter, thank God. I manage to get back into drive and, after running over several plastic trash cans, I've got control.

I hit the gas again and watch as the bleeding Tiger disappears in the rearview mirror. The truck nearly comes up onto two tires as I take the turn to get us on the highway.

Justine is glued to the side mirror. "I don't see him. No one is behind us." She lets out a shaky breath. "Now what? We can't go to the Hill. We'll lead him right to the kids. The police? Will they protect us?"

I glance at Meredith and Camille, but apparently, I'm the one who has to tell her.

"The police can't keep us safe," I say softly. "It's probably more dangerous. We don't even know who he works for."

"Plus, we'll arrive in a stolen truck from the scene of a triple homicide," Camille says, staring out the passenger window. "Not ideal."

I take the on-ramp to 95-S and speed this big boy up.

"Where then?" Justine asks a little too calmly.

I don't answer because I don't want to fight about it.

"Where?" She demands it this time.

"The only place we can go." I reach for the radio. "Let me focus on driving this tank."

The opening guitar riff of "When Doves Cry" begins, and Prince is the lone voice as we rumble down the nearly empty highway.

I grip the steering wheel as the guilt returns, a sharp pain in my chest. I swallow thickly, knowing I don't deserve the tears to relieve it.

This is not the life I wanted. This is the life I left. And Romeo, damn him, brought us all the way back.

Maybe I turned a blind eye one too many times. Because you can start to feel like you're safe when you're in a house on the other side of town. When you only swing by the Hill for Sunday dinner. But how far did I really go? And what did I really leave behind, and what did I never have the courage to face?

The highway splits, and I take the exit toward East Greenwich. Justine tenses, but she doesn't say anything. Maybe she knows we should be glad we have anywhere to go at all.

My eyes burn as I think of Arti and Tino. Hell, even Donna, crazy as a loon, but definitely didn't deserve that nasty namaste.

As a girl, I saw people dragged behind wise guys' cars down Atwells Avenue. That feels like it was witnessed by someone else when I'm behind the wheel of a new car on the East Side of town. But not so far in an armored truck with fresh bullet holes.

It's not that I'm judging my sisters or my father or anyone who gets in the life to make their own possible. But Romeo, God bless him, he knew there was more. He was smart enough to go after it. He'd known I'd kick his ass if he didn't.

I was never as far as I told myself. To get away, I had to work hard. But to stay away, that's where you make tough choices. To stay on the right side. And not look the other way.

I justified every backslide as a choice I made for my sons. As if playing dirty in a good neighborhood made me any different.

Here I am again.

I slowly take the turn down a long dirt road, no longer packed with cars and hustling valets, though there are a couple of Crown Vics right before the final turn onto the driveway. I ease the giant truck into the circle drive right as "Somebody's Watching Me" plays.

"What's Sal going to do?" Justine slams off the radio. "Poison us too?"

I grin at her because that was pretty funny. Then I turn off the truck. "If we don't find an answer here, sweetie, we're dead."

"I don't think he'll let us in," says Meredith. "I wouldn't."

"Four desperate broads in a stolen truck with a killer on their tail." Camille straightens her fur collar, lightly spattered with blood, then heaves open the passenger door. "How could he say no?"

I glance at my face in the mirror and see blood along my hairline. Probably from glass or maybe Arti or both.

We stand at Sal's doorstep, blood on our coats, some of it ours, and nowhere else to turn. I swallow thickly and knock on the door.

"Yeah?" says a deep voice on the brown rectangular intercom.

"Miss me?" I call.

"Krissie?" Sal says, sounding worried. "Be right there."

I run my hands through my hair, which is hopeless, and dab at the blood.

The door swings open, and Sal is in his tuxedo pants, white undershirt, and open, red silk robe. "Look what the cat dragged in."

"Too soon," I say, my throat tightening as I picture necks exploding. "We were just at Donna's shop. I've got some bad news."

The grin on his face falls. "Arti?"

"I'm sorry." I put my hand on his arm. "He got Tino too."

"Damn it," Sal says. "I should have listened when that crazy broad said she needed more muscle. This is on me."

"Nothing was going to stop him." I squeeze his arm.

"He blew up Donna," Meredith says. "Car bomb. Then tried to kill us."

Sal curses under his breath and pulls out a handkerchief. He dabs at my forehead, then stills. "My wolves aren't howling."

We all glance around. "Do they normally?" Camille asks.

"When someone pulls up? Absolutely." Sal drops the handkerchief and puts his hand on his waist, revealing a gun. "Something's wrong."

"The Tiger," whispers Justine.

"Get inside, now," Sal says. "Hurry."

He doesn't have to tell us twice—he holds open the door,

and we rush past him. We stand in the dark, cave-like entryway. I turn to check on Sal, but he's blocking the doorway, hands raised in the air.

He's found us.

But it's a woman's voice that slices the air. "FBI! On your knees!" Sal drops down, and the woman leads a SWAT team into the entryway with their weapons drawn. "Hands up for you too, ladies!"

We obey, and Meredith gasps beside me. Her gaze is on the bossy FBI lady, now cuffing Sal under his giant oil painting while she reads him his rights.

"Frankie?" Meredith steps toward the woman. "What are you doing here?"

"Oh, shit!" I mouth at Camille and Justine, who seem equally shocked.

Bartender no more, Frankie has on FBI gear, including a bulletproof vest and a Smith & Wesson pistol aimed right at Sal's head.

"Cardinale," says an agent to Frankie. "Got the ID on the truck they were driving from Providence PD. Came from an active crime scene. Police found two bodies, one car bomb detonated, and another car bomb undetonated in a vehicle registered to Robin Calder."

"Cuff them too then," Frankie commands with a steely gaze toward Meredith. "But this one's mine."

JUSTINE

I would always choose silence. If it were me shackled in the middle of a sunken living room, surrounded by officers aiming loaded weapons at me, my palms would be open and my lips would be closed. I was a lawyer's wife. How many times did I hear Jack lament some client running his mouth to the wrong person? *Pleading your case is for the courtroom*, he always said. Cops don't want to hear anything aside from confessions.

The second handcuffs came out, I knew to keep my mouth shut.

Salvatore Ponterelli's lawyers are all dead. Maybe that's why he heeds no such counsel. Instead of listening to the officer reciting his Miranda rights, *the wolf* howls denials, emphasizing each with some combination of the seven dirty words that can't be aired on television.

The worst of his profanity is aimed at the only female agent in the room. Her name, according to the badge she flashed, is Francesca Cardinale. Though judging from the bits of information between f-bombs, she was known to Sal as the *chiacchierone* bartender with the heavy pour, which explains why she looks vaguely familiar and why Meredith's mouth hasn't closed since the woman stormed into the room screaming *FBI*.

"I shoulda known by the way you was always flapping your gums with the customers, asking questions and making doubles." Sal shakes his head as if he's disappointed with himself. "You were trying to get people liquored up and loose-lipped."

Sal's shoulders move as he speaks since his hands are clamped behind his back. The sight of him struggling to communicate sans gesture seems to pain Krystle. Like the rest of us, she stands beside an officer with her wrists tied together in front of her stomach. But her expression isn't shocked like Meredith's or relieved like Camille's and, likely, my own. Krystle stares at Sal with her lips parted and hands clenched beneath her new bracelets as if she wants to say something—or slug someone—in his defense.

"Fuckin' A, Frankie." Sal says the woman's name like it's another epithet. "And after all I've done for you. Just the other day when you was begging like an ugly *comare* to come to my New Year's Eve party, talking 'bout how you had nothing to do and really needed the cash."

"Thanks for the invitation, by the way." Francesca smirks. The smug expression refreshes my memory. She was Meredith's friend wearing the painted-on leather dress. "The tips sucked, but I got plenty of evidence."

"You don't have shit," Sal counters. "What the fuck did you do to my girls?"

Francesca looks at Meredith. "He means the wolves," Meredith explains.

"Don't worry. They're just tranquilized." Francesca laughs. "They'll be up and about in a few hours, which is more than I can say for you. This time, you're going away, Sal. We've known for some time that you used the Wolf Den to launder money. No way a strip joint sandwiched between a pair of auto body shops was pulling in the kind of income you were claiming on your tax returns. But we didn't want to give Sal Ponterelli a little slap on the wrist for cheating Uncle Sam. The U.S. Attorney wanted to know where the money was really coming from. And now we do. It's Italians like you that give the rest of us a bad name, you know."

"Yeah? That's exactly what I was thinking about you. So you, what, saw some coke at a party?" Sal's nostrils flare. "When guests come to my private residence to play, I don't make them empty their pockets."

"Actually, you do."

The quip comes from Meredith, who has apparently picked her jaw up from the floor.

"Everyone is a consenting adult, sweetheart." Sal grins at Meredith as though he knows some of what she herself has *consented* to at his parties. "I'm nobody's daddy."

The last word triggers something inside me. Maybe it's because it recalls my dead husband and my now-fatherless child. Or perhaps it's due to the fact that, despite all the terrifying images of the past few hours—Donna Moldova's car exploding, mobsters' necks spouting blood, glass shards flying at my face, Krystle's crazed driving—I still see red dribbling down my three-year-old's chin. I still feel him writhing as I wrestle with his terror. I still suffer the swell of guilt, knowing that chemicals were eating away at my child's insides while I was playing lounge singer at the damn piano just a few feet away. Whatever it is that sets me off, I can no longer stand quietly on the sidelines while the mobster who dumped the chemicals that sickened my son and so many others claims he's innocent.

"You poison people," I shout. "And not only with coke. You poison people with the garbage you dump. There are children suffering—nursery school kids dying—because you buried carcinogens in the ground. Because who cares about some poor kids in government housing, right? Who cares about a bunch of Black and brown babies? They get sick. You still get paid."

Somehow, the expression that raises Sal's thick, dark brows and draws down his full mouth doesn't appear angry. If he didn't raise wolves to torture his enemies, I might think that my accusations actually hurt him.

"Hey, I don't know what you're talking about. I don't kill kids." Sal's Adam's apple bobs as if he's swallowing something difficult. "Black, brown, yellow, white—don't matter to me. Children are against code. I only deal with adults."

He turns his attention to Krystle, who's still bleeding from a nasty gash at her hairline. His dark, downturned eyes seem to plead with her. "I don't know what she's talking about, Krissie. You know me."

Krystle opens her mouth to respond, but I don't give her the chance. "It's on your land!"

My voice reverberates, bouncing off the room's marble floor before getting lost in its high ceilings. The agent beside me jostles my arm. I'm adding heat to a pressure-cooker scenario. But I can't help myself.

"You mean the mall land?" Sal again focuses on Krystle. There might be a dozen FBI agents in the room, but there's only one person whom he cares to convince. "How are people sick? No one has even built anything on it yet."

"The land your family *donated* is right across from it," I explain. "People live there now. Kids live there."

A vein throbs in Sal's muscled neck. "My parents donated that land in the '60s, when I was a kid. The city built on it. Nobody ever said anything about poison."

"There had to be an environmental analysis of that land too," I counter.

"No way." Sal's attention is finally on me. His tan brow is scrunched into waves. He really seems not to know what I'm talking about.

"The EPA wasn't founded until 1970," Francesca pipes up. She frowns at me as though I might have tried to upstage her big money-laundering, drug-dealing arrest with a bunch of nonsense. "There wouldn't have been any environmental studies."

I gesture with my chin to the agent holding both Camille's elbow and her purse. "We have a report that says the future mall site is poisoned with carcinogens. It's not a stretch to think all the kids getting sick next door, on land the Ponterellis also owned, are being affected by the same buried chemicals."

Camille stares down the man guarding her side. "It's in my bag." She directs her explanation to Francesca. "The findings are from an environmental testing agency: Vista Corp."

Francesca's eyes go large at the company's name. She turns to one of her colleagues with a rifle trained on Sal's torso. "Vista Corp. Wasn't that where the guy whose car exploded on the I-95 worked?"

The male agent nods while keeping his eyes and his gun on Sal. "Yeah. It didn't look like an engine failure, but there was so little left that forensics couldn't tell."

Francesca turns her attention back to her prime target. Her head tilt asks the obvious question.

Sal holds up his cuffed hands. "I don't know nothing about no report or Vista whatever or environmental bullshit. I know that I had land, and the city needs a mall to bring jobs to the area. It's a win-win." Sal turns to face Krystle, his big body pulling one of the agents holding him in the process. "Ask that developer Martin Ellis. He said it was the perfect place. To hear him tell it, there isn't a single parcel available in Providence where he could build a big shopping center without more red tape."

"So if it wasn't Sal who hired that psycho to get the report, who else would kill to keep it quiet?" Camille asks.

The click in my brain almost feels audible. A key engaging a lock. Martin Ellis hired the Tiger to obtain the report and bury it, which meant burying our spouses.

"Martin Ellis was determined to build his mall no matter what," I say, directing my appeal to Francesca.

Though I'm the one who verbalizes it, my fellow widows have clearly assembled the same puzzle. I see the realization on their faces, the recognition of the common enemy who has been there all along, hiding behind his expensive suit and fancy business cards.

"He had the plane blown up," I add. "He hired the man who came after us, the one who just killed three people. He might have even been involved in the car explosion with that guy from Vista Corp."

"He's killing off anyone who knows about the report," Meredith shouts.

"I can't believe he tricked me." Camille's blue eyes burn like the hottest part of a flame. "He had me believing that the mob was trying to pull one over on him—that he only wanted the report to avoid getting duped into purchasing unusable property."

Francesca's gaze darts from Camille to myself to Krystle and, finally, to Meredith. "I'm still not sure what's going on."

Meredith's eyes narrow. "I can explain better if you uncuff me."

Francesca nods to the agent charged with restraining her former coworker. Meredith's cuffs release with a loud click. She rubs her wrists and then brings her hands to her hair, glittered by glass fragments.

"You know that Robin and their husbands were killed in a plane crash before Christmas," Meredith says, focusing on Francesca. "Their law firm was putting together a deal to build a mall on Sal's land. That's what the money Sal took from us on New Year's Eve was for. The firm was paying Sal for the land on behalf of Ellis Corp. and taking fees for negotiating the deal. But the firm—"

"Jack," I interrupt. My husband was Ellis Corp.'s main lawyer. If the FBI is going to make a case against the developer, I won't have them sully his name in the process. "Jack ran a due diligence report on the land to make sure his client wasn't buying something unusable."

"It's standard practice with property deals," Camille adds as Meredith withdraws the document from her purse. "Peter did those things all the time. He probably recommended Vista Corp. The letterhead says it's a Rhode Island company."

Meredith flips through to the pertinent RESULTS page. "The report came back that the land was corrupted with all kinds of carcinogens and needed substantial remediation before it would be safe to build. That kind of thing can take decades. But we found a forged one, which Ellis Corp. must have intended to give authorities so that construction could start." Meredith raises her chin, looking Francesca directly in the eye. "And we couldn't let that happen."

Francesca runs a finger down the text as she reads. "So this original report says the land was poisoned?"

"That's what we've been saying." Aggravation spikes my tone. The FBI agent isn't processing everything fast enough. She needs to comprehend that there's a highly trained murderer on our hides. If he can't get to us, he might go for JJ, Kimberlee, and Rom—even if they are being protected by Krystle's mobbed-up relatives. We can't save them with our hands cuffed, standing around in Salvatore Ponterelli's living room. "Ellis hired a contract killer called the Tiger. He's the one who's after us for the original report. He must know that we have it now, since we went to confront Donna. He wants us dead."

"The Tiger killed Donna Moldova." Camille's voice breaks on her hated boss's name. Her sadness makes sense to me. I know all too well how possible it is to hate someone and still not want them harmed, especially not the way Donna went out—the same way Jack died.

Krystle cuts in. "He killed Romeo. He murdered all our spouses. He blew up Donna. He executed Arti and Tino. He won't stop until we're dead too."

The entire room looks at her and the man to whom she addressed her speech. Tears sting my eyes. I realize with some horror that they're not just for Jack but also for the men Krystle has just mentioned—the mobster friends for whom big, strong

Sal is also fighting his sadness. I saw these people shot in cold blood as they tried to protect us. I watched a man's neck explode and his aorta spray the last of his life onto my clothing.

Sal's brown eyes become muddy with unshed tears. "You'll wait for me, Krissie?"

Since I've known her, Krystle has always moved fast. But I've never seen her move with such speed. In a blink, she's wrested free of the FBI agent who'd had her elbow and sprinted past Francesca. She stands before Sal, her face tilted upward.

Either Sal's guards loosen their grip, or they never had a good hold on him before. His chest and chin lower toward Krystle. Their lips connect.

Krystle rocks backward. Despite his restrained arms, Sal manages to draw her upright, seemingly by the connection of their mouths alone. When they break away, the air in the room seems to finally escape.

The agents spring into action, pulling him toward the exit.

"How long do you plan to be away?" Krystle shouts after him.

"Depends on my legal counsel," Sal calls over his shoulder. "I lost my best guys."

Krystle stands straighter. "I'll get the firm's top associates on it. Rom will work his ass off. He has a debt to repay. I'll make sure he does it."

Sal chuckles despite the two men yanking him from his home. "You're making him work for it now?"

"I'm making everybody work for it," Krystle yells back.

In spite of everything, I smile. Jack and I once had that kind of playful banter. God, I miss it. I wonder if Camille is thinking the same thing.

I turn toward her, but Camille's not watching Krystle. Her attention is entirely taken up by Francesca.

"I can get you Martin Ellis." She assumes her full height, topping the male FBI agent at her side. "He thinks I still believe him, and he's waiting for me to deliver the report. Let me wear a wire when I bring it to him."

JJ's face flashes in my mind. With Camille helping to take down Ellis, maybe I can grab my son and run. The FBI will be on to him and the Tiger. They'll have bigger problems than me and my three-year-old.

But my husband died trying to bring that report to light. I can't let Camille carry that burden alone.

"I want to help too." I raise my restrained hands. "The Tiger has been particularly focused on me since the beginning. I can be of use."

I feel a sudden heat to both my right and left. Krystle and Meredith have squeezed between where Camille and I remain guarded, forming a tight semicircle flanked by FBI agents.

"He killed our family." Krystle shakes her cuffed fists. "And families fight for their own."

CAMILLE

I tug on the visor of Justine's white Mercedes and check my reflection, even though I know what I'll find. Makeup, flawless. Hair, big and bouncy. But not even Kevyn Aucoin could do anything about those dark circles under my eyes or cover up the new ditches a crash diet of grief and terror has carved into my cheeks.

I flip up the visor with a disgusted sigh. "When this is over, I swear I'm eating the biggest burger you ever did see, and then I'm sleeping for a week."

"Same here," Krystle says from the back seat. "Only I'm having two burgers, both of them with fries. And a chocolate milkshake. Extra-large."

Justine groans, her hands tightening on the wheel. "Can we please stop talking about food? I'm so nervous, I might throw up."

She's not the only one. My stomach has been churning since yesterday evening, when two beefy FBI agents spent the entire night banging around downstairs, guarding the doors and windows so the Tiger couldn't slip inside and slit my throat. It would have taken a tranquilizer to knock me out. I didn't sleep, not even for a second.

I clutch Jack's briefcase on my lap and think through the plan, which we've discussed and debated from every angle. A sting under the guise of a business meeting. An attempt to sweet-talk Martin Ellis into a confession so the microphone in Jack's briefcase can send in the feds.

I run my finger over the tiny hole drilled into the bottom, feeling the microphone head flush to the leather. A thin wire leads to the secret compartment, where a transmitter is duct-taped to the felt.

"What if he sees the bug?" Justine says as if she knows I'm thinking about it too.

"He won't." Meredith sounds more confident than she looks, pressed between Krystle and JJ's booster seat, which Justine said was too complicated to remove. She did brush off the Goldfish crumbs before we piled it high with our purses. "He's going to be too busy patting us down to examine the briefcase, and if not, Camille will distract him. She knows to hold the thing so the mic is facing the right way."

"What if he's aware of the secret compartment?" Justine asks.

"He's not."

"He might be," she argues. "I still think the FBI should have created some contingency for that."

It's the one flaw in our plan, the big, fat bluff we're going in praying he won't call. If Martin Ellis is a James Bond fan, we're toast.

Krystle leans forward to pat Justine on the shoulder, the bracelets on her wrists jangling. "Just breathe, sweetheart. Everything's going to be fine."

Nobody dares contradict Mama Romero, so we drive the rest of the way in silence, the tires humming on the pavement beneath us.

On Allens Avenue, Justine slides the Mercedes into a spot along the curb, and the four of us step out in a flurry of dry-cleaned furs and sculpted suits. Anybody who sees us might think we've gone a little overboard with the boardroom attire, but Martin is from New York. He won't take us seriously unless we look the part.

A brisk wind skating up the Providence River chases us into Martin's office, a red-bricked mercantile building spitting distance from the mall site. The inside is squeaky clean and as nice as an old building can be, with slapped-on paint and scrubbed floors and light bulbs dangling from the nineteenth-century rafters. Clusters of mismatched desks are scattered around the edges of the room, topped with computer monitors so new they're practically wearing price tags. A battered black conference table stands in the direct center, decorated with a giant bowl stuffed with every Little Debbie cake known to man.

"Ladies." Martin stands against a far wall in a navy pinstriped suit, arms spread in welcome, and I see now what I was blind to before. His eyes are too sharp, and a flicker of malice disrupts his handsome brow, a flash of static in the signal. "I didn't realize this meeting was going to be a group effort."

Jack's briefcase vibrates in my fingers, but I manage to match his smile with a flirty one of my own. "The girls and I are a package deal these days. Too depressing to be all alone. Besides, what I'm here to talk about concerns them too. I hope you don't mind."

"Not at all. And I hope *you* don't mind if my associate pats you down."

His associate, the Tiger, the murderous creep, steps out from behind an enormous ficus. He stalks toward us, a predator on the prowl, and I position myself for the intercept. I slide the briefcase onto the conference table and the chinchilla from my shoulders, tossing it over a chair.

Me first.

The Tiger complies, but he's no gentleman. His hands slide all over my body, fingertips pressing in places they have no business pressing. He tugs on my blouse to explore the bare skin of my waistline. Dips a finger into the sensitive skin between my breasts and drags it under the lace of my bra, coming dangerously close to my nipples.

Martin moves closer, shifting to get a better view. He's enjoying this.

So is the Tiger. His lips twitch in what I suspect is a grin.

"What's your name, sugar?" I ask.

He kicks my feet apart so a hand can slide up my skirt.

I try not to squirm as his fingers skim my panties. "It's just that I usually like an introduction before I let a man feel me up."

He grunts, patting me on the hip. "Barbie's clean."

I take a step back, putting some much-needed air between us.

The Tiger turns to Krystle, who gives him a withering glare. "Try any of that on me, mister, and you're likely to lose a limb."

Martin sinks onto the edge of the conference table. Six feet, maybe less, between him and the briefcase. I come closer, sultry movements that grab his attention. "Martin, sweetheart, you can't really think we'd be stupid enough to bring a weapon. I already told you, I'm only here to deliver the report."

"In this line of business, you can never be too sure."

"I guess the construction industry is really cutthroat these days, huh?"

He laughs. "You'd be surprised."

The Tiger declares Krystle clean, then repeats the process with Meredith and Justine, whom he saves for last. With her, he takes his time, but Justine doesn't make so much as a squeak. She just stands there, her mouth a flat line, breathing slow and steady through her nose. No wonder Jack couldn't quit this woman. There's a lot more to her than what you see.

After what feels like an eternity, the Tiger steps back, and Meredith reaches for Justine's hand.

I perch a hip on the table smack between Martin and the briefcase. "It's the strangest thing. When we were searching for this report, we found a couple of different versions floating around."

"That *is* strange," Martin says. "But the one I'm looking for has a notary seal."

"Oh, that's right. You mentioned as much, didn't you? With everything going on, I must have forgotten."

"Stop playing around, Camille. Did you bring the right one or not?"

"I did."

"Then give it here."

Not a question. A demand. But I can't do that yet. Frankie was very specific. As soon as I hand over those papers, I lose my leverage. I am not to give him *anything* before he gives me a confession.

I reach for the briefcase, then pretend to reconsider. "It's awful complicated, this report of yours."

"You read it?"

I nod, then shrug. "Fat lot of good it did me. Like trying to read Chinese or something. The least you can do is tell me what all that scientific jargon means."

"Don't you worry your pretty little head about that, sweetheart. Leave the business stuff to me. Now hand it over."

Frustration rises, a leaden balloon in my chest. He's giving me nothing, giving Frankie and the eavesdropping feds nothing, and we're running out of time. I try to slow my heartbeat with a few deep breaths, allowing a few seconds to *think*, but the only thing I can come up with is a last Hail Mary pass. I dart a glance at Krystle, thankful she's the praying kind.

I place a palm to the center of the briefcase, the leather soft against my skin. "One word I did pick up on, though, is *toxins*. It seems the dirt under that future mall of yours is teeming with those nasty things."

Martin eyes me with a frown. "You misread it. This is complicated stuff. You must be confused."

"You're probably right, but let me ask you this. If it's true about the toxins, what happens when that mall is stuffed to the gills with people, breathing dirty air and sucking on bubblers pumped through poisonous ground? I'm no scientist, but I can't imagine that would be healthy. Would you let your kids hang out there?"

"I don't have kids."

"Your mother then."

"My mother lives on the Upper East Side. Why would she come all this way for a Podunk mall? She doesn't even like the Gap."

Behind me, Krystle sucks an insulted breath. There's not much in her wardrobe that comes from the big-box chain, but like me, she's probably considering the bigger implication: that Martin Ellis looks down on us, that he doesn't give a shit what happens to our friends and family, so long as they're shopping at his mall.

I smile at Martin, my expression all sugar. "So your plan is to hang the Ocean State out to dry by leaving cancer clusters in your wake? That doesn't seem right."

"How about you quit with the goddamn lectures and give me the report."

I lift my hand from the briefcase, looking up at him through my lashes. "Okay, but I think you should know that it was Jack who hid it."

"Jack." Martin puffs a sarcastic laugh, pushing off the table. "Now there's a sanctimonious prick for you. That man had no right to be lecturing me about anything, not while he was fucking around with the likes of you." He turns to Justine, and he has the audacity to look apologetic. "Oops. Didn't mean to let the horny cat out of the bag, but it's true. Jack was sleeping with your friend here."

Justine is unflinching. She raises her chin. "Yet he was more honorable than you. He wanted to stop this deal from happening."

Martin's brows nosedive, slamming together in a sharp V. "Your husband should have remembered who he was working for. I am the client. The client is king. And look, I understand you're in mourning, but the plane crash that took your husbands was an accident, no matter how hard you and the investigators try to prove otherwise." He gives her a close-lipped smile.

I feel the first, violent pulse of panic. I picture Frankie and the others huddled around the monitor in some van around the corner, wondering what the hell they were thinking, sending in a bunch of amateurs to take down a professional. What, do they give classes in deflecting blame at criminal school?

I step to the table and release the brass latches with a flick of my thumbs, pausing before lifting the top. "Fine. You want to know what the girls and I think? We think you intend to build that mall no matter what's in this report, and our spouses were getting in the way. They dug in their heels, so you and Tony the Tiger here decided to blow them up before they blew up your deal."

A hand lands on my shoulder and shoves me aside—the Tiger, not pleased at the comparison. I teeter and slam into Martin, who doesn't have time for me now that the briefcase is unguarded. He shoves me toward the table and lunges, right as the Tiger holds the report over his head like a trophy.

Martin's eyes gleam at the notary seal. "That's it. That's the one."

The Tiger grins too, and I guess that's the good news, that they're both too focused on their victory to pay much attention to the vessel. Meredith sidles closer to the table and flips the briefcase closed.

Martin grabs the report, beaming. "I can't believe it. You bitches actually did it. You came through. I would say you're not as dumb as you look, but you did make one mistake. A very big one."

He doesn't elaborate, but he doesn't have to. His eyes gleam in a way that tells me he's enjoying this. He *wants* us to be scared. He's getting off on being in charge.

Krystle sees it too, and she takes a step back, muttering the words we're all thinking: "Time to go."

"Yeah. Too bad we can't stay." Meredith gives me a look, tipping her head toward the exit.

But I can't move, not with Martin's arm slung around my shoulders. Justine's eyes flash panic, matching mine. Now that he's got the goods, no way he's letting us go. Where the hell is Frankie?

Martin's arm is a rock-hard noose around my neck. "This has been fun, gorgeous, but let's go." He juts his chin at the Tiger, and I see the gesture for what it is—silent marching orders. The Tiger moves to his right, a barrier between the others and the door.

Shit.

Martin gives a mighty tug, and it's like going up against a professional wrestler. He drags me easily to a door along the back wall, then opens it and shoves me inside. Behind me, the Tiger is still rounding up the widows, their heels clacking in protest on the floorboards, so they don't see my face when I get a load of the room or the alarm and shock and horror that open my mouth in a scream.

Smooth concrete walls. Floor covered in wall-to-wall plastic. A folding table topped with knives and saws and power tools.

And standing in the corner, Robin Calder dressed in head-to-toe white.

MEREDITH

At first, I think she must be a ghost, floating under the harsh light hanging in the center of this empty room. In that pristine white suit, the fire of her hair against her ice-pale skin, Robin looks too beautiful to be real.

"Darling." She rushes toward me, ignoring the others. "Are you all right?"

Then she presses her lips to mine, and it knocks the breath from my chest. She's real. This is really happening.

Robin is alive.

She's alive, and she's working with Martin Ellis. With the Tiger. My mind ties itself in knots, trying to fit the pieces together.

But the only thing I still know for sure about Robin is that no one can force her to do a damn thing.

"Why?" It's the only word I can get out. I feel like my throat is full of broken glass. I'm not going to cry—not in front of that smug asshole and his leering psychopath pet. Not in front of the other widows, after everything we've been through.

I want you to have everything, darling. That's what Robin whispered in my ear when I signed the paperwork that made our relationship official. *I'll take care of you, I promise.*

Was she planning this, even then? Planning to betray her partners and leave me behind?

"I'm so sorry, Meredith." Robin strokes my hair, the same way she used to in bed, and I shiver. "I'm sorry I had to lie to you, to let you believe—"

"What about killing our husbands?" Krystle stabs a finger at Justine and Camille. "You sorry for that, you psycho bitch? Everything my Romeo did for you, and you dump him into the ocean like he was nothing?"

Robin pulls away from me. "I didn't kill them."

"They did." I point to Ellis and the Tiger, and *God* how I want to be right about this. "They sabotaged the plane. They planted those car bombs."

"Car bombs?" Robin looks over at Ellis. "What car bombs?"

"On the BMW," I tell her.

Robin's gaze narrows at Martin. "I told you to leave her alone."

"They kept getting in the way," he says with a shrug. "And she was always with them."

"He had Donna Moldova blown up in her car," I explain,

hoping this is all a surprise for Robin. That she's shocked or outraged. "See! They're out of control."

A smirk twists Ellis's too-handsome face. "It was just business."

So are we is the unspoken implication. Whatever Robin's plan is, whatever control she thinks she has over these men, I'm not convinced it's enough to get us all out of this room alive.

"So what if you didn't bring down the plane with your own two hands?" Camille says to Robin. "Didn't you realize the other partners were in danger?"

"You knew enough not to get on the plane," Justine adds. "How could you stand by while they boarded, knowing they might never land?"

Krystle shakes her head. "All this time, you let Meredith think you were dead. How could you hurt her like that?"

"What choice did I have?" Robin says simply. "You have to understand my point of view. Romeo and Peter and Jack, the second they started waving around that report, they were doomed. And once Ellis moved the meeting to New York and chartered that plane under Romeo's name, there was nothing I could—"

"You could have warned them!" Justine shouts.

"I *did* warn them." Robin fixes her with a frigid stare. "Right from the beginning. Romeo and Peter, they might actually have listened to me too. If not for Jack."

Justine presses her lips together. Camille wraps an arm around her shoulders.

"Jack convinced himself he was some big hero," Robin says. "Riding in on a white horse to save us all from ourselves by demanding Ellis stop the mall deal, or else we'd go to the authorities. Convincing Romeo and Peter to put morals over money for the first time in their goddamn lives. I told Jack he was putting himself in danger—putting you in danger too, Justine, and your little boy. He refused to listen. Men that handsome, they're so used to getting their way, aren't they?"

"Jack *was* a hero," Justine says. "He had his faults, but he made the right choice in the end. He was willing to put his career at risk, everything he worked for, to expose the truth."

"And what good did that do him?" Robin snaps. She takes my hands in hers. "It's over now, darling. I know it's been difficult, but we have everything we need. Ellis paid me more than my share of the deal, and we have enough to start over, just the two of us."

She always had a master plan. Of course she did. Even playing dead, Robin stayed in control. This whole time, she's been pulling the strings from beyond the grave, certain this will all work out: she'll get the money and the power and the girl. Happily ever after.

"About that…" Ellis takes a few steps backward. The Tiger doesn't move a muscle. "I know what we agreed to, Robin. But she knows too much now. They all do."

Robin's expression hardens. "You gave me your word."

"And you told me they wouldn't suspect a thing." He's almost to the door now. "Just a trio of housewives and a stripper, yet somehow, they've figured all this out. What's to stop them from talking? They could still ruin everything."

Ellis grabs the doorknob. The Tiger takes out his gun.

"We had a deal, Martin. You swore Meredith would be safe." Robin turns back to me, growing frantic. "You're not going to say anything, are you, baby? Tell him. Tell him you'd never talk."

She's trying to save me. Only me. Donna was right. Robin will cash in Krystle, Justine, and Camille like poker chips if it'll get her the big win she wants. I know laying down my life won't save my friends. It's the same choice Robin faced that night in New York: do the right thing and die for it, or trade the moral high ground for a chance to stay alive.

What would Robin say if she knew I'd already talked plenty—to an FBI agent no less? Some good it did me. If Frankie and her SWAT guys were going to burst in and rescue us, surely they would have done it by now. We're on our own.

"Deals change." Ellis shrugs, then smooths his suit back into place. "Like I said, it's just business. You of all people should understand that." He nods to the Tiger. "Let me know when you're finished."

Then he's gone, the lock clicking into place behind him.

Robin looks desperate, something I've never seen. I'm suddenly aware of the huge room. The plastic covering the windows. The long metal table with saws and handcuffs and knives. This a torture room. This is where we die.

The Tiger raises his weapon. "Down on your knees," he growls.

The other widows and I exchange a look as we sink to the floor. We outnumber him, but we all witnessed how quick he is with that gun back at the jewelry store. He took Arti and Tino out in seconds, at a distance. We're locked in here, nowhere to run, no weapons unless we can get to that table all the way on the other side of the room. Robin might take a bullet for me, but she'll just as soon push the other three in the line of fire.

"Close your eyes." Though Robin is speaking to me, she doesn't look my way. Her gaze is locked on the Tiger. "Don't watch, darling. It'll all be over soon."

I'm done doing what she tells me. I'm done living by her plan, following along blindly. So as the Tiger levels his pistol at my throat, I keep my eyes wide open.

KRYSTLE

The Tiger points his gun at Meredith's neck.

Bam.

A gun explodes, a powerful reverberation on the concrete walls before the sickly sound of metal into skin. My scream isn't the only one, and before I open my eyes, I know someone is dead.

The scent of blood is overwhelming so close by. There's a quietness after death, and my whole body shakes as I find the strength to find out the truth.

Meredith.

From where I'm huddled on the ground, I search for her. There's a panic in my chest, something near when my Rom was missing. I blink tears away as I search for stubborn, smart, and brave Meredith.

I can only see Robin with eyes wide as if in shock. Her arm

outstretched with a sleek silver gun, barrel still smoking, and aimed right where the Tiger was standing.

I stifle a sob, so terrified that Meredith is on the ground with her throat torn open like Arti and Tino.

Camille is huddled next to me and grabs my arm tight. We are trembling together, searching the room.

There's a glare behind Robin where one of those industrial lights blasts like a spotlight. Meredith steps from behind her, eyes wide at the fresh pool of blood spreading toward her and Robin.

Meredith collapses into her, clinging as if she saved her life. Which she did, thank God.

Justine stumbles over to the source of all that blood. The Tiger's body. "He's dead?"

"He better be," says Robin coolly, sliding her arm tighter around Meredith's waist.

Justine sucks in a shuddering breath. "It's finished. Oh, thank God."

Her shoulders begin to shake in relief, but I'm not feeling a drop of it yet. One problem solved, another big one—Robin returned from the dead—still in front of us with a smoking gun.

Camille elbows my side and motions me to look on the ground. The Tiger's weapon has fallen on my side of the body, almost within arm's reach.

Meredith's terrified eyes track mine, then the waterworks. "You saved my life, Robin." She nearly crawls inside Robin's still impeccably white jacket. "Thank you, baby." She kisses her long and hard.

It's now or never. I heave my body forward and spread my arms wide. The gun is within my grasp, but so is all the blood.

Robin yells for me to freeze, so I do the opposite. I twist to miss the blood, my arm raking the gun into my chest. I grip it tight and roll up to my knees as a bullet fires in my direction. Meredith screams, and Robin curses at her for messing up her aim.

"Please don't hurt them," Meredith begs, still pulling on Robin's arm.

The concrete next to me is smoking where the bullet barely missed. She's still looking calm and in control, even as she tried to kill me. Even as she tried to make my boys orphans.

The gun is still warm in my hand as I go up on one knee and aim the weapon at Robin. "All right, bitch. I think this is called a standoff."

"Hardly," Robin says with a laugh. "There are three of you I could shoot."

"You only have three bullets left. Better aim fast and true," Justine says outta left field.

"How the hell do you know that?" I stammer.

"Her gun is a Walther PPK. It's in Jack's favorite movie," Justine says casually. "Holds six rounds."

I shake off my surprise and make a note to ask about Justine's movie trivia later over margaritas—if we survive. "Listen, Robin," I say, trying not to let all the hatred bubble to the top. "The FBI are right outside. You were defending Meredith when you shot Tiger. We all get that. But you shoot one of us, that's a whole different story."

She rolls her eyes and wraps an arm around Meredith's waist. "Of course the FBI are outside," she says, completely unsurprised. "That's why I have an exit plan. One that leads us out of Providence forever."

I see conflict in Meredith's eyes. I'm sure I'd look the same if Romeo was the one giving me a second chance at a life with him. I glance at Camille and Justine, thinking either of them might take that deal if they had the chance. Wouldn't they?

"What do you want?" I ask Meredith, not dropping my gun but making sure she knows it's not on her. "If you still love her. If you want to be with her. You can go."

Justine steps toward Meredith as if to stop her but pauses. "You can't trust her." Her voice is soft, as if her words are coming from her own pain.

"You're not a widow anymore," Camille says. "If you can't live without her, here's your chance."

Meredith blinks a few times at the three of us. Then her gaze finds Robin. "I want to be with you."

I let out a small sigh—disappointed, sure, but also worried. I can't see things ending well for Robin, no matter how smart she thinks she is. But if that's where Meredith sees her future, I'm not going to stop anyone from going for the brass ring, no matter how tarnished.

Robin strides over to pick the report off the ground. "This will never see the light of day." She turns to Meredith, nodding toward a door in the corner just past the table with a murder weapon smorgasbord. "We have to hurry. You are coming with me?"

"Yes. This is what I want. I want you."

Robin leans in and kisses Meredith, who backs them up, kissing deeper, until they bump into the murder table. She pulls back, both of them gasping for air.

"I want you…but you're dead," Meredith murmurs, running her cheek against Robin's. "I *am* a widow. What we had died with that plane. If it ever existed at all."

Robin's eyes go wide. "What?"

Meredith pulls a knife off the table and presses it to Robin's throat. "Drop your gun. It's all over."

I want to cheer, but instead, I scurry over behind Meredith and keep my weapon on Robin, who doesn't move. "You heard her. Drop it."

Robin's eyes shine with angry tears from this betrayal. Tears we all know well. "I love you, darling," she says against Meredith's temple. "I did this for you."

"No, you didn't. If you really knew me, if you really loved me, you'd know I'd never want any of this. I only wanted you. Us." She lets out a shuddering breath. "But it's all dead. You killed it."

Robin hisses as the knife at her throat draws blood. "I find the one stripper with a heart of gold." She drops the gun onto the table.

Justine dashes for it and quickly aims it at Robin.

As Meredith releases the knife, tears fall down her face in thick black streaks. Camille puts an arm around her shoulders as if she knows sometimes doing the right thing hurts worse than the wrong one. Then she hands her some handcuffs from the table. "I imagine you've done this before?"

Meredith smiles through her tears and gently turns Robin, who puts her hands down. It occurs to me that if they'd been married, Robin might have worn a suit like this on their wedding day. That in some way, maybe she'd thought this would be the first day of the rest of their lives.

Meredith tightens the cuffs and then steps away.

"The door is locked. We need to signal the FBI." Justine aims the gun at a window, blasting through a plastic curtain.

Bam.

The glass shatters like a bomb went off. "That should do it," she says with a firm nod.

Camille points toward the door we came in, and Robin starts to move that way. We walk around the murder table, where the Tiger is splayed on the floor.

"At least he's dead," I say as I pass him. "Doubt there's a widow to mourn that sick bastard."

Justine pauses and leans over the body. "Thank God, he's—"

His eyes snap open before she finishes. We scream as he grabs Justine's ankle, pulling her down into his blood on the floor. I try to aim my gun with a trembling hand, but he's got Justine around the neck as they writhe and kick for control. There's no way I can safely shoot him.

"He's choking her!" Camille screams.

Justine is turning blue, and I realize she only has one hand around his arm to pull him off. That's when I see the other, still clutching Robin's weapon.

Bam. Bam.

The gun goes off twice, right into the Tiger's gut. His eyes are wide as blood pours out of his grinning mouth. Justine shoves him off her, and he drops to the floor. There's only the sound of her ragged breath and heels as she stands over him. Then pulls the trigger one more time.

Bam.

This one explodes in his throat. "Fuck you," Justine says.

I give a whistle, since it's the first time I've ever heard her curse. Or shoot a man, while we're counting.

She lets the gun drop. "Guess I miscounted. There were four bullets."

We all stand around her, staring at his vacant eyes, finally able to believe it's over. I skip the sign of the cross.

Outside the room, there's the unmistakable sound of the SWAT team descending. Martin is yelling on the other side of the door where he locked us in here with that killer. The metal scrapes as its hinges are rammed and the door flies open. Frankie rushes inside with her weapon drawn and finds us, a handcuffed Robin, and a very dead Tiger.

The four of us glance at one another, still shoulder to shoulder, ready for whatever is next. Justine and I drop our weapons. Then we all put our hands up together.

JUSTINE

I'm searching for a red house. Though I have the address, making out numbers from my driver's side window is damn near impossible. They're all posted to cement stairs hidden by parked cars or, worse, affixed to shared mailboxes squeezed between front doors. It's easier scanning for a color as I roll the Mercedes down the strange block.

JJ sees the place first. He shouts from the back seat that it's the one behind the flowers, and I find myself smiling. Not only is a glorious crabapple in full bloom, but my son's enthusiasm shows me how well his throat has healed over the past four months.

Some act of providence has left an empty parking space right in front. I pull the car forward. "This is it," I call behind me. "Don't unbuckle until the car is stopped."

Since turning four, JJ has learned how to disengage his seat belt and most child locks. Fortunately, he's a natural rule follower, so I don't fret much about him getting into things. Even so, I still keep all the cleaning products on the pantry's highest shelf.

I park the car and reach for the manila folder on my front passenger seat. It contains the necessary documents and a legal pad with a list of a dozen names. By the time the week is out, I intend to add at least forty more.

Behind me, JJ's belt unclicks. I ask him to wait inside for me to round the car, open his door, and release him to the sidewalk. Such caution isn't strictly necessary. The Tiger is dead. I watched the light leave his eyes for a second time after pressing the trigger, an act that my muscles remember more than my mind. He was choking me and I reacted. There was no conscious thought on my part, no decision to kill him. But maybe deep down, I knew the only way to keep my son safe—to live without incessantly looking over my shoulder—was to make certain the Tiger would never threaten us again.

I take JJ's hand and head to the steps. He skips the several feet, happy to be tagging along for the first time in a while. Usually, I don't bring my son on law firm business. I leave him at nursery school or with his grandparents. Sometimes, Kimberlee watches him. I'm pretty sure those nights are JJ's favorites.

Just as I'm about to ring the bell, my host flings back the door. "Come on in!"

There's a lightness to Raquel that I haven't seen before. It's in her bright smile, the way the expression not only parts her lips but also pinches her eyes.

I step inside. Immediately, I sense the difference from her last apartment. The air feels warm but not humid or stale. There's a faint, sweet smell from the crabapple beyond the cracked windows. It's possible to breathe easy in here.

The living room is considerably larger too. Her love seat and entertainment center float like two islands on a seafoam carpet. Waves of sunlight waft onto the floor, undulating with the sway of the crabapple's branches. Bathed in this sparkle is Denise.

Now I understand the real reason for Raquel's happiness. The child beams as JJ steps around my legs. Bright pink barrettes cling to the tight curls covering her head. Both her big, brown eyes focus on my son.

I can't hide my awe. "It really worked."

When Raquel and I spoke on the phone, she said the surgery went well. I assumed she meant that the cancer had been put in remission at the cost of her daughter losing the damaged eye. Never did I imagine Denise would be cancer-free and seeing out of both beautiful irises.

Raquel knocks on the wooden doorjamb. "That laser is simply amazing. The tumor is totally gone." She lowers her voice. "And to think that last year, I was simply praying for God to save her life, even if it meant she'd be blind."

Though Raquel whispers this last part to avoid scaring her daughter, there's no need for hushed tones. JJ and Denise are already in the midst of their own giggly conversation. "Let's get toys," Denise squeals, grabbing my son's hand and running with him down the hall.

"It's incredible," I say. "She seems to have so much energy. It's just so…"

My voice breaks before I can find the right word. The silver lining to losing Jack is that Denise and other kids have a new lease on life. Had Jack, Peter, and Romeo succeeded in simply stopping the mall construction—say, by convincing Ellis to build on another area—the polluted land might never have come to light. The attention from the crash spurred the city into investigating all the Ponterelli-owned properties by the river and pushed them to relocate the families living there. It's a comfort to know that our husbands didn't die for nothing.

The tears bubbling in my throat are visible on my friend's cheeks. "The oncologist says there's no evidence that the cancer metastasized beyond her retina. Once we stopped exposing her to those chemicals, I guess the chemo was able to take effect and shrink the tumor to the point where they could zap everything." She grabs my hand and squeezes. "I'll never be able to thank you enough for all you did."

After uncovering the pollution, the firm pushed for the relocation of Raquel and her neighbors with both carrots and sticks. No politician wants to be known for forcing poor, sick kids to remain in subsidized homes that are killing them. When I threatened to go to the press, the city council was all too happy to swoop in and *save* its suffering constituents.

The real coup was getting the city to take action without also making anyone waive their right to sue. Krystle, by way of Rom, was responsible for that. After getting him cleaned up in rehab, she had her eldest son working day and night to figure out all the ways he could force the city to act without making the tenants sign anything against their interests.

"I'm actually here to talk about how the firm can still help," I tell my friend. "There are folks who made a ton of money either dumping those chemicals or looking the other way. And they should pay."

Raquel gestures to the couch. I take a seat and open the manila folder on my lap. As she sits, I hand her the class-action notice.

"My husband's law firm." I clear my throat, swallowing my mistake. The firm is owned by the widows now. "We're bringing suit against several dozen companies involved in the dumping as well as individual city councilmen for failing to enforce environmental laws."

Raquel scans the document as I speak. "Don't they say you can't fight city hall?"

"Times are changing. You can hold everyone accountable—even in Providence."

"For how much?"

"It depends on how many people got sick." I pass her my legal pad with the names I've already signed up. "I would have come to you first, but I knew your plate was full with work and Denise's surgery."

Raquel runs her finger down the list. Her eyes open a little wider when she comes across somebody she knows. "Michelle's on here."

"Robbie had to have brain surgery. She's really hoping a payout could go toward his college fund."

Raquel raises her arched eyebrows.

"If we win, the jury sets compensation," I explain. "But we're going to be demanding multiple millions at a minimum."

"Millions? Can we get that?"

"Believe me, these folks have it."

At least four million should be earmarked for our clients as far as I'm concerned. That was the amount of the illegal-dumping fine in Salvatore Ponterelli's plea bargain.

The deal was considered a victory by both groups, according to Krystle. The city got to cry that the Wolf was paying one of the highest illegal-dumping penalties in history as well as donating his poisoned land to the city. And Ponterelli, for his part, only had to hand over the four million we'd given him for a deal that didn't happen and a parcel of land that he no longer owned.

Raquel passes back the notice of intent. She keeps hold of the legal pad.

"It's your choice," I continue. "But I have to believe any jury would sympathize with what you and Denise went through. You two suffered so that others could save a buck on their garbage disposal."

Raquel nods along with my argument. The sight of her

agreement empowers me. Helping people feels better than entertaining them, and I've actually been using many of the performing arts skills that I developed in college. I need to grab people's
attention and keep it while I deliver my argument. I need to
empathize with my clients.

Lately, law school is at the top of the list when I think of
what I want to do with Jack's million-dollar life insurance benefit,
which finally came through after the police ruled the partners'
deaths homicides and pinned the crash on Ellis. I make a mental
note to ask Rom about the LSATs after the press conference
today at the former mall site. Apparently, we're the guests of
honor.

"Okay then." Raquel extends her hand for the pen that I've
already slipped from my purse. "I'm in. Where do I sign?"

The construction site recalls a burial ground. It's all the dirt and
grass, I think. Or maybe it's the way that Krystle, Meredith, and
Rom huddle to the right of a small podium, each dressed in dark,
stoic colors that painfully contrast with the pastel day. There's
something about the stance of Krystle's younger sons that also
begs the comparison. They flank the group, backs straight in dark
suits, pallbearers prepared for duty.

I can't shake my somber feeling as I approach the small procession. I guess it's because I'm flying solo—a press conference
isn't an ideal environment for a fidgety four-year-old. JJ is with

Jack's parents, both of whom have promised to turn on the television so he can see his mom on screen. When I left him, Jack's mom hugged me, and his dad said that I made him proud. I nearly bawled. Killing Jack's murderer has ingratiated me to his family in a way that neither our marriage nor JJ's birth managed to do.

"It's a fine day for a press conference," I quip. "Beautiful weather."

Though I think I've kept my voice light, Krystle knows me well enough to sense something is off. She pulls me closer to the group, offering a shoulder pad to lean on.

I sense she might also need someone. There's a stiffness to her demeanor, that strong front that she puts up when she's feeling emotional. I know her well now too.

"You went out to Cranston today?" I guess.

A pained smile confirms my suspicion. The small city is the location of the state's largest maximum-security correctional facility and Ponterelli's home for the next few years. The plea deal, which allowed Providence to take his poisoned property and our four million, still made him a *guest of the state* for the next five years.

Prison time was a bitter pill for the mob boss to swallow. Ponterelli believed all the years of paying off Providence's elite should have inoculated him against any charges. Rom had to explain that an FBI investigation couldn't be ignored, regardless of how many local judges or prosecutors were in the Mafia's pocket. If the state didn't send its largest narcotics trafficker away for a bit, it would lose all credibility in its war on drugs.

"How is he?"

I hate to ask, but even behind bars, Ponterelli's happiness has come to determine more about my own well-being than I'd care to admit. The firm relies on business from his legal enterprises— the garbage union, the construction union, and other connections. We don't want Salvatore Ponterelli stewing behind bars about the raw deal his lawyers worked out. Plus, Ponterelli's mood *really* matters to Krystle. Being her friend and business partner demands a certain willingness to acknowledge the good in "bad" people. She's flexible that way.

"He's not at the Ritz, but he's all right. It's not the same inside for guys like him as it is for regular people. We had a nice dinner. There was a pasta course cooked by this wise guy who used to run a restaurant before he got pinched for running numbers." She places a hand on her chest. "Sal told me he sliced the garlic for the steak. Can you believe he cooked for me?"

I force a smile, even though Ponterelli getting off so easy annoys me. The guy demanded four million from us in the wake of our spouses' deaths and then scared us all into paying it. His punishment should be harsher than a one-star vacation funded by taxpayers and his own palm grease, if you ask me. Under the bargain Rom worked out, Ponterelli becomes eligible for parole after two years. I have no doubt he'll serve the minimum.

"The garlic sauce was beautiful too," she continues. "He cuts it with a razor blade, since they can't have knives. The slices are so thin that they liquefy in the pan with just a little olive oil." Krystle sniffs. "It's just hard always saying goodbye."

"I take it that he's still happy with his representation?"

"What's he got to be mad about? If you're in the mob, serving time comes with the territory."

I suppose Krystle's right because, to my knowledge, Ponterelli hasn't pulled any business from Romero, Tavani, and Kelly. We dropped the Calder. Given Robin's *accessory to murder* charge, it seemed best to take her off the letterhead. Her legal troubles might get even worse if the prosecutors side with Martin Ellis. From the little that Frankie has told Meredith, the two are competing for who can rat the other out to the feds faster.

Meredith was fine with the change. She prefers being a silent partner, and she has enough on her plate with the Wolf Den. The proceeds from selling Robin's posh town house were just enough to buy the club from Sal, who can't really run it from prison. Robin transferred the property and her interest in the firm to Meredith after her own incarceration, likely out of fear that Krystle, Camille, or I would try to take it in a wrongful-death lawsuit. Not that we would have. We all feel that Meredith has earned her share.

Thinking of Meredith makes me realize that she's no longer beside us. She's walked over to the other side of the podium, where nearly everyone wears a suit and a name tag. Most of them are from the Environmental Protection Agency or a local group that's been agitating to clean up Providence Bay. Whom could she possibly know in that crowd?

The sight of familiar brown curls answers my question. Francesca's over there in her FBI windbreaker and steel-toed boots. I wonder how a relationship can work out between the owner of a mobbed-up strip joint and a senior agent with the bureau? What do they talk about over dinner?

Judging from the way Francesca slides an arm around Meredith's waist, I guess it doesn't matter. And good for her. I lost Jack and my trust in him on the same day. For Meredith, ripping off the Band-Aid was painfully slow. She deserves some happiness.

"Are we late?"

I turn to see Camille striding toward us with Kimberlee following close behind. Maybe it's all the hanging out that the two of them have been doing, but Kimberlee is starting to look like she could be Camille's biological child. She's traded the heavy eye makeup for a fresher face that showcases her natural beauty. She's also dropped some of the attitude.

"I had to grab Kimberlee from her mother's," Camille explains, doling out a cheek peck to both Krystle and me as her stepdaughter heads toward a seat.

I don't flinch as Camille's lips brush my skin. This has become a standard greeting between us. Surviving a kill room together has a way of making other disagreements seem petty.

Krystle raises a brow as if she knows that isn't the only reason for Camille showing up so late.

"And I had a little bitty job," she adds. "The Branford divorce."

At the request of the firm's family attorney, Camille has started a side business that's proving very valuable: catching cheating husbands. Rhode Island allows no-fault divorces, meaning that all assets are split down the middle—unless wrongdoing can be proven. And Camille has a talent for finding proof that our clients' marriages aren't disintegrating from mere *irreconcilable differences*.

"That was over by lunch though," Camille adds. "Really I'm late because I had to run and grab Kimberlee. Can you believe her mom wasn't going to take her to see this? I can understand not wanting to cheer me on, but this is about so much more than that. It's about more than congratulating *us*. They're honoring her father."

As soon as Camille says it, the sadness hits me again. This press conference is recognizing that the law firm prevented countless Providence residents from being exposed to carcinogens. We may be the future of the firm, but it's our spouses' legacy. This event is a reminder that they didn't live to see it.

A crowd of onlookers has gathered, and the television journalists have exited their news vans. They march toward us, holding microphones, leading their camera crews in our direction like horses to water.

The sight of them stirs something in the name-tag crowd. A man emerges with papers in his hand. I see Meredith separate from Frankie and rejoin our side of the dais. She gives Krystle and me an acknowledging nod before turning to Camille. "You bringing that client by later?" Meredith asks. "I have everything set up in the champagne room."

I don't hear Camille's whispered response as the man with the papers strides over to the lectern. Everyone present hushes. The camera operators train their lenses on the speaker, who identifies himself as the director of the EPA.

Camille lets out a low whistle. Like me, she'd probably assumed that only the state folks were coming out for this. This conference is more important than I realized.

"Now I know some people think the Environmental Protection Agency is a bunch of folks hugging trees, shouting about the importance of the black-footed ferret." The audience chuckles. "We do care about animal extinction. But our efforts to preserve the environment are also about saving ourselves. Industrial processes have unleashed chemicals that can sicken us—that can kill us. The laws we enact are not about hampering business but about preserving human health."

The director continues on like a lawyer, making his case for why "ordinary Americans" should sacrifice some economic good for public health. I realize that he's trying to explain why it's more important for Rhode Island to remediate this site at a time when unemployment remains stubbornly high, sacrificing a job-creating shopping center. No doubt some residents would take the risk of cancer if it meant a biweekly paycheck.

"The law firm of Romero, Tavani, and Kelly."

The director gestures to us. On cue, the crowd claps.

"They realized the threat to public health of building on a site that could have endangered the lives of hundreds of thousands of residents. Senior citizens could have died. Our children could have developed cancers."

I fight the urge to grab the microphone. Children *did* develop cancers. They went through chemo. Some may even have died. Unfortunately, the government is not going to admit dropping the ball during this carefully orchestrated PR event. Our lawsuit will have to force its hand.

The director drones on, congratulating the EPA for enacting illegal-dumping laws. I start to tune out. Camille, Krystle, and Meredith appear to be doing the same. The smiles on their faces have fallen into straight lines.

"We will transform this dangerously polluted site into a place where kids can play," the director continues. "We will take this corrupted dirt and make it clean. We will install water treatment plants that will enable us to remediate chemical runoff before it ends up poisoning our once beautiful Providence River. This site you're all standing on may look rough now, but we will make this land shine."

I hear the words "rough" and "shine" and feel my eyes well. It's like Jack is calling to me from the grave, apologizing from the great beyond, telling me that he still sees my sparkle.

I close my eyes and think of all I intend to accomplish. In my mind, I answer him. *I see it, Jack. I see it too.*

THE WIDOWS

I t sounds like the opening of a joke: Four widows walk into a bar.

The problem with that joke is *they* are the punch line.

But no more.

The two founding partners' wives, who once hated the sight of each other, now rarely go a day without laughing together.

The other two women, who felt alone and ostracized, have never been more embraced.

All four widows. Now partners. The heart of the firm.

Their lives are different. Their loves are different—for the most part. But it all ended the same.

At a back table in Hemenway's, overlooking the Providence River, the widows raise a glass. First to the partners, then to themselves.

People say all kinds of things about these women. At least they're still young. At least they're rich, now that the life insurance money came through. But how sad to be left alone, widows all.

They are young.

Young enough to start over, which they've realized has nothing to do with age and everything to do with determination and support.

They aren't as rich as everyone thinks, but that doesn't scare them either.

What good is dirty money? Or money just dropped in their laps? What matters, what makes it mean something, is that they work hard. That they earn what they have the right way, day after day. That they live those values and pass them on to their children, not just hand them a blank check.

They are certainly widows.

But what that means is that they've loved and lost. There is no shame. Not when they consider all they have now that they didn't have before. How it goes beyond a shared law firm or what side of town they live on.

They have friendships forged in the fires of desperation and thriving in the growth of their new lives. Surviving on their own would have been impossible. And they'll never be alone again.

The headline will read: FOUR WIDOWS SAVE PROVIDENCE FROM TOXIC MALL.

The widows wish they'd had a chance to say goodbye. Last words instead of last rites:

I forgive you.
I will always love you.
We saved your legacy.
We saved each other.

Read on for more from the Widows!

Look for

DESPERATE DEADLY WIDOWS

available now in audio from Audible
and coming in 2025 in paperback and
e-book wherever books are sold.

PROLOGUE

Want to know the secret to success? How to get that Ferrari, that Tiffany, those designer silks decorated with 24 carats? Well, it's not hard work, sugar, or setting goals or managing your time—none of that psychobabble crap peddled in Brian Tracy compact discs. It's money, pure and simple. Cold, hard start-up capital. Cash is king, any which way you can get it: beg, borrow, or steal, that's the only way to the American Dream. Of course for some, you don't even have to lift a finger because you were born with a silver spoon or, better yet, a gold one jammed right into your entitled mouth.

Money not only paves the way for whatever the hell you desire but that silver spoon? Well, it's something to sell when it's time to buy a ticket out of trouble. 'Cause second chances don't come cheap. It's simple math: the fatter the wallet, the less morals matter. Fortunes are made convincing good people to forget their principles.

And once that fortune's in the bag, baby, people will pay for a peek. Folks will buy into any Ponzi scheme and pie-in-the-sky vision, provided it's being sold aboard a private plane or eighty-foot yacht. Throw on a captain's hat, every man becomes Hugh Hefner.

Money—real money—is possibility. Choices. The power to decide for oneself whether to take the high road, the low road, or pave another way altogether.

And whatever that road is, money ensures other people will get right on it. You lead; they follow. Even when it's simply a direct route for more dollars to end up in *your* bank account.

Money is reinvention. Slip enough bills into the right hands and robber barons become philanthropists. Philanderers become family men and faithful public servants. Money holds the magic to becoming someone else entirely.

But what to do if the family forbears didn't set sail with Columbus, intent on riches at any cost? If they came in cargo vessels with only the clothes on their backs for warmth, starving from famines and poverty, seeking safety from violence?

If they came in chains, heavy with the trauma of losing their freedom? Or had to endure the perpetual loss of everything they'd built their lives upon? If they'd watched the fruits of their labors consumed by others—stolen, not only from them but from their descendants?

What if they didn't set sail at all? What if they were already here? What if they're still here, despite all the odds, and their very presence reminds us what it cost to build the U-S-of-A?

Well, all is not lost. If you don't come from money, there's another secret to success, albeit not as surefire.

Being out of options. Having no other choice.

Nothing's a bigger driver of success than desperation.

And nothing's more dangerous, sugar, than a widow with nothing left to lose.

CAMILLE

I am getting too old for this shit.

I stand against the bar at the edge of the strip club and wonder if this is it then, if I've officially aged out. George Michael blaring in the speakers, a thumping bass line so hard it vibrates deep in my bones. The swirling disco lights above my head, barely breaking through a room that's dark as sin but blinding me with an occasional lightning bolt to the face. All these men, large and small and bald and potbellied and thin, businessmen in fancy suits and mobsters with Popeye arms. Every type of man you can think of, leering at the waitresses and lap dancers and the topless brunette riding the pole.

And so far, not a single one of them has noticed me. God, what a depressing thought.

I suppose it doesn't help that the room is filled with gorgeous women in various states of undress or that all of them are younger than me by a mile. I take in their smooth stomachs and perky thighs, their tight foreheads without even the slightest hint of a line, and a surge of something bitter burns in my throat. A lady never reveals her age, but I'm no lady and these girls make me feel like a grandma.

"The room's all set up for you. The champagne is chilled and waiting."

I look up to find Meredith leaning against the slick bar. Former stripper, fellow widow, and owner of this fine establishment. The Luna Lounge, Providence's only female-owned strip club. These past few years, she's also become a dear friend, one of the best I've got, and no one is more surprised about it than we are. The kind of drama we survived together will do that, I guess—stitch together a kind of unbreakable bond.

I give her a saccharine smile. "Only the best for Mayor Tom."

The vippiest V.I.P. in the champagne room, by far. He's supposed to arrive any minute now, via a back door that will lead him straight into the private area. A big fish, with an even bigger payday. The two bouncers guarding the door will make sure nobody gets in there but me.

The champagne is expensive, but Meredith will give me the bottle at cost. She knows as well as I do that a lot is riding on tonight, and for all the widows. When two years ago the plane carrying my husband and his law-firm partners exploded over the icy Atlantic, so did our cushy lives. All those shopping trips, all the flashy vacations and sparkly tennis bracelets just because…

they were suddenly a thing of the past. And in their place? The widows and I were handed the keys to a law firm on the verge of bankruptcy with a four-million-dollar debt to the mob. Let's just say we're lucky to be alive—but the point is, we've been paying our own way ever since.

Meredith plunks both elbows on the bar and leans in. "He requested Luxe tonight, you know. My best dancer and not just because she earns the most tips. Her lap dances are the stuff of legends."

"Honey, by the time I'm through with Mayor Tom, he'll be asking *me* for a lap dance."

She purses her lips, painted a dark red. "I have no doubt. Though watch out. Word on the floor is that he's a real perv."

Oh, I know. The Mayor and I go way back to a previous life, to long before he got elected. Parties. Benefits. Political fund-raisers, even though everybody in town knows that Davenforth money bought him that seat. Before my late husband, Peter, boarded that plane, he and Tom ran in the same circles. They don't call him the Playboy Mayor for nothing.

"I wouldn't need all these schemes if you'd just let me set up a camera. One little shimmy from anyone here and he'd pounce. And I'd have more than what I need to take him down." Meredith gears up for a protest, but I've heard her arguments before—and dozens of times. I wave her off with a hand. "I know, I know. Your club is fancy now."

Fancy might be a bit of an overstatement but still. Ever since

Meredith took over this place, the club is tight as a drum. No more strippers snorting lines of coke behind the bar, no more shady mobster deals decided in the back rooms. No more shenanigans from anyone, at all, ever, otherwise they get tossed to the curb and blacklisted. But the Luna Lounge is still a strip club, and half the men in here are married. Hidden cameras would kill Meredith's business.

But it sure would help mine—gathering evidence for the city's wronged wives to prove their husbands are liars and cheats. Rhode Island allows no-fault divorce, meaning all assets are split down the middle—unless I can give the wives ammunition for divorce court. A photograph of her husband with his hands up another woman's skirt, for example, or a tape recording of him explaining all the ways he plans to pleasure his mistress later that night. Anything that provides undeniable proof there were more than just two people in the marriage.

And it turns out I'm good at my job. After all, I know from experience what motivates a man like Mayor Tom to get handsy with a woman who's not his wife. I know how to whip him up with whispered promises in his ear, how to answer his indecent proposals with a smile that will make him forget all about the woman waiting for him at home. I'm not proud of how I gained this knowledge or the people I hurt along the way, but I figure at the very least, sticking it to Providence's most devious philanderers will clean up some of my karma.

"Miss Camille?" I twist around to find one of the bouncers,

a sweet man named Mikey, towering above me. "The limo just pulled up."

That's my cue. I slide off my barstool. "Showtime."

Meredith straightens, slapping me hard on the ass. "Go get him, hot stuff."

I make my way across the dimly lit room, and the girls clear a path. They know I'm Meredith's friend, and they spin with their drink trays and grinding dance moves in the other direction. At the edge of the stage, a dark corridor leads me to a plain wooden door marked with two clinking champagne flutes lit up in pink lights. I reach for the handle, right as the DJ fades into a song that I couldn't have planned any better: "Need You Tonight" by INXS.

There is no need for Mayor Tom to *slide over here*, as he's already seated smack in the center of the sole red velvet couch, his big body spread to take up most of it. The King of Providence on his throne.

I stand for a moment in the doorway, letting him drink me in: My hair, perfumed and curled into shiny waves that tumble down my back. My bejeweled heels, as high as any stripper's. These few well-placed strips of fabric that are masquerading as a dress. It wasn't easy hiding a microphone in this skimpy thing, and I pause to let him appreciate the effort I've made, with a smile that says it was all for him.

"Camille Tavani." A slow grin spreads up his face. "Fancy seeing you here."

He pats the couch cushion next to him.

Bingo.

READING GROUP GUIDE

1. Female competition and friendship are important themes of
   this story. Which friendships did you find the most compel-
   ling? Which were the most unlikely or surprising?

2. Eighties references abound in this book. Were there any
   mentions that prompted a walk down memory lane or
   inspired some fashion or music choices for your next party?

3. The authors' inspiration for this book was some of their
   favorite campy '80s and '90s comic thrillers like *Married to
   the Mob* and *The First Wives Club*. What did you think about
   the balance between comedy and tragedy in the book?

4. When the four women are tragically thrown together, they
   each have major judgments about one another. Sometimes

it's easier to be mad and hateful than deal with real feelings around betrayal, loss, fear, and loneliness. What moments stood out to you as being vulnerable about their real feelings? And what was the result?

5. Much of this story is based on real events of the 1980s—from Providence's thriving Mafia scene to the early days of enforcing environmental regulations. How did the 1985 time stamp impact the plot, and would it work the same today?

A CONVERSATION WITH THE AUTHORS AND WIDOWS

Krystle: All right, where the heck did this crazy idea come from?

Vanessa: My brain, I'm afraid. At least the premise of four women taking over a law firm in 1980s Rhode Island, where I live. I always loved group projects in school and—

Krystle: Yowza.

Vanessa: Yeah, but in this case, I was right. I admired Cate's, Kimberly's, and Layne's books and thought we could write something really fun together. The vision was campy, with murder but also friendship. And there was a pandemic, and I was maybe a little lonely. A lot lonely.

Layne: I was so not a group project person.

Meredith: [*snorts*] I can appreciate that.

Layne: I thought why not give it a try. Writing this book ended up being a blast. We each wrote a character: Cate/Justine, Kimberly/Camille, Layne/Meredith, and Vanessa/Krystle.

We brainstormed ideas for an outline of the story. Our process was to write one chapter from our character's point of view every week while reading and editing the other coauthors' chapters as we went along. Ten weeks later, we had a whole book. It was collaborative in the best ways.

Meredith: Well, you got to create me, so that helped. By the way, why a stripper?

Layne: I wrote my thesis on burlesque and striptease in graduate school.

Meredith: Hang on. You can go to college for stripping?

Krystle: Guess we better start calling you Professor Stripper Tits.

Meredith: Oh yeah? Know what I'm going to call you? How about—

Justine: Moving on. I may have started out as an exhausted ex-model housewife, but I like how my character really grew into her own. And I got my revenge.

Cate: That was important for me to see you finally have victory over that psychopath and get to connect with your forgotten talents. I also loved the research in the story. The suitcase, the weapons, even the environmental regulations were fascinating to include in the plot. It harkened back to my financial reporter days.

Justine: Did you have lounge singer days? Because I really enjoyed singing on that piano.

Cate: I was in an original rock band, in fact. We were signed to an indie New Jersey–based label and toured around the tristate area. I love how you used music to express something deep in your heart, and it ended up creating a connection with Camille. You really came a long way in this story.

Meredith: So did I. Looking back at that will-reading scene with Uncle Vin, that was a really scary moment for me. Though the leather lapel blazer almost made it worth it. And wiping that smug look off Rom's face.

Layne: Writing that scene was tough, and you're welcome on the blazer. It was definitely the most difficult of any of our chapters. We had a lot of plot to summarize and a lot of characters who didn't want to be in the same room. But I was very proud of how you stood up for who you were that day and demanded what was rightfully yours.

Camille: [*pours Kimberly a glass of sweet tea*]

Kimberly: [*sniffs*] Is there bourbon in here?

Camille: A lady never tells. Now, sugar, we need the truth. Besides being the most gorgeous character you're ever created, am I your all-time favorite?

Kimberly: You're the most entertaining, that's for sure. I got to have fun with you in ways I never do with my other characters whose stories are a lot more serious. And I love watching you evolve from a man-eater into a loving and loyal friend.

Camille: Bet you loved writing the clothes too.

Kimberly: That was also a lot of fun. You do have some serious style. The closet scene with you and Justine has a special spot in my heart.

Justine: Yeah, and it really turned around how I saw Camille. Well, and good wine helped our relationship too. We found a much-needed understanding of each other and how our lives were entwined. I'm curious though. What's next for us?

Camille: Yeah, authors, any hints? We don't get in too much trouble in the next book, do we?

Krystle: Maybe instead of a murder mystery, it's a romance? Set somewhere tropical? With an expense account?

Kimberly: Well…we can't say too much about the widows' next adventure, but a word of advice: don't drink the champagne.

ACKNOWLEDGMENTS

The four of us authors would like to raise a very large martini to our editor, Shana Drehs, at Sourcebooks, who believed in bringing *Young Rich Widows* to print. We have loved working with the whole Sourcebooks team, including Cristina Arreola, Anna Venckus, Molly Waxman, and the production, marketing, and sales teams.

Thank you to our fantastic agents, Sharon Pelletier, Jamie Carr, Nikki Terpilowski, and Paula Munier. You have been a dream team supporting this project and our wild ideas.

Thank you to agent Victoria Sanders and Lara Blackman, our editor who acquired this idea for Audible Originals and gave the four of us the greatest gift—an excuse to work together and learn from one another.

Grazie to the city of Providence and particularly the first season of the podcast *Crimetown*, which delves into the city's checkered past and served as an inspiration for so many aspects of this story, including the wolves at swinger parties (that really happened!).

Finally, it's been particularly meaningful to have this book centered on female friendship and empowerment set in the 1980s, shared with readers by Sourcebooks, which was founded by CEO Dominique Raccah from her home in 1987, where she has guided the company to be an absolute powerhouse in publishing. We are so honored to be among your authors and share this story with your many, many readers.

ABOUT THE AUTHORS

Kimberly Belle is a *USA Today* and international bestselling author with more than one million copies sold worldwide, with titles including *The Personal Assistant* and *The Marriage Lie*, a Goodreads Choice Awards semifinalist for Best Mystery & Thriller. Kimberly's novels have been optioned for film and television and selected by LibraryReads and Amazon Editors as Best Books of the Month and the International Thriller Writers as nominee for Best Book of the Year. She divides her time between Atlanta and Amsterdam.

Layne Fargo writes dark, dramatic stories that support women's rights—and also women's wrongs. She's the author of the thrillers *They Never Learn* and *Temper*, and her next novel, *The Favorites*, releases in 2025. Before becoming a full-time writer, Layne worked as a dramaturg, a librarian, and a knowledge manager, and she still loves going down a good research rabbit hole.

She lives in the Rogers Park neighborhood of Chicago with a rescue pit bull and cat who are best friends, the only man she never wants to murder (well, almost never), and way too many books.

Cate Holahan is a screenwriter and *USA Today* bestselling suspense novelist of six standalone thrillers, including *The Widower's Wife*, named to *Kirkus Reviews*'s Best Books of 2016, and *Lies She Told*, a September Book of the Month Club Selection. Her books have been optioned for film and television. Her original film, *Deadly Estate*, premiered on Fox's Tubi in March 2023, and her latest film is *Dancers on the Darkside*. A biracial female writer of Jamaican and Irish descent, she is a member of the Author's Guild, Sisters in Crime, and Crime Writers of Color. She lives in New Jersey with her husband, daughters, and dogs.

Vanessa Lillie is the author of the Rhode Island–set bestselling thrillers *Little Voices* and *For the Best* and the creator of the Audible Original coauthored bestselling book *Young Rich Widows*, which was an International Thriller Writers Best Audiobook nominee, and a sequel, *Desperate Deadly Widows*, forthcoming. Her latest book, *Blood Sisters*, launches a new suspense series featuring a Cherokee archaeologist. She also had a weekly column in the *Providence Journal* about life during the pandemic. Vanessa is an enrolled citizen of the Cherokee Nation of Oklahoma living on Narragansett land in Rhode Island with her husband, third-grade son, and bossy pugapoo. Say hi on Facebook or Instagram @vanessalillie.